FEE, FI, FO, FUM . . .

The Fabergé egg awaited her, beneath its glass case, and she smiled as she approached. It was even more beautiful than the first time she'd seen it, so beautiful her heart caught in her throat. Oh, she couldn't wait to see it by the light of day, to study each and every gem as it sparkled in the sunlight.

"Boy, you picked the wrong man and the wrong night," a voice came from behind her. She peeked over her shoulder, seeing a giant of a man reaching for a pair of trousers that hung over a hard-backed chair. She paused. Damn. Not only was the man tall, he was well-built.

At least he didn't recognize her. If she could just slip past him while he pulled on his pants . . . She spun around and ran straight for him, then cut sharply to the right to dart past as he stepped into one trouser leg. She almost made it, too, but a quick and strong hand shot out and grabbed the back of her shirt.

"Hold on there," her captor drawled. He pulled her back and away from the door, jerking on her shirt so that it tightened around her. She continued to pull against him, hoping that his hold would slip and she could make her getaway. The grip tightened, and she could feel the heat of his hand at her back.

"Fiddle," the man whispered softly, an element of surprise in his voice. "I do believe I smell an Englishwoman."

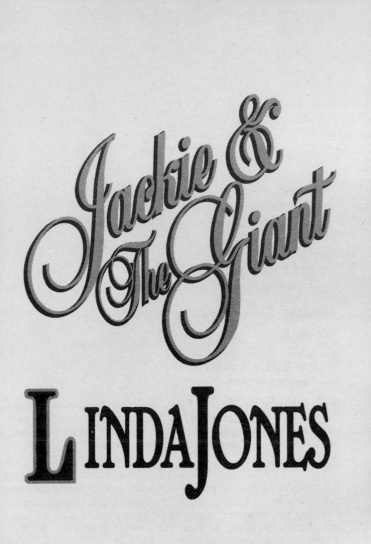

Jackie & The Giant

Linda Jones

LOVE SPELL BOOKS NEW YORK CITY

LOVE SPELL®

August 1999

Published by

Dorchester Publishing Co., Inc.
276 Fifth Avenue
New York, NY 10001

ISBN 0-505-52333-7

The name "Love Spell" and its logo are trademarks of Dorchester Publishing Co., Inc.

Printed in the United States of America.

To my youngest son, Steven,
who makes sure I keep my feet on the ground and my eyes
on the stars. Even hockey players never grow too old for
fairy tales.

Chapter One

1895

The man locked his doors! Here in rural Alabama, a hundred miles from nowhere, this paranoid man named Rory Donovan secured every one of his doors and windows at night. Every single one! Jackie knew it to be true because she'd checked, circling the plantation house and silently trying every door and every window.

Well, she wasn't going to give up simply because this job wasn't easy. If only she had a set of false keys like the ones Mina used to carry, she'd be in that house right now, climbing the stairs to the master bedroom where there rested, she'd heard tell, a Fabergé egg on a bed of black velvet.

If she had that egg in her hands she could retire. Over the past few years, she'd been able to save a tidy sum, but it wasn't quite enough. Not to make her feel completely secure, absolutely certain that she'd be set for life. With the Fabergé egg in her possession, security would be hers at last. The cottage she dreamed about would be hers, and she'd gladly leave this chancy profession to others who were more daring than she.

Jackie placed her hands on her hips and lifted her head to the gallery that encircled the second floor. Washed in moonlight, the square two-story plantation house was colorless, hushed, and imposing. White-pillared and classic in design, it was a Southern castle, a monument to a time and a lifestyle long gone. There was elegance here, and majesty . . . and money.

There wasn't enough light for her to see very far beyond the gallery railing, and that concerned her for a moment. For all she knew a sleepless resident of this house could be standing in the shadows above, waiting and watching. A smile crossed her face. It was going on three in the morning, so that wasn't likely.

Taking a deep and silent breath she approached one of the narrow columns that girdled the house. This burglary was turning out to be a bit more work than she'd intended, but the prize that awaited her was worth any effort. This was definitely her last job, she reminded herself as she clasped the white column and hoisted herself up. She'd said that before, once when she'd been almost caught, and again a few months later when she'd decided she had enough money to get by on if she were very frugal. In the end, she'd always decided that the time wasn't right for retirement, but tonight she meant it. Truly.

The black trousers had definitely been a good choice for these early morning hours; she never would have been able to work her way to the second-story gallery in a cumbersome skirt. Her progress up the column was slow but steady, and when her arms and legs got tired she thought of the Fabergé egg. It was gold, she'd heard, bedecked with more gems than even the grandest lady would wear. Pearls, rubies, sapphires. Diamonds. Ah, she absolutely adored diamonds.

A peek onto the gallery through the slats of the railing confirmed her suspicion that no one was about at this hour. All was as quiet and gray and peaceful here as it was below. A dismal thought occurred to her, but she brushed it aside. Surely Donovan was not so paranoid as to lock the French doors on the second floor?

Once she'd hauled herself onto the gallery she sat with her back against the column she'd climbed, catching her breath and ordering her heart to be still. It only took her a moment to restore her breathing, but her heart was slow in obeying. As she sat there, she thought about this Rory Donovan and his fine house and his

Fabergé egg. Sally said he'd won it in a poker game in Nashville, taking the prize with four aces from a Russian prince or duke or some such who'd thought—wrongly—that he had an unbeatable hand.

Some people had all the luck. It wasn't the first time Jackie had made that observation, and it likely wouldn't be the last. From her position against the column, she looked down the wide gallery. Rory Donovan was one lucky son of a gun. He had this plantation—Cloudmont, it was called—more than his share of money, and according to Sally he'd been blessed with the gift of beauty as well. He wouldn't miss the egg. At least not for long.

Jackie rose to her feet silently and made her way to the nearest opened French door. She peered beyond the lace curtains that danced softly in the breeze to see a small boy huddled under his covers, a shock of hair unruly against his pillow and a tattered blanket clutched in his little fingers. She smiled, but only for a moment.

She knew of entire families who lived in houses smaller than this room. The bed was wide and had a tall, ornately carved headboard, and the matching wardrobe would have held everything Jackie owned, and more. There was a fine rocking chair, a large rug, and a desk for rocks and books and other boyish treasures.

This was one lucky kid, Jackie reasoned as she made her way along the gallery to the next room.

The French doors to this chamber were closed tight, and a quick look through a pane of glass showed her that the room was deserted. Sheets were draped over its contents, and in the moonlight the covered furniture looked vaguely like a family of ghosts. She shivered once and walked on, rounding the corner. Taking small, silent steps she walked to the very end of the gallery and stopped just short of the next door. This was the place; she knew it. Even though she hadn't yet glimpsed into the room, her heart told her this was the place. A treasure beyond her wildest dreams awaited within.

She peeked around the door to see a scene similar to the one in the first room. All was gray and dark, but her eyes had adjusted to the night and she could see well enough what lay before her. A man slept in a massive four-poster bed, a quilt pulled well above his waist, his hair tousled on the white pillow upon which his head rested.

Sally had been right; from what Jackie could see by the pale moonlight, he appeared to be very handsome. Physically, Rory Donovan had been blessed with regular, strong features and thick hair that curled just slightly. His chin was square, his jawbone prominent, and his shoulders wide.

Without a twinge of conscience, she stepped around the open French door and into the room. Once she was inside she stood very still.

15

Some people were such light sleepers that the very presence of another person in their room awakened them, and before she went too far she had to make sure that Rory Donovan was not so sensitive.

She stepped into a shadow and watched the figure on the bed for movement, listened for a change in breathing before she moved on. It simply wouldn't do for Donovan to wake and catch her. Even asleep he looked far too strong, and far too fast.

When it became clear he hadn't been disturbed, she turned her attention to the rest of the fine bedchamber. It was a large room, airy and elegantly furnished and free of clutter. There was a dresser and a tall wardrobe fashioned from the same dark wood as the four-poster bed, a massive wing chair upholstered in a dark fabric, and against the far wall there was a glassed display case sitting on a low table. That case held the object of her desire.

She crossed the room silently, her eyes on the egg that had brought her here. Even by the scant moonlight that made its way through the French doors on two walls, it was magnificent, finer than she'd imagined, more exquisite than she'd dreamed. Gems formed an elaborate pattern on the golden egg, twisting and twirling in an almost exotic design. How could she not smile?

Here was her retirement, her way out of this crazy life, a chance to begin again.

A harmonica had been carelessly left on the display case. She glanced back at the man on the bed. Did he play? She didn't know him, except from Sally's descriptions, but for some reason she couldn't imagine him playing such a thing. Sally said he was a charmer, a carefree man of the world, but in sleep he seemed much too serious and imposing for a frivolous endeavor such as playing a harmonica.

She lifted the instrument with every intention of putting it aside so that she could lift the glass cover, when something struck her as being odd. She held the harmonica up so that it caught more moonlight. Gold. The man had a gold mouth harp! Without another thought she slipped the harmonica into the front pocket of her trousers.

Her hands were on the case's glass cover when she heard Donovan stir. Just to be safe, she dropped down and placed her back to the wall, pulling herself into a tight ball and making herself as small as possible. She was in the shadow of the wing chair, well hidden. If Donovan should arise from his bed he wouldn't see her. *He wouldn't.* She closed her eyes and said a little prayer. Who was the patron saint of thieves? Dammit, Mina would know.

Her prayer went unanswered. Rory Donovan sat up slowly, running lethargic fingers through his short hair, rolling one shoulder as if he had a crick in it. That's it, she thought. Work out those kinks, lie down, and go back to sleep.

17

Her silent instructions were no more effective than her prayer had been. Donovan sat there for a minute, and then he tossed his quilt aside and sat up, throwing his legs over the side of the bed and rolling his shoulder once more as if it pained him. He rotated that bare shoulder yet again, sending the muscles on his back into an undulating dance that fascinated Jackie.

All better, now, she thought, breaking out of her spell. Lie down and return to dreamland, Mr. Rory Donovan.

He was an uncooperative mark, deciding instead to stand. Mercy! The man slept as God had made him, bare from one end to the other. In silent admiration she followed the process as he unfolded himself from the side of the bed, stretching to an incredible height. Good heavens, the man was probably six and a half feet tall! Sally had said he was tall, but Jackie had assumed he might reach near six feet. Since Mr. Clark, Sally's gregarious father, stood no more than five feet six inches, and Sally was an inch shorter than Jackie at an even five feet, Jackie had assumed that anyone more than five-eight would qualify as "tall." But this was incredible; Rory Donovan was a veritable giant! Heaven help her, she couldn't allow this man to catch her.

He stepped to the door where his long and completely naked body was washed by moonlight. This was a disaster of major proportions. Not only was he tall, he was well built. There

wasn't an ounce of fat on the man. His legs
were long and lean and hard, regrettably tailor-
made for chasing clumsy or unlucky thieves,
and as he lifted a hand to his hair again she
saw that it was large as well. Large and powerful. His back was to her, thank God for small
favors, but she had already seen more than
enough. Oh, she could not get caught here.

A sudden and gentle breeze washed over that
naked body, ruffling the fine hair on his head
and the curtains that framed him.

Jackie closed her eyes and tried her best to
remember who the patron saint of thieves was.

He should be sleeping. It had been a long day,
a hard day, and he hadn't had a good night's
sleep in more than a week. Rory looked out
over the well-tended lawn beyond the gallery
railing, a sight that usually had the power to
soothe him. This was home, after all, his land,
his legacy, the place that harbored all his
memories.

Cloudmont was a well-run community, and a
walk around the gallery, when he chose to sur-
vey his property in that manner, would show
him a stable and barn and carriage house, all
of it enclosed by a white Tennessee fence. The
kitchen beyond the house and the covered
brick walkway that connected the two build-
ings were always silent at night. On that brick
porch pies cooled and jams were put into jars,
and Rory drank his coffee there on many afternoons. Farther beyond were the smokehouse,

the woodhouse, and Nell's raised cottage. The flower garden thrived, as did the vegetable garden. All was well here.

Tonight, Rory remained at the doorway rather than walking about the gallery and admiring it all. The sight wouldn't comfort him, not the way it once had. Yes, all was well here, but changes were coming. They were inevitable, but he wasn't ready. Just recently he'd decided to accept the fact that he might never be ready.

Kevin needed a woman's soft touch. The boy was six years old, and since Margaret had died long before his first birthday, he had no memory of her. No memory of the woman who had given birth to him, nursed him, cuddled him, sang lullabies when he cried. The chills came, as they always did when he allowed himself to think of his late wife, and he ran an impatient hand over the offending goose bumps on his arm.

He should marry again, for Kevin's sake. He should do his duty and provide the boy with a family that consisted of more than an inattentive father figure and a crotchety housekeeper. Nell did her best, but she had to run the household and she was getting on in years; he couldn't expect her to take charge of Kevin full time as well.

Nannies had come and gone in the past five years. Just in the past two years one had married and moved to Virginia, another had gone to live with her ill sister, and three had simply quit, declaring their charge was beyond redemption. Kevin *was* a handful, he'd admit that much.

Marriage was the most logical solution, but Rory didn't want to get married, not ever again. In the past few years, he'd worked diligently to make sure that those who had daughters of a marriageable age knew good and well that Rory Donovan was not looking for a *wife*.

Something odd tickled his nose, a hint of a fragrance that didn't belong. He closed his eyes and took a deep breath in an effort to identify the scent. It was pleasant, and made him think of beautiful women and soft hands. The tension left his body, and he let his mind wander free. For a few precious seconds he didn't think of Kevin or marriage or of anything but the faint odor that tickled his nose.

"Fiddle," he whispered to no one in particular. "I smell lavender."

Nicholas of Myra! It came to her in a flash, the memory of Mina saying a special prayer to the patron saint of thieves. Jackie said her own quick prayer as Donovan turned to face her. Before she thought to close her eyes she got enough of an eyeful to know that he was as impressive downstairs as he was up. She never panicked, but there was an unexpected flutter of fear in her heart.

She kept her eyes closed and held her breath in the childish hope that perhaps if she couldn't see him, he wouldn't see her. Soft footsteps approached, and she opened her eyes just enough to see the legs and feet coming toward her. The sight did nothing to still her heartbeat. Oh, she had a feeling she couldn't run fast enough. . . .

Donovan didn't discover her, though he lowered himself into the wing chair that shadowed her. Blast! If she breathed too hard he would hear her!

He stretched out his long legs, leaned back in the chair, and took a deep breath. "Lavender," he whispered sleepily.

Jackie cursed silently in the shadow of the wing chair, barely breathing, making very certain that she didn't so much as move a muscle. Rory Donovan, bare as the day he was born, sat not much more than a foot away. A lift of her eyes gave her a view of his forearm so clear that she could see the tiny hairs there. Straight ahead, his long legs and big feet stretched out forever and a day, long legs and big feet she would practically have to step over to make her way out of this room if he didn't get back to bed soon.

Nicholas of Myra apparently wasn't a very attentive or effective saint. It soon became obvious that Donovan had no intention of going back to bed. His breathing gradually became deeper and more even, the hand that hung over the arm of the chair relaxed, and once again he whispered "lavender" before he began to snore.

She'd dabbed a very small bit of lavender-scented water behind her ears hours ago. Another gift Rory Donovan apparently possessed, in addition to his good luck and beauty, was an uncanny nose. Fortunately for her he didn't quite trust what his senses were telling him.

Her breathing was slow and silent, and she remained motionless in her hiding place until every muscle screamed at her to move, and an inconvenient itch appeared in the center of her back. She ignored the rebellion of her body and tried to think of something to take her mind off her discomfort; the ocean, a bawdy song Mina was fond of, the magnificent prize that awaited so near that if diamonds had a scent she'd be able to smell them the way Donovan had smelled her own lavender water. That was the thought that finally soothed her. The smell of diamonds.

When she was certain Donovan slept soundly, she stood slowly. Her muscles were tight and cramped from sitting for so long, but she ignored the pain. She could only spare a glance for the egg that had called her here. There was no time, and opening the case while Donovan slept this close by would be too fool-hardy for her to attempt. Besides, the house-keeper was usually up and about well before five, which didn't leave Jackie much time to make her escape.

Jackie stepped very cautiously forward, spar-ing only a brief sideways glance for the man in the chair. Donovan slept soundly. Big and hard though she knew him to be, he looked very vul-nerable at the moment, sleeping in his chair and dreaming of lavender. She very pointedly looked at his face and ignored the area between his legs. Still, since she'd never had the opportunity to study a man quite this closely and safely, it seemed a sin to waste the opportunity.

Her perusal of the manly instrument God had given Rory Donovan was purely academic, she told herself as she glanced down. She stared for a moment, wishing the shadows didn't fall just so. Well, it certainly didn't *look* threatening in its current state.

Her curiosity satisfied, she looked at his face again; to make sure he wasn't waking up, she told herself. His peaceful expression hadn't changed. If she'd had more time she might have been compelled to watch him a while longer.

Holding her breath, she stepped past Donovan's legs, lifting her own feet much higher than necessary to make absolutely certain she didn't brush against him. She needn't have worried; he didn't stir.

At the French doors she paused and looked over her shoulder. Her eyes fell longingly on the Fabergé egg, and for an instant she wanted it so badly she was certain she really could smell the diamonds. The odor was crisp and clean and tantalizing, and it tempted her mightily. She sighed. Not tonight.

She spared another glance for Donovan and a smile crept across her unrepentant face.

"I'll be back," she whispered softly. Silently, clad in black that allowed her to blend into the shadows, she stepped onto the gallery. "I'll be back."

Chapter Two

Nell had breakfast waiting when he stepped into the dining room. Ham and eggs and grits steaming, biscuits tender and coffee strong, it was just what he needed to get the day started after yet another long night.

This house would have fallen down around his ears long ago if not for Nell. She'd joined the household after marrying Will Logan, Cloudmont's now long-deceased foreman, nearly thirty years ago. There had been Logans at Cloudmont almost as long as there had been Donovans.

Rory couldn't understand why Nell stayed on, even now. She had sons in Texas and in Mississippi who were doing well, and she could've retired years ago to be with them and their families. He never asked her why she didn't leave. Without this little bit of a woman he would have been lost long ago.

Rory went through his first cup of coffee quickly, as usual, and Nell was there to refill his cup. She frowned down at the dark stream of coffee and muttered something unintelligible under her breath. She was, like many of this region, of Scots-Irish and Indian descent, openly claiming the Cherokee blood that was evident in her high cheekbones and dark hair, which had only recently become shot with silver. Her temper, however, was pure Irish. He really should ask her what was troubling her this morning, but found he didn't have the energy.

But there was one question he did want answered. "You hired on a new girl last week, didn't you?"

Apparently, it was the wrong question to ask. "Why, yes I did." She placed the coffeepot forcefully on the table.

There was a constant stream of helpers in and out of Nell's kitchen, young girls who came early in the morning, six days a week, and left as soon as supper was prepared. The good ones usually left too soon, to get married; the bad ones quit, scared off by Nell's demanding ways.

"And a fat lot of trouble that Corinne is turning out to be," Nell continued. "Here I am needin' just a little help in the kitchen, and what do I get? Some whiny little girl who cries when she cuts her finger peelin' taters, and cries when her no-count fella decides to go to

Tuscumbia for a few days, and cries when I tell her she's goin' to burn the biscuits if she don't get them out of the oven. I tell you, she's more trouble than she's worth."

Before he advised Nell to fire the girl and hire someone else to help her out, he asked, "Does she by any chance wear a lavender scent?"

Nell looked at him like he had lost his mind. Hell, maybe he had. "Not that I recall," she said curtly.

She waited for him to explain, raising one eyebrow when he didn't speak immediately. "I smelled a hint of lavender in my room last night, and I thought maybe you'd had one of the girls cleaning in there—"

"Mister Rory," she interrupted with a tone that held no room for argument. "I am the only one who touches your bedroom. Lordy, with all them fancy geegaws you got I wouldn't dare send Eleanor or Corinne up there to clean. Not that I don't think they're honest girls, mind you, but that Eleanor is downright clumsy, and so far I can't say that Corinne's any better." She leaned a little closer and lowered her voice. "And I can assure you I haven't taken to wearin' lavender as I make the beds and dust the furniture." After a short pause she laughed heartily.

Rory turned his attention to the food on his plate. "I probably dreamed it," he mumbled. It hadn't seemed like a dream at the time, but right now it was a memory as vague as the dream that had followed as he'd slept in the chair. He waggled a fork in Nell's direction. "Fire that new girl if she's not working out."

"Good heavens, I can't do that," Nell said, clearly horrified at the very suggestion.

He hated to ask, but he knew it was required. "Why not?"

"Corinne's a sweet thing," Nell said as she made her way toward the door to the brick porch and the kitchen beyond. "Why, if I don't teach her how to make biscuits and how to keep that fella of hers in line, who will?"

He had a few minutes of quiet before Kevin came bursting into the dining room, his bright red hair standing out at all angles even though a small tamed section indicated that he'd tried to comb it. His shirttail was tucked in crooked, and his shoes were untied. Rory glanced at the boy and then returned to the business at hand: eating.

"Mornin', Pa," Kevin said as he took his place three chairs down.

"Mornin'," Rory didn't even lift his head. He couldn't help feeling angry, still, over the incident that had led to the departure of the last governess; something to do with a collection of worms in a desk drawer.

Nell appeared a moment later with Kevin's breakfast and a glass of milk. "Good mornin', Mister Kevin," she said with a broader smile than she'd had for Rory. "Why, just look at that hair. What a fine figure of a man you are this mornin'."

Kevin returned her greeting and the smile,

revealing a gap where his front teeth had been just a few weeks ago. Then he dug into his breakfast, shoveling it in as if he hadn't eaten for days. Nell smiled on, taking these terrible table manners as the greatest compliment.

"Pa?" Kevin asked almost shyly between bites of scrambled egg. "Can we go fishing today?"

Rory shook his head. "I have too much work to do." His voice was unnecessarily sharp, and he realized it as the words left his mouth. But it was too late to take them back. "You can fish at the pond."

"The good fishing's down by the river, and I can't go to the river by myself."

"No, you can't," Rory confirmed.

Ever hopeful, Kevin tried again. "Maybe we can go tomorrow."

Rory shook his head again. "This is going to be a busy week for me."

Nell made a short, derisive snorting noise from her position by the door. Rory didn't respond, but he did give her a sharp glance. Two against one, wasn't that how it always was? They didn't realize how hard he worked to provide for them, to make this place grow, to make the fortune his father had only dreamed of. He didn't have time for fishing.

True, the investments he'd made in coal and iron took little of his time, but he was establishing Cloudmont as a first-rate livestock farm, and that took dedication and hard work. What land wasn't sharecropped out grew cotton, but he wasn't active in the farming. There were hired hands for that work, and an indispensable foreman who had come in after Will Logan's death more than ten years ago. These days Rory's time and passion were reserved for his thoroughbreds.

Rory knew Nell didn't blame Kevin for the antics that drove away caretaker after caretaker; she'd deemed them all worthless from the beginning. She looked at Rory now as if he should ignore the mounting pile of correspondence on his desk and forget about the new stallion to go fishing with an irrepressible six-year-old.

"I won't be here for supper," he said while he had her undivided attention. "The Clarks have invited me for this evening."

"Too bad," she said, making it clear by the tone of her voice that he wouldn't be missed. "I'm making fried chicken, and biscuits and gravy, and snap peas, and there will be chocolate cake for dessert."

All his favorites, and she knew it too well. Kevin voiced his approval, and seemed to forget that Rory didn't have time to go fishing with him.

Jackie looked critically over her reflection in the cheval glass. The white dress and simple hairstyle helped, but she wouldn't be able to pass herself off as seventeen for much longer. She might not know where or exactly when she'd been born, but she did know that her seventeenth year had come and gone quite a while back.

The Clarks had been a gift, surely. Anyone could have stumbled upon her at that resort and offered assistance, but the meeting with the Clarks had been serendipitous. She would have been satisfied with a place to stay for a few days and perhaps a small collection of jewels. That was the usual outcome. But she'd been at the Clarks' home for almost a month now, sleeping in this elegant chamber that was plush with red velvet and hints of gold, living a life of total leisure and loving it.

When they had mentioned Rory Donovan's luck at the tables and his fabulous prize, she knew it was more than chance that had made her choose that resort and that moment to pull her scam. It was destiny, fate, divine intervention. . . . At that thought she glanced quickly upward, promising silently that she wouldn't forget Nicholas of Myra again.

She wouldn't try for the Fabergé egg tonight, tempting as it was. After a long night where she got no more than three hours' sleep she was tired, and besides, it seemed bad form to try two nights in a row. She'd wait another day or two, and then she'd try again.

A dab of lavender water behind her ears, that was all she needed to complete her preparations for the evening. Sally had been twittering and giggling all afternoon about some mysterious dinner guests, so Jackie had gone all out, styling her hair in a fashionable psyche knot and choosing the white China silk gown with many ruffled petticoats, young-looking puffy sleeves, and yet another ruffle at the low neck. It was a good thing she didn't have much of a bosom, since what little she had practically spilled over the neckline.

She met Sally at the top of the winding staircase that led to the ground floor. Sally had gone all out herself, with her pale pink satin gown showing off her hourglass figure and a sprig of silk flowers in her blond curls.

Jackie took a deep breath, preparing herself. "You look simply marvelous." She'd been affecting the English accent for so long now it was almost second nature. "Whoever these mystery guests are, they must be quite special."

"Oh, they are." Sally took both of Jackie's hands in her own and squeezed as she giggled once again.

"I am simply dying of curiosity." *I couldn't care less.* "You must tell me." *Let's get this over with.*

Sally slipped her arm through Jackie's and they descended the spiral stairway. "You have become such a special friend to me."

"And you to me," Jackie answered. Why was her heart suddenly in her throat? She had no time or patience for sentiment, but she couldn't deny that perhaps there was a touch of truth in that statement. Sally *was* her friend . . . for now.

"Wouldn't it be wonderful if you could stay here forever?"

Jackie knew she wouldn't stay anywhere forever . . . at least not until she had enough money saved to buy her own cottage. The thought of that nonexistent cottage soothed her in troubled times. Lately she'd been thinking that it should be somewhere near the water, perhaps.

"I can see you're giving the notion serious thought," Sally said softly. "It would be wonderful, wouldn't it?"

"Yes," Jackie said just as softly.

"If you married someone from this area, why, we could be best friends forever. We could give parties together, barbecues and picnics and grand balls. We could visit on Sunday afternoons and raise our babies together. . . ."

"Babies?" Jackie asked, unable to hide the horror in her voice. She quickly recovered. "Goodness me, Sally dear, I haven't even a prospect of marriage. Speaking of babies seems to be quite a leap."

At the foot of the stairs, Sally turned a coy smile to her new friend. "Papa has invited several eligible bachelors for dinner. Surely there will be one—"

"Sally Clark!" Jackie had to take a deep breath. "Oh, you didn't." She raised a demure hand to her chest. "You know how shy I am in the company of strangers."

"You'll be fine," Sally said with a reassuring pat to Jackie's arm.

Jackie couldn't tell Sally that she had no intention of marrying anyone—ever. She wouldn't bow to any man's whims or bear any man's children, she could never place her trust or her body in any man's hands. She was her own woman, and always would be.

Still, there was nothing wrong with playing along for the evening. This might even be fun, if she wasn't so tired. Right now she'd much prefer an evening in bed with a cup of tea and a mountain of pillows to flirting and deceitfulness. As it was, she had no choice but to endure.

"Mama invited three gentlemen to have supper with us, using a couple of old excuses about talking politics with Papa and talking cotton and the like. Now, you keep your hands off Telford Wilkins. He's mine," Sally said with a smile. "He doesn't know it yet," she added, "but he is spoken for." She flashed a grin that was all teeth and dimples. Poor Telford didn't stand a chance.

"Noted," Jackie said with businesslike precision.

"Clint Marsh is a nice young man," Sally added in a soft voice as they headed for the parlor. "His place is small, but he has cattle and crops and a very nice house. Papa thinks he'll go far. He's very handsome, too, with dark hair and eyes and an aristocratic nose, I noticed when I saw him last. Since he's twenty-three he's just the right age for you, don't you think?"

"Perfect," Jackie said without enthusiasm as

the opened parlor door loomed closer. Cut flowers filled the entryway, arranged artfully in vases that rested on pedestals and polished tables. Portraits of the Clarks' ancestors lined the hallway. She'd been given a name and history to go with each and every solemn face, but right now she could remember nothing of these long-dead men and women.

Voices came from within, hinting that at least one of their guests had already arrived. She was becoming accustomed to these Southerners' distinctive voices, the drawn out vowels and the honey-sweetness, the words that rolled off their tongues so easily. She listened carefully, since the ability to pull off an accent like that might come in handy someday.

Except that she was going to retire once she had that Fabergé egg. She had to keep reminding herself of that fact. "So we have Telford, who is spoken for, and Clint, who is perfect for me. Who is the third lucky bachelor?"

"I don't think he's right for you," Sally whispered. "He's too old, and he's a wicked ladies' man with a charming smile and a wandering eye. His father was a scalawag, and of course blood can't be denied, no matter how much money a man might have."

Blood can't be denied. Jackie's stomach flipped over unpleasantly. "Of course."

"Still," Sally sighed, "Mama seems to think him redeemable, even though he has a scandalous reputation with the ladies." She sighed again, a long-practiced exhale. "He is dreadfully handsome, but I want my husband to have eyes for me and me alone, and of course you deserve the same commitment."

Jackie was having fun with this, now. She raised a hand into the air where it danced airily for a moment. "Then we shall dismiss this third bachelor without another thought. A scalawag, you say?" She made a lazy chopping motion with her hand. "Off with his head."

Sally giggled, and Jackie had to laugh herself. Dammit, she liked this little girl. Sally was eighteen years old, beautiful, rich, sheltered: everything Jackie had learned to hate. But she was so full of life and joy it was hard not to like her.

"I guess we'll have to turn all our attentions to Telford and Clint and leave Rory to Papa."

They had reached the parlor door, where Jackie stopped abruptly. "Rory?" she said softly. "Not the Rory Donovan you've told me so much about."

"The same."

Damnation! How was she supposed to look the man in the face and not laugh? Perhaps she should blush instead. Last time she'd seen him she'd been carefully studying everything God had given him.

Ah well, she'd never been given much to blushing, and she did wonder what he'd look like clothed.

An eager Telford Wilkins was in the parlor talking to Mr. Clark, and Sally led Jackie to them with a bright smile and a muted giggle.

Stepping into this finely furnished and very formal parlor gave the scene an air of fantasy for Jackie. Here, among deep green velvet and finely carved wood, among porcelain figurines and cut flowers and brightly lit lamps that chased away the night, she became someone else; a girl who didn't exist. She mouthed low, shy responses to Wilkins as she was introduced, and then she gladly stepped aside, leaving Sally to work her charms on her intended beau.

Jackie didn't have long to wait before Donovan arrived. She stood at the far side of the room, before a forest green velvet fainting couch, and studied the man as he walked into the room. His clothing, unimaginative and austere, fit his form very well. She'd known he was tall, but standing next to Mr. Clark and a pasty Telford Wilkins, he was a titan. If she had a lick of sense she would be terrified, but when his eyes lit on her she gave him a coy smile that would have made Sally proud, had she been able to wrest her eyes from Wilkins.

No wonder Sally preferred Wilkins. Telford blushed when she spoke, dropped his eyes when she batted her lashes, and downright shook when she smiled. She'd have that poor boy wrapped around her finger before he knew what had hit him. Jackie predicted a long and happy marriage for the two of them.

Rory Donovan, on the other hand, must have been made of stone. The only aspect of his appearance that might be called soft was his warm, slightly curly dark blond hair. The lines of his face were sharp and harsh, and his eyes were narrowed in a calculating manner. His body was tall and broad and solidly built; she knew too well just how solidly built. There was an interesting air of control about Donovan, as if every movement, perhaps even every breath, was planned.

He showed not the slightest interest in her sweetest smile, and he hadn't so much as glanced at her cleavage. Ah, hard as he appeared to be she knew he wasn't made completely of stone, didn't she?

Mr. Clark insisted on dragging the poor man across the room to make the proper introductions. While Donovan made the journey willingly, it was clear he had no interest in Sally's little friend.

"Rory Donovan, this is our houseguest Miss Jacqueline Beresford," Mr. Clark said formally.

Towering over her, Rory mouthed the proper greetings and bowed over her hand in a gentlemanly fashion. Mr. Clark moved away as their last guest arrived, leaving the newly introduced couple alone.

Donovan was bored. Jackie could see it in his restless eyes, in the firm set of his mouth as he did his gentlemanly duty and entertained her with small talk. He had not yet become annoyed, but she could tell he'd much prefer to be having a manly discussion with Mr. Clark, or even with Telford Wilkins. . . .

Ever the gentleman, he welcomed her to Alabama and then asked her what she thought of their weather. She was making a statement on the humidity when a frown marred the perfect example of indifference on his face. He leaned slightly forward, fixing honey-brown eyes on her face.

"You wear lavender," he said softly.

They'd seated him next to the Englishwoman, and Rory smelled a rat. It was a sweet-smelling, lavender-scented rat, but vermin just the same.

Mavis Clark was much too jovial this evening, and the dinner conversation revolved not around crops and stables, as Rory had expected, but around the two young girls. It was a trap, a blatant and hostile husband trap, and Sally and her friend Jacqueline were the bait.

Sally sat between her mother and Telford Wilkins, and Miss Beresford sat between Clint Marsh and Rory. She was a little bit of a thing, and when he glanced to the side he could see right down the front of her frilly dress. He did his best not to glance that way any more often than was necessary. Fortunately, she directed her verbal charms to an attentive Marsh.

If only she didn't smell like lavender, he could have disregarded her. The faint scent teased him, and he kept turning his head her way even though he had every intention of ignoring her and this ridiculous and obvious trap. Mavis should have known better. Good God, even if he was seriously considering another marriage it wouldn't be to a mush-brained child who looked at the world in a wide-eyed and innocent way.

If he'd made a trip to Miss Ellington's house in Huntsville or to see Vera in Birmingham within the past two months perhaps he would-n't be feeling so restless in Miss Beresford's presence. Yes, he was definitely overdue for a visit. Miss Ellington's girls provided comfort for a price, and they never asked him to talk about himself, to be charming, to kiss them. Vera was always glad to see him arrive and just as glad to see him go in a day or two.

He put Vera and Miss Ellington's house from his mind, and looked at the girl beside him. Her hair was so dark it was almost black, but it was much too warm to be true black. It was the deepest sable brown, thick and silky and well behaved—unlike her friend Sally's blond curls. Her eyes were the oddest shade of blue, icy pale in the center and rimmed with a blue like sapphires. They were most extraordinary.

His eyes fell to her exposed bosom. She did-n't have much to offer there, but what she did possess was pale and soft and shapely. He had the urge to reach over and run his fingers against that flesh just above a girlish ruffle, to see if it felt as silky as it looked. The very thought was enough to make his mouth go dry, and his stomach knotted in a not altogether unpleasant fashion. Yes, it had definitely been too long if he was having salacious thoughts about a seventeen-year-old who was barely a woman.

Clint asked a question that silenced the Clarks and the lovely Englishwoman. "You met the Clarks at a seaside resort in South Carolina. Were you a guest there yourself?" It was an innocent enough question, but Sally's smile faded and Walter Clark stared at his plate. It was Mavis who nodded to their guest and asked, "Would you like to tell the story?"

The girl at his side looked demurely into her lap and grasped her small hands there. After a moment she lifted her head. "I don't mind sharing my experience, but I think I'd prefer that Sally tell it, if she doesn't mind. I do tend to get," she fanned herself with long, pale fingers, "a little overly emotional."

Rory managed to contain a *harumph*. Miss Jacqueline Beresford didn't know Sally Clark at all if she thought the girl would mind telling any story.

"It was on our fifth day there," Sally began dramatically, leaning forward and lowering her voice as if there were someone lurking around a corner, listening. "We were returning to the hotel when we saw Miss Beresford. She was sitting on her trunk with her head in her hands and she was sobbing most horribly."

At this, Miss Beresford dropped her head, and Rory was gifted with a view of the back of her long neck and a few strands of escaping dark hair.

"I couldn't just pass by," Sally said, a touch of horror at such a prospect clear in her voice. "We stopped to see if we could be of any assistance, and she told us she'd been cruelly abandoned by the lady she was companion to, and all because the lady's husband had made an unwelcome and improper advance." Sally's voice displayed the proper amount of indignity. "They had given her a sum of money to make her own way back to England, but a pickpocket had robbed her right there in front of the hotel, leaving her destitute and alone and so very far from home. Can you imagine?"

Marsh and Wilkins made appropriate exclamations of outrage. Still, Miss Beresford didn't lift her head.

"We very quickly became good friends," Sally said, and a sweet smile signaled the end to the traumatic part of the story. "There was plenty of room in our suite, so she stayed with us for a few days. We found that we had so much in common, it was quite the miracle. Of course we insisted that she come home with us when our stay at the resort was over."

"Of course," Rory muttered, put off by the thought of picking up a stray while on vacation.

The stray in question lifted her head, then, and turned those remarkable blue eyes on him. They were filled with tears that did not fall; they sparkled like blue diamonds. Young or not, she was everything feminine, delicate, alluring. Well, perhaps in the right circumstances one might pick up . . .

"I wish she could stay here forever," Sally said as she finished her story.

With those words, the truth hit Rory right between the eyes. He'd known this was a trap, and that both the young ladies were of a marriageable age and Mavis had matrimony on her mind for her girls. But there was more.

Yes, that was the point of this dinner; a husband was to be found quickly, very quickly, for the young Englishwoman so she could stay close to her new friend. A single tear trickled down Miss Beresford's perfect and pale cheek before she turned away.

"The Clarks have been very kind to me," she said in that peculiar accent of hers. "While it's most generous of Sally to wish that I could stay indefinitely, I know I cannot. England is my home," she said wistfully as she wiped away that tear.

"Since we're such special friends, she lets me call her Jackie," Sally continued. "Isn't that a wonderful nickname?"

"It is," Marsh agreed quickly. "Might I have the honor of calling you Jackie?" Rory tried very hard to contain a disbelieving snort. Clint was falling so fast and so hard that Miss Beresford would probably have a ring on her finger before the month was out.

"Of course," she said, recovering from the emotional remembrance of her abandonment rather quickly.

This was all so cozy and sweet, it was more than Rory could stand. "I once knew a horse trader named Jackie," he said as he speared a piece of overcooked beef. "He had a bad leg and one eye that was given to wandering this way and that." He waggled his fork back and forth as an example, before taking it to his mouth to bite into the meat, which was dry and leathery. Maybe, if he was lucky, Nell would put aside a plate of fried chicken and a slice of chocolate cake for him.

He looked up to see that all eyes were on him. Sally and her mother had been offended, and Mr. Clark looked fatherly and stern. Telford and Clint were shocked at his bad manners.

Miss Beresford's eyes were fixed on him, as well, but she didn't seem to be the least bit offended. If he didn't know better he'd think she was holding back a smile. In that instant, as she leaned slightly toward him and he caught another whiff of lavender, he was certain that there was more to Jackie Beresford than met the eye.

She had something to say. Her mouth twitched with it, her eyes sparkled with intelligence and humor. But the moment passed and she leaned back and away from him, and in another moment she turned her attention to Clint Marsh and the conversation resumed.

Rory struck up a discussion with Walter Clark, ignoring Mavis's censuring stare. Why was it that every happily married woman fancied herself a matchmaker? He'd tried marriage once before, and it had ended without warning in death and incredible pain; Margaret's death, another death he refused to think about, his own pain.

He pretended to be contented most of the time, and if he was occasionally a bit too sociable with the ladies, or exaggerated his reputation to a man who he knew couldn't keep a secret, well, it served his purpose. He wasn't interested in getting married again, and he wasn't about to play dangerous games with a husband-hunting child, no matter how fetching she might be.

To his right, Miss Beresford laughed lightly at something amusing Clint Marsh had said, and the silvery sound sent an unexpected tingle up his spine. Rory ignored it and her, and he started making plans to be out of town on business when the nuptials were celebrated.

Chapter Three

Jackie adjusted the dark leather cap that covered her hair as she gazed up at the gallery of the fine Donovan home. All was dark and quiet, as it had been on her last visit. Tonight she was again a part of the dark and the quiet, in her black clothing and soft leather shoes.

In the three days since the dinner party, Clint Marsh had called on her three times. He was beginning to look at her with an altogether much too serious glint in his dark gray eyes, and that meant there wasn't much more time to waste. Marsh was becoming bothersome, more ingratiating and more irritating with each visit, and Jackie was ready to move on. As soon as she had the Fabergé egg she could pack her bags and bid the Clarks farewell. Usually she slipped away in the night with her loot, grateful to be making her escape, but she couldn't imagine leaving without saying good-bye to Sally.

She was growing much too soft for this game, Jackie thought as she climbed toward the gallery, her black-clad legs wrapped tightly around the column, her arms hanging on and inching her upward. Friends were not for someone like her; bonds were impossible, ties unthinkable.

She pulled herself over the railing, and as before, she had to sit for a moment to catch her breath. The night was warm, the scents on the air that surrounded her sweet and rich. How had Rory Donovan smelled a little bit of lavender water over the heady perfume of a multitude of spring flowers that filled the night? Just her luck, she thought as she rose to her feet.

Donovan slept as he had on her last visit. She could only hope that he slept more soundly on this night. She watched his slumbering figure for a long moment before stepping into the room, waiting for any sign that his rest was less than deep and complete. He didn't move at all.

The Fabergé egg awaited her, beneath its glass case, and she smiled as she approached. It was more beautiful even than the first time she'd seen it, so beautiful her heart caught in her throat. Oh, she couldn't wait to see it by the light of day, to study each and every gem as it sparkled in the sunlight.

She wouldn't keep the egg for long, of course. She'd sell it for a bloody fortune and retire to her cottage. In the past she'd always thought of her retirement near a lake, but she was thinking more and more of the ocean, lately. She could see it, a cottage where she could open the windows and hear the sea at night, and walk on the sand by day when it suited her. She envisioned a small home, just right for one, with a garden, perhaps, and lace curtains in all the windows. Her cottage, her life, would be clean and colorful and peaceful.

Her hands rested on either side of the glass case that covered the egg, gripping steadily as she lifted. Nothing happened, so she tried again. The glass was immobile. She lowered her face closer to the foundation of the case only to discover a small lock. Damn that distrusting Donovan!

She stared at the egg for a moment longer. In her mind it was already hers, though she was no closer to having it than when she'd first heard of Rory Donovan and his gambler's luck. A single finger touched the glass, tracing the image of the treasure within. It was a truly magnificent piece of work.

Her first clue that all was not well was a creak so faint that she might have missed it had she not been holding her breath. She didn't move, hoping that she was wrong, praying once again to Nicholas of Myra. Without straightening her spine or moving anything but her head, she glanced over her shoulder to see that Rory Donovan now stood at the end of his bed, arms crossed as he watched her.

Nicholas of Myra was a lousy excuse for a saint!

"Boy, you picked the wrong man and the wrong night," Donovan drawled as he reached for a pair of trousers that hung over a hard-backed chair.

At least he didn't recognize her. If she could just slip past him while he pulled on his pants. . . .

She hadn't stirred at all but to turn her head, so perhaps he would be surprised when she made her move. She spun around and ran straight for him, then cut sharply to the right to dart past as he stepped into one trouser leg. She almost made it, too, but a quick and strong hand shot out and grabbed the back of her shirt just as she reached the French doors.

"Hold on there, kid," Donovan drawled. He pulled her back and away from the door, jerking on her shirt so that it tightened around her. She continued to pull against him, hoping that his hold would slip and she could make her getaway. The grip tightened, and she could feel the heat of his hand at her back.

Trapped! Donovan held her shirt in one of his big hands, and no matter how hard she tried she couldn't get away.

"Fiddle," he whispered softly, stunned amusement in his voice. "I do believe I smell an Englishwoman."

The element of surprise was just what she

needed. She fell back against his chest, and
then burst forward and out of his grasp, brushing past a wafting curtain and rushing onto the
gallery. She couldn't look back. If she did, he
would have her; she knew it.

With one leg over the gallery railing, she
chanced a glimpse at the open doors. Rory
Donovan was making his way through the
opening, his body too big for the small doorway, his trousers up and held together with one
hand clenched at the waist. The other hand he
shook at her as he ordered her to stop.

She threw her other leg over the railing and
clasped the narrow column that would lead her
to the ground, but in her haste she let go of the
railing too soon. Her grasp on the column was
not as firm as it should have been, and instead
of scooting safely to the ground she slipped a
couple of feet and then lost her grip and fell. In
an instant, every curse word Mina had ever ut-
tered went through Jackie's mind, and one actually made it out of her mouth. The ground
came up hard, and she had one brief glimpse of
Rory Donovan peering over the gallery railing
before the stars and his face faded and all was
black.

Rejecting his first instinct to go over the rail
and follow the little thief, Rory dashed down
the stairs and exited the house through the parlor doors, buttoning his trousers as he went.

She lay flat on her back on the ground, still
as death and fading into the shadows as if she

were about to melt into the ground and disappear. He knelt beside her and touched her throat, feeling for a pulse. When he felt it beating against the tips of his fingers, strong and steady, he experienced a surge of relief.

Her silly little hat had fallen off, and her hair was spread around her like a dark halo. Surrounded by the night and dressed all in black, her pale face stood out like a welcoming beacon.

He touched her cheek, softly at first, and then he drew back and slapped her lightly. He'd feel better when she was awake. At least he thought he would. She didn't respond the first time, or the second, but the third time he slapped her cheek he was rewarded with a wrinkling of her nose and a tightening of closed lids, as if she didn't want to open her eyes.

"Come now, Miss Beresford," he said softly. "You're caught, well and true. Might as well open those pretty eyes and get it over with."

She did as he asked, opening one eye and then another. Just in case she decided to run again, he grabbed one of her wrists and held on tight.

"Are you hurt?" he asked as she glared up at him.

She took a deep breath before answering. "Of course I'm hurt," she said in that strange and formal accent of hers. "I fell all the way from the gallery. Bloody fool," she muttered.

"You or me?"

"What?" she snapped.

"Who's the bloody fool, you or me?"

She took another deep breath, and it seemed to hurt her. "You, of course."

"Of course."

He should have been expecting her to make a break for it but she caught him by surprise, yanking her hand from his and shooting to her feet. It was a foolish mistake. He was quicker, and hadn't just taken a nasty tumble from the second story.

She hadn't taken two steps in the direction of the mimosa trees before he had her, and this time he clasped both arms around her and held her back against his chest. No wonder he'd taken her for a boy! She was a tiny thing, much smaller in her pants and shirt than she'd appeared in her fancy white dress a few nights earlier.

"Now, now, Miss Beresford," he rumbled. "Do you really think I'd let you get away so easily?"

Her answer was a sniffle, which was followed by a loud, dismayed, pleading sob. "I beg you, Mr. Donovan, let me go. I . . . I was desperate for a way home, and when Sally told me about your winnings I . . . I suppose I saw an easy way back to England." There was that desolate sob again. Why didn't he believe it?

Keeping a firm grasp on her at all times, he spun Miss Beresford around so he could see her face. It wasn't easy to see her in this light, but she turned her face up to him, presenting him with tear-filled eyes and trembling lips washed in moonlight.

"Where'd you get the clothes?" he asked, flicking one finger against a billowing black sleeve. The dark costume fit her pretty well, and was perfect for clandestine maneuvering.

"I stole them from one of the stable lads." Her voice shook. "Oh, my desperation has brought me to the lowest level I can imagine, stealing from people who have only been kind to me, sneaking about in the night like a burglar. Whatever was I thinking?" She blinked, twice, and tears rolled down her cheeks. She laid one of those wet cheeks against his bare chest and sobbed again.

Without wanting to, he found one hand in her hair, patting gently as he soothed her. "There now," he drawled softly. "Don't cry. There's no harm done." She sniffled and hiccuped and rubbed her cheek against his chest. Damn, he wished she wouldn't do that.

She lifted her face to him, a too-young, too-sweet face that was pale in the moonlight. "Then you'll let me go?" she whispered shakily.

He hadn't kissed a woman in five years. Sex was one thing, but mouth-to-mouth contact was too intimate. He didn't want to be that close to anyone, ever again. Still, he had an inexplicable urge to kiss this slip of a girl. She looked so vulnerable, so tempting, and he was somehow sure that a kiss would soothe her. Perhaps it would even soothe him. His hand went to the back of her head, and he laid his palm on a neck that was soft and warm, threaded his fingers through silky hair, and he lowered his lips toward hers with every intention—

She kicked him and flew backward and out of his arms, all signs of the suffering and distraught lass gone. "Get your hands off me, you bastard!" she hissed, just as she turned and began to run.

The girl was no match for him, but she was quick. She took off across the lawn, heading once again for the mimosa trees and the stand of cedars beyond. No doubt she thought she could hide there, foolish girl. She ran hard, but her short legs couldn't possibly outdistance his long ones, and he had her in his grasp again before she'd gone far.

"Let me go," she insisted, sounding more frantic than before.

She hit him with her elbows, kicked back at him with little, dangerous feet, and still he didn't release her. His senses returned to him, even as she did her best to sweep his feet out from under him and they both toppled to the ground. She wriggled and fought like a cat, but there was no way he would let her go again. She ended up on her back once again, and Rory straddled her with his knees on either side of her waist and just enough weight on her to keep her still.

"Now," he breathed, in control once again. "A thought occurred to me, as you kicked me in the shin for the third or fourth time. You were in my house a few days ago, weren't you Miss Beresford?"

"And if I was?" she asked breathlessly and not without anger.

"You made off with a gold mouth harp, I believe. I thought Kevin had borrowed and misplaced it, as he sometimes does, but it was you, wasn't it?"

"Yes," she admitted softly, surprising him with her honesty.

"It's the lavender that gave you away."

"I know."

At least she was being honest, for the moment.

"I'll return the harmonica, I promise. Just . . . just let me go and forget this happened."

She was truly frightened now, much more frightened than she'd pretended to be earlier. She shook beneath him, and the trembling of her lips appeared to be uncontrollable. There were no tears in her eyes this time, just fear.

"I don't know if I can do that or not," he said honestly. "You are, after all, a burglar. You have broken into my home and stolen from me, and I don't see how I can pretend that didn't happen."

She took a deep breath, steeling herself he was sure. "You're going to send me to jail, aren't you?" she asked softly. "You're going to lock me up the same way you locked up that Fabergé egg."

"I should."

She wasn't quite as frightened, now. She feared jail less than she feared—what, that he might kiss her? That didn't make any sense.

"But I think maybe I have another solution," he whispered. She tensed again, and balled her fists at her sides. Every muscle in her body stiffened. He could see it, feel it, as he knelt above her.

"I'm sure you do." Little more than a breath passed her lips.

The ground beneath his knees was soft and damp, and the air that washed over his bare torso turned cool. Suddenly he was convinced that he didn't need this. Miss Beresford was going to be more trouble than she was worth.

He should do as she asked and let her go. No harm had been done, after all, and she had seemed—for a moment or two—contrite.

He should, but he wouldn't. "You see, I need a governess for my son in the worst way. If you take the job I'll pay you well, and you can save enough to go home in just a few weeks. A good honest job, Miss Beresford. What do you say to that?"

Poppycock. That was the first word that came into her mind at the offer, but she kept it to herself. Governess? A kid? Was he crazy?

But Donovan had her in an awkward position. She could barely move, she could barely even breathe, since a half-naked man sat on top of her.

She rather liked looking at Donovan naked, but only from a safe distance. For a moment, earlier, she'd been certain he had other thoughts on his mind. She'd seen lust in his eyes and he'd lowered his head as if he were trying to kiss her. No way was that going to happen. When he'd mentioned a way to work this out, she'd been sure he was going to suggest something vile and degrading, but he hadn't. Luckily for her he didn't look as if he had any improper thoughts in his mind at the moment.

If all he wanted was a governess, she could play along, for now.

"I don't have much experience with children," she said sensibly, "but I would be willing to try. An honest job; that's such a sensible solution to my dilemma."

He gave her a triumphant half-smile. "Good. Tomorrow afternoon you report here with your bags."

In spite of her position she gave him a warm smile. She ached all over, and she had a feeling that by tomorrow morning she would be sore and miserable. The plunge from Donovan's gallery was going to take its toll. She showed none of her discomfort, but did her best to lift her chin haughtily; a difficult task since she was pinned to the ground.

"Of course, Mr. Donovan," she said in her most aloof English accent. "Now, since we've come to this agreeable solution, do you think you might remove yourself from my person?"

He didn't remove himself, but leaned forward so that his face hovered much too close to hers. She could no longer see him well, since that face was now in shadow, but she recalled the strength of his hard features too clearly. He thought himself a commanding man, and for now she would allow him that illusion. She was not in a position to argue. She was not in a position to do anything but agree, but as soon as he released her—

"Don't even think about running, Miss Beresford," he said lowly, as if he read her mind. "If you do, I'll hunt you down, and believe me when I say I *will* find you. I don't care if I have to spend the rest of my life and every dime I have, I'll do it."

Her smile faded. "I have no intention of running," she lied. "But if I did, why on earth would you bother yourself chasing after a harmonica thief?"

Donovan didn't answer right away, and that worried her. He was giving the question too much serious thought. His breath came deep and even, his chest rose and fell, and his thighs remained tight around her.

"Because I don't like to lose," he finally whispered. Within those simple words was an unspoken promise she knew he would keep, a vow that was sacred and dark. If Rory Donovan had his way she would be effectively jailed in this house until the time that he saw fit to release her.

Jackie didn't think the time was right to inform him that she didn't like to lose either.

Chapter Four

It was just after dawn when Jackie crept down the spiraling staircase of the Clark home carrying a single bag. She ached all over, but her shoulder was especially sore. There was a huge bruise there, and another on her hip. Dragging herself out of bed had been difficult, but what choice did she have?

She hated to leave so many nice clothes behind, but she wasn't about to drag her trunk all the way to Florence. The town was a good distance away, and her tapestry bag was heavy enough. It contained three good dresses, the necessary underthings and accessories, a gold harmonica, and a few pieces of jewelry, including a pair of diamond earrings.

They were small but beautiful earrings,

teardrop diamonds—her favorite. Thinking of them caused a small knot to form in her stomach. Ridiculous! She'd never felt guilty about stealing from a rich woman before. Mrs. Clark had lots more, bigger pieces, more elaborate, eye-catching jewelry. She'd probably never even miss the earrings, and Jackie could sell them and finance the next job.

At the doorway she glanced back just once. The wide entry hall, with its marble floor and high ceiling, with its portraits and porcelain and mahogany occasional tables, reeked of wealth and privilege. Wealth and privilege had always been the hallmarks of her enemies, but there were no enemies here.

These people had been truly kind to her. Mr. Clark had never behaved inappropriatly, Mrs. Clark had never made her feel obligated, and Sally . . . well Sally was probably the only friend Jackie had known since she'd left Baltimore.

Jackie turned her gaze to the closed door before her. How silly she had become. If Sally Clark knew who her "special friend" really was, where she'd been, the things she'd done just to survive, her attitude would change in a heartbeat.

With that thought in mind, she quietly opened the front door and left the Clarks behind. She stood on the front porch with her bag in hand and surveyed the green expanse beyond the wide white columns before her; the lush grass and ancient trees, flowering bushes, pink and lavender and white and yellow, were all lovingly tended. Everything here was so still, so unhurried and clean and lovely. It was like a dreamland where nothing was sullied by the harsh realities of life. She would have liked to stay a little while longer, to pretend for a while that an existence like this was possible for her, for anyone.

But thanks to Rory Donovan she had to make her way out of Alabama like a thief. She pursed her lips unhappily at the thought. Who she was and what she did rarely bothered her conscience. She was a survivor, a player in the game of life. She never went hungry, no man owned her and no woman ruled her, and if the price she paid for her freedom sometimes seemed too high, well, the feeling passed quickly.

She took a step forward, intent on walking to Florence—a good long trek—and taking the train she'd arrived on a month ago back to South Carolina. Before she knew it she'd descended the steps and was on her way. This strategy had worked well in the past; it would work well again. Her shoes were comfortable, her traveling outfit black and austere. She could pass herself off as a grieving widow, this time. She'd been getting damned tired of pretending to be seventeen.

"Going somewhere, Miss Beresford?"

She spun around and there he was, six-foot-plus, wide-shouldered and long-legged Rory

Donovan, leaning against the wide column of the Clark house as if he'd been admiring the view himself. His pose was casual, his arms crossed over his chest and one booted ankle crossed over the other, but there was something very *un*-casual in the gleam of his eyes and the set of his jaw.

He'd been there all along, hidden and furtively silent as she'd stood on the front porch and prepared herself for the journey ahead.

"What are you doing here?" she snapped.

"I had a hunch, and apparently it was a good one," he said as he pushed away from the column and came toward her. Damn him, he was tall, and his supreme confidence was evident in the lazy but purposeful steps he took with those long legs of his. In two strides he was there, towering over her and *tsk*-ing softly as he took her bag from her hand. "Really, Miss Beresford, you weren't planning on leaving without saying good-bye, were you?"

She would deny it, lift her chin and look him square in the eye and come up with a tale he'd believe. But as soon as she locked her eyes to his she knew there was nothing she could say to convince him that his hunch had been wrong. She'd been caught by Rory Donovan. Again.

"It seemed worth a try," she said honestly. "I don't think I'll make a very good governess. You see, I don't particularly care for children."

"You'd prefer jail?" he drawled softly.

"No."

He smiled at her, a humorless and unattractive grin of victory as he raked his eyes up and down, perusing her as if she were a mare he was thinking of purchasing for his stables. "Black does not become you, Miss Beresford," he said lazily. "I do wonder that you seem to care for it so dearly."

A hundred responses came to her mind, but none that an English lady would dare to utter. So she smiled demurely and silently plotted against Rory Donovan, envisioning all sorts of bodily harm she could inflict upon his person. Ah, but violence was not her way and never had been. She'd never harm a hair on Mr. Donovan's head, but she would gladly take his Fabergé egg and anything else of value that struck her fancy, when the time came.

"It seems you have me at your mercy."

"You won't try to run again?" he asked, openly suspicious of her easy surrender.

"I'll be governess to your son until I've earned enough to make my way back to England. I'm quite sure you'll let me know when my time in your employ is done." And when she left the Donovan house she'd have the egg and more.

"Very good," he whispered.

They both lifted their heads when a window above opened noisily.

"Good heavens," Mrs. Clark said, drawing

65

her heavy wrapper close and leaning slightly out the window. "Whatever are you two doing out at this time of the morning?"

Donovan faced the woman above, and he activated his charm suddenly, as if a switch had been thrown. He smiled, displaying deceptively boyish dimples in a hard face, and there was a twinkle in his eyes that was most assuredly visible even from Mrs. Clark's high perch. "You must forgive me for being overanxious, and for stealing your lovely houseguest away."

Mrs. Clark smiled widely, positively beamed as she blushed and lifted a pale hand to her breast. "Oh my." No doubt she thought her matchmaking had paid off handsomely.

"You see," Donovan drawled, "Miss Beresford has just most graciously agreed to be my governess."

"Governess?" Mrs. Clark repeated, her smile dying quickly. "But I thought—"

"Governess," Jackie said, before Mrs. Clark could finish her sentence and embarrass them all.

It was either the smartest or the stupidest thing he'd ever done, and he wouldn't be sure which for a while.

Rory walked the short distance from the stables to the house. There were letters of inquiry to answer, the latest statement concerning his iron investments to peruse, and he did wonder how Kevin and Miss Beresford had gotten along on their first day together.

He was fairly certain she would still be there. She now believed his threat to hunt her down if she ran, a threat he'd reiterated this morning as they'd made the trip from the Clarks' house to Cloudmont in his best phaeton.

Miss Beresford likely wouldn't last long as a governess. She obviously did not want to be here, and she'd told him straight out she didn't care for children, much. But her presence, however short, would perhaps give him time to locate and hire a more suitable woman for the position, someone stern and tough who would take Kevin well in hand. A few weeks should suffice, and then he'd gladly send Miss Beresford on her way.

Rory entered the house quietly, listening for the everyday sounds of the household running smoothly. Nell and her girls kept busy, cleaning this big house and cooking for themselves and two hungry men. From early morning until sunset they bustled about the place, humming and cleaning, baking and doing the laundry. In the daytime hours the house was never still.

He entered directly into his study through the French doors, which were opened to allow the breeze to circulate. A delicious aroma greeted him first, something sweet and spicy that had probably been put on the big table on the brick porch to cool. The breeze carried the familiar and comforting fragrance through the open doors and throughout the house. All was quiet, and then he heard the soft voices from the room next door, a small library he'd converted into a schoolroom for Kevin. These were the voices he'd been listening for.

"I don't like to read." Kevin insisted.

Rory moved to the doorway of his study so he could better hear the voices. He'd listened to the other governesses, one stern and another cajoling, and he wondered what Miss Beresford's approach would be.

She surprised him. "Neither do I," she said sadly. "This morning's history lesson went well, but we can't devote the entire day to the American Revolution and tales of the Indigo Blade. What do *you* propose?"

Kevin didn't hesitate. "Fishing!"

Miss Beresford didn't immediately veto this suggestion. There was a short span of silence while Kevin—and Rory—awaited her answer. "I don't think your father considers fishing to be an educational activity." She sounded rather disappointed, as if she'd rather go fishing herself. "How about a try at mathematics?"

Rory stepped into the hallway so he could hear their voices more clearly.

"Do you like mathematics?"

"I like it better than reading," Kevin conceded sullenly.

"Let's try this, then," Miss Beresford said. "If you catch four fish on Monday, and five on Tuesday, how many fish do you have?"

"How big are they?" Kevin asked seriously, and Rory smiled to himself as he quietly stepped closer to the schoolroom door.

He was close enough to hear Miss Beresford

sigh. "What difference does it make?"

"If they're little I'd have to throw them back, and if they're really big Miss Nell will fillet them and we'd have lots for dinner—"

"Big enough to keep," Miss Beresford interrupted, "and for the sake of counting let's keep them whole."

He could see them now. Miss Beresford had shed her awful black gown for a more becoming and simpler blue dress. She stood behind her large desk, and Kevin was seated at his smaller one. They faced one another across the room, each intent on their subject and . . . and each beautiful in their own way. Bringing her here hadn't been a mistake, he knew at that moment.

Kevin held up both hands and bent each finger slightly as he counted, mouthing the numbers. "Nine," he finally said. "That was easy."

The new governess crossed her arms. "Aren't you clever?"

Kevin beamed. "Yup."

"I think as a reward we should take ourselves fishing," Miss Beresford said, relief in her voice. She seemed as anxious to escape the schoolroom as Kevin was. "I've never been fishing before," she confided in a lowered voice, "so you'll have to teach me."

"Sure!" Kevin smiled, and Rory felt a catch, a twinge of a promise of pain in his heart. The boy was so open, so eager to be loved and wanted.

"We'll make it an educational outing," she

said sensibly. "We'll count all the fish we catch."

Kevin saw him then, and eyes went wide as he spoke. "Pa! What are you doing here?"

Miss Beresford turned slowly, deliberately, and the look on her face was stern and cold. She looked him up and down, taking in the faded jeans and the battered boots and the sweaty shirt that had once been white, with obvious disdain.

"Me and Miss Jackie are going fishin'. Do you want to come with us?"

Miss Jackie turned to her student. "That's Miss Jackie and I," she corrected primly. "And I'm sure your father has other activities planned to keep himself occupied this afternoon."

"I do, as a matter of fact," he agreed.

"Mucking out stables, perhaps?" she said softly.

Rory ignored her. "Kevin, if you're going fishing you'd better go change your clothes. If you come home with another pair of good trousers ruined Miss Nell will have your hide and mine, too."

In a flash Kevin was past him, through the door and down the hall, and in a matter of seconds his little feet pounded on the stairs.

There was a moment of awkward silence. He had the feeling Miss Beresford would have fled the room herself if it hadn't meant passing close by him.

"How's it going so far?" he asked, not quite

ready to turn around and leave her behind.

"Fine," she said.

"Fine? After one day most governesses say Kevin is uncontrollable, incorrigible, and one even said he was diabolical."

"Ridiculous," she said softly. "Kevin is extremely active, I'll give him that, and I can see where that might be a problem for someone who's accustomed to dealing with children of a more sedate manner." She seemed to mull over the situation. "He's very bright, I think."

"You think?"

An expression of annoyance crossed her face. "Yes, I *think*. I told you I'm no governess, so what do you expect from me?"

He didn't answer.

"He's possessed of a great deal of energy and curiosity. I suppose to some that might be a bother, but in truth he seems to be a normal and active little boy."

Rory was glad to hear his own opinion voiced by someone else, even this seventeen-year-old would-be thief.

"Now if you'll excuse me," she said, waving him aside before she approached the doorway. "I suppose I should change clothes myself."

He backed away, a single step that effectively blocked the doorway more completely. "He calls you Miss Jackie."

"It's my name, after all," she snapped.

"Might I . . . ?" he hesitated. "After all, you will be living in the house. Perhaps I should

71

call you Jackie."

With a sigh she approached him, and with a small, soft raised hand she gently pushed against his chest. He could've stood firm, but he stepped aside and allowed her to walk past. "Only my friends call me Jackie," she said as she passed.

"I'd like—" he began, ready to make the first gesture of friendship.

"No," she said firmly, glancing over her shoulder once. "Absolutely not."

She would not be Rory Donovan's friend!

Jackie watched Kevin's back and the pond beyond. She'd given up her own awkward efforts at fishing after a few fruitless minutes, but was content to sit and watch. Every muscle in her body ached, particularly her back and her left shoulder. But once she found a position that put the least strain on those muscles she was quite comfortable here on the ground, with a blanket beneath her and her calico skirt and plain white blouse cool and comfortable.

This was a beautiful place, lush and green, wild and eerily silent. Clover and violets grew all around, and nearby trees shaded moss so bright a green it nearly hurt her eyes to look at it. She could almost pretend that it was a magical land, with unicorns and fairies hidden in the trees beyond the pond and a rainbow in the sky above. Here it would never rain or grow cold, and when it was warm as it was today, a cool breeze like the one that washed over her now would always be present. Here there was peace and safety, always.

She would have enjoyed the afternoon and her unusual fanciful thoughts if Rory Donovan didn't keep encroaching, his face and his voice intruding into her mind uninvited. How dare he ask if he could call her Jackie, intimating that they might become friends? If he thought he could turn his charm on her he was much mistaken. She was here because he demanded it, a prisoner as surely as if he had called the law.

Of course, in jail there wasn't likely to be quiet ponds and sunshine, or redheaded boys with freckles and gap-toothed wide smiles.

Kevin, who had talked her ear off for most of the day, and who'd had a difficult time staying in his seat in the schoolroom, was now perfectly content to stand on the bank of the pond and fish.

Everyone should have a childhood like this. Kevin had surely never been hungry, and he'd certainly never been taught how to pick a man's pocket or cut a woman's purse from her wrist without detection. Those were skills Jackie had possessed by the time she was not much older than Kevin. Even before that, she remembered Luther—the man who'd raised her—making her stand alone on a street corner and cry until someone stopped to see what was wrong. Then he'd come along to claim her, playing the relieved father or uncle as he picked the pockets of a man kind enough to stop, or cut off the jewelry of a well-meaning lady. Their attention was on her, and so they never caught on—until later, of course.

She doubted Kevin had ever had to lie quietly on his bedding on the floor and listen while his father entertained his lady friends. She and Luther had lived in one room from her earliest memory until the day she'd run away. He'd thought himself a ladies' man. And in truth, he'd always had one woman or another.

Several nights a week he'd brought one home with him, and on Luther's bed they'd bucked and wriggled and moaned. Jackie had always pretended to sleep, her face to the wall and her body very still. She'd tried to block out the sounds, to think of something else and fall asleep, but on too many nights she hadn't heard anything but the sounds from that bed.

One night the woman Luther had brought home with him had a change of heart. She'd said she was sorry, but she just couldn't go through with it. Jackie remembered feeling a moment of relief, but it hadn't lasted long. Luther hadn't taken no for an answer. He'd forced the woman to the bed and taken what he claimed she owed him while the woman sobbed.

Jackie had heard Luther's women moan before, but not like this. It had been horrible, as if a wounded animal fought on that bed. Jackie'd tried to block out the terrible sounds, covering herself with the blanket and pressing her palms against her ears. It hadn't been enough, though. She hadn't been able to block out the sounds of Luther's hands slapping the woman's face and body, the sobbing and pleading, and finally the soft and helpless crying.

The second time Luther had taken the woman she didn't make a sound, and somehow that had been worse.

Jackie had remembered that night two years later, when Luther had decided she was old enough to warm his bed. He would train her, he'd said, and with her looks she could bring in a good income warming the beds of others. After he'd taught her all the tricks of the trade, of course.

She'd run away that night. Luther had tried to stop her, chasing until he'd caught up with her, throwing his arms around her and clapping his hand over her mouth when she tried to scream. Jackie had bitten him hard, and in surprise he'd let her go. She'd run and she hadn't looked back. Not once.

A few days later Jackie had found Mina, who'd taken her in. It was Mina who'd taught her to read and write, to speak correctly, to smile and cajole and steal properly. By her reckoning, she'd been about thirteen years old.

Jackie knew who and what she was now: a thief and a con artist who didn't dare stay in any one place too long. But no matter how low she was occasionally forced to sink, there was one part of her that remained untouched. She'd never let a man do to her what Luther had wanted to do. There had been times when it would have meant easier living, to lie back and allow a man to use her . . . but she never had. She'd held onto her virginity as if her very life had depended on it. One part of her soul was pure, no matter what else she did.

Looking around, Jackie realized that the beauty of this place didn't enchant her any longer. There was no freedom here.

Kevin finally caught himself a fish, and his shout of joy broke the silence so abruptly that Jackie jumped, a little. Once the fish was freed from the hook, Kevin spun around and displayed the poor creature proudly. Jackie couldn't help but wrinkle her nose.

"It's a disgusting little beast, isn't it?" she observed from her comfortable seat, leaning back on her hands and squinting against the sun.

"It's a beauty!" Kevin said defensively. "See?" He came closer, intent on displaying his catch. "It's a keeper."

"That's quite close enough," Jackie said when Kevin and his fish were directly before her. She couldn't help but grimace as she watched its gills working. Of course she'd seen fish before, but they'd always been long dead. "It's still alive," she whispered. "Perhaps you should throw it back."

"Throw it back?" He insisted on holding the slimy-looking fish out, thrusting it close to her face. The fish twisted suddenly, slipping out of Kevin's hand and falling smack dab into Jackie's lap, where it twisted and flopped unhappily.

Jackie couldn't help it. She squealed as she

jumped to her feet, ignoring the protests of her bruised muscles and a throbbing shoulder.

Kevin laughed, and when he straightened after collecting his fish from the ground, she caught a glimpse of the most wickedly satisfied grin she'd ever seen on a child.

Perhaps she should scold Kevin, whether the dropped fish was an accident or not, but she didn't want to do anything to take away the expression of pure joy on his face.

"You," she said softly and with a smile of her own, "will pay for that." She only had to take a single step forward before he took off. She merrily gave chase, running after Kevin and being careful to keep a constant span between them. They ran in a big circle, in the sun, into and out of the shade, back into the shade and around a big tree. He held his fish away from his body with one hand, and as he ran he laughed and laughed until Jackie found she was laughing with him. Laughing with no real reason, laughing until she was nearly out of breath, and still she ran. The unexpected laughter took away the pain in her muscles and made her forget the dark memories that had robbed her peace just moments earlier.

With a burst of energy she gained on Kevin, wrapped her arms around his waist, and lifted him easily from the ground. He laughed even harder as they came to a halt.

"You can't get away from me," she said breathlessly. She walked, with Kevin held tightly and awkwardly before her, to the edge of the pond, and without her saying a word he tossed the fish into the water.

"He'll be even bigger next time," he explained as Jackie dropped him to his feet. He looked up at her, and she couldn't help but smile at his freckled face so red from exertion, at the dark brown eyes so wide and innocent. His ears were too big for his head, and they stuck out prominently. In combination with the gap-toothed smile and red hair that wouldn't be-have, they made for a wonderfully goofy picture. "You run pretty good," he said, "for a girl."

"For a girl?" she said indignantly. "I'll have you know that a girl can run every bit as fast as any little redheaded boy."

He took the statement as a challenge, turn-ing on his heel and taking off toward the house. They ran all the way home.

Every day of her time at Cloudmont Jackie had found something new to explore. On this after-noon her natural curiosity led her into a flower garden that was allowed to run slightly wild. It appealed to her even more than the Clarks' well laid out and tended garden—and she had come to adore the Clarks' garden of roses and camellias.

Here there were daffodils and Japanese quince, periwinkles and hyacinths. There were lush nooks and crannies beyond the winding brick path, and flowers that looked as if they'd grown wild, fighting their way into a flower bed where they didn't belong. Rather like herself, she thought with a smile.

Kevin was sleeping, and on this warm afternoon she simply wasn't tired enough to do the same. She walked past the flowers and into a small orchard. Apples and peaches and plum trees formed a fragrant and colorful corridor of blossoms. Kevin had told her how, when the time was right and the harvest was good, Nell and her helpers would make jams and preserves and pies galore.

She circled around and found herself heading for the white fence that encircled Donovan's domain. She was safe enough, she supposed, since all she saw were a number of horses grazing contentedly in the enclosure.

She stepped onto the lower slat of the fence, which was not particularly low, and held onto the top, peering into the green pasture and studying the animals that seemed oblivious to her presence. Jackie knew nothing about horses, but she could tell these were fine specimens. They were sleek and powerful, strong and beautiful.

And, from all she'd heard, these were Rory Donovan's passion. Nell and Kevin had both mentioned his love for the animals, but even if they hadn't, she would have known anyway. He spent so much time here at the stables, doing menial jobs hired hands could very well do while he sat back and kept his hands and his clothes clean. He was always up and about early, anxious to get to his work.

She had to admit, grudgingly, that he cut a dashing figure in his old blue jeans and battered boots and plain white shirts. In them he was even more striking in appearance than he'd been in his fine evening clothes at the Clarks' dinner party.

Of course, nothing could compare to the night she'd first seen him, when he'd been wearing nothing at all.

"Beautiful, aren't they?"

The familiar drawl, so close to her ear, startled Jackie so completely she jumped as she jerked her head around, and without warning she lost her balance and fell backward and off the fence.

Powerful long arms caught her, and she found herself staring up into the face she'd been daydreaming about. How embarrassing!

There was a twinkle of amusement in his pale brown eyes, as if he knew what she'd been thinking. Impossible!

"I didn't mean to startle you," he said softly.

"Well, you did." Her tone of voice was cold and accusatory, as distant as she could make it, given the circumstances.

He held her quite securely, and this close to Donovan—as close as she'd been the night he'd captured her and made her his reluctant governess—she could see details that had escaped her before. Stubble on his cheek, flecks of gold in his eyes, the beginnings of wrinkles around those eyes.

"I apologize," he said with a small smile that teased her with the hint of dimples in those stubbled cheeks.

"You can put me down, now," she said haughtily, and he did, slowly and carefully. Even after he'd deposited her on her feet he stood too close! The fence was behind her, and Donovan was planted firmly before her. She was trapped again.

She'd tried very hard, in her days at Cloudmont, to stay away from Rory Donovan as much as possible. He made her nervous, and she'd sworn long ago not to let anyone make her nervous! It was as if he knew too much, as if he saw right through her. Perhaps it was his sheer size, and then again maybe it was because he'd tried to kiss her that one time. He'd been a perfect gentleman since, but still. . . .

"Lovely animals," she said, spinning away from him to lean on the fence and face the pasture. With her back to Donovan she felt a little stronger.

"Yes, they are." He stepped up to lean on the fence beside her.

She could run, now, but then he would know she was a coward, and that simply wouldn't do. Instead, she sneaked a glance at his face. Gazing out over the pasture he seemed at peace, and not a threat to her at all.

Stepping onto the lower slat once again

brought her almost face-to-face with him. She held on tight. "This is a happy place," she said softly.

He wrested his gaze from the horses to glare at her. "Is it?" Oddly enough, he seemed to doubt what had only been meant as a compliment.

She was saved from further discussion by the arrival of a man on horseback, and for once—for the very first time—she was glad to see Clint Marsh bearing down on her with a wide smile plastered on his face.

Clint dismounted and tossed the reins to Alvin, the young man who was a permanent fixture at the stables, and with his long stride he headed for Jackie and Rory.

Rory sighed, as if tired. She'd heard this sigh before, when Kevin asked too many questions of him or when Nell went into one of her tirades about Corinne or Eleanor. He simply didn't want to be bothered.

Before Clint reached the fence where they stood, Jackie leaned slightly toward Rory and whispered, "He has a magnificent nose, don't you think?"

Rory raised his eyebrows in obvious distress. "I've honestly never noticed."

Good. If he was going to keep her off balance, she'd have to do her best to return the favor.

Chapter Five

Miss Jacqueline Beresford had been living at Cloudmont for more than a week. Kevin adored her and Nell liked her, declaring Miss Jackie the first governess with backbone who had come into this house. Sally had stopped by three times, and so had Clint Marsh—to Rory's consternation. They all called her Jackie, and she accepted their friendship and adoration with warm smiles and enchanting conversation.

Rory couldn't help but notice that she still didn't seem to like him much. She had not been pleased when he'd joined her to watch the horses that afternoon a few days ago. He could almost believe that she would prefer to take a fall than to allow him to catch her again. Pity.

Whenever he walked into a room where she

entertained her friends or laughed with Kevin, her smiles invariably disappeared and her charming conversation was silenced. It was becoming quite annoying.

From his study window he watched a scene that had become familiar to him. Kevin and his governess were running toward the house, laughing as they passed beneath the big oak, running in loops and circles as they approached the house, perhaps not quite ready to end the game. When had he last seen Kevin so happy? It was an easy question to answer: never.

Much of Jackie's hair had fallen from the neat style she'd begun the day with, and it now danced around her head, wisps of dark hair that even from this distance looked silken. Her red skirt whirled as she ran, and she laughed heartily as she finally caught up with Kevin, scooped him up and spun him around. Even from here, Rory could hear their merriment.

There were moments when Miss Beresford looked no more like a proper English lady than he himself did.

"They do make a pair, don't they?"

Rory didn't show his surprise at being interrupted, as he turned to face Nell. She was carrying a tray that held a tall glass of lemonade and a plate of cookies. He had to smile; she had a tendency to treat him as if he were still no older than Kevin.

"She's the first governess he's liked at all," Rory admitted. "But I don't think he's learning much."

Nell brushed off that concern. "They spend all morning in the schoolroom, with them books and numbers. That's plenty enough for a boy Kevin's age, I reckon."

"Maybe," Rory conceded softly.

Nell joined him at the window, and they watched as the happy pair approached the house. Jackie now held Kevin before her, her arms about his waist and his spindly legs dangling. The kid wiggled and giggled with every step she took.

Nell was silent for a long while, but Rory knew she had something to say. He could almost feel it. Finally, she gave in and blurted, "I think you ought to marry her."

"What?" Rory thundered, looking down at his housekeeper. Of all the things he might have expected to hear, that wasn't even on the list.

"Well, you can bet your bottom dollar she's not going to be a governess forever. She's not at all like those sour women you hired before her," Nell said with a twitch of her nose that displayed her distaste at the memory. "Jackie's bright and pretty and full of life, and if you don't snatch her up, someone else will. I guarantee it."

"She's seventeen years old!" Rory hissed. "Not much more than a child. If I ever do decide to marry again I imagine I'll pick a grown woman."

"I was married at sixteen, and many young ladies are married at seventeen and even younger. You're just thirty-two, Mister Rory, and I don't see as how fifteen years difference is an impracticable one." The grin that spread across Nell's face was wide. "Besides, if Jackie's seventeen then so am I."

Rory narrowed his eyes at his uncannily observant housekeeper. She seemed so certain, so . . . confident. "What makes you say that?"

Nell continued to smile. "Oh, just this and that. She might be acting like a child right this minute, but most of the time she don't move like a child, or talk like a child, and if you look in her eyes she don't have the eyes of a child." Her smile faded. "Sometimes I look into those eyes and I think maybe she didn't laugh much before she started chasing Mister Kevin around the house."

He was inclined to agree with Nell on that one point, though he was reluctant to agree with anything else she said. Why would Jackie lie about her age? As for marrying her, he wouldn't even consider such a ridiculous notion, no matter how much Kevin liked her.

"It's past time you started thinking about getting yourself a wife and Kevin a mother," Nell gently prodded.

"I'll never marry again, you know that," Rory answered without looking down. Nell's eyes had a tendency to see too much.

She harumphed and grumbled, and shifted uneasily from one foot to another. "If I thought you'd loved Miss Margaret so dearly that her death broke your heart, maybe I could accept that decision without question. But I was here from the day you brought your bride home 'til the day you buried her, and I know better."

"Nell," Rory whispered, knowing where this conversation was heading. "Don't."

"I think I know . . ."

It was a greater effort than anyone would ever know, but he turned a brilliant smile to his meddling housekeeper. Secrets buried deep were best left buried, unspoken horrors best left unspoken. "There's no mysterious reason for my decision not to marry. Why should I tie myself to one woman when there are hundreds, thousands of beautiful women in this world that I haven't yet encountered?" She was playing dirty, and so could he. He leaned down, placing his face closer to hers, and he lowered his voice. "Why, just last year when I was in Birmingham on a business trip I met a widow who is capable of assuming the most amazing bodily positions. The lady is double-jointed, I'm sure, and she is always rather anxious to display her many noteworthy skills."

Nell's expression didn't change.

Rory winked at her. "I believe she has a sister I haven't yet met. The prospect of discovering for myself if she possesses the same skills as her sister, why, it leaves me breathless with anticipation."

There was a long moment of uncomfortable silence, but finally Nell shook her head and turned away. She muttered under her breath as she walked past the desk where she'd left his tray of lemonade and cookies, and when she reached the door she turned and glared at him.

After a brief pause she almost broke a smile. Almost. "Mister Rory, you play the womanizer almost as well as Miss Jackie plays seventeen."

Jackie tucked Kevin in, and in just a couple of minutes he was sound asleep. The heat of the afternoon and their outdoor activities often exhausted him. They exhausted her, too, if she were to be honest. Ah, but it was the most wonderful weariness. Some afternoons she took a nap herself, hunkering down in the soft feather bed in her room next to Kevin's and sleeping deeply.

But this afternoon she wasn't particularly tired. Since she wasn't in the mood for an encounter with Donovan, it would definitely be best to stay in the house. She'd explored much of the Cloudmont grounds. Surely there were places in this big house she didn't yet know well.

Nervously fingering the full skirt of her blue and white striped dress, she crept into the hallway and looked longingly toward Rory Donovan's bedchamber.

There were four large bedrooms, as well as a small lavatory that Kevin told her had recently been added, on the second floor of the manor. Each bedroom was on a corner of the house and had two doors that opened onto the gallery. In three of the bedrooms, Kevin's and

Donovan's and her own, the doors were open nearly all the time, and there were doors at either end of the wide hallway that were kept open as well. In the heat of the day there was usually a breeze to keep the place cool.

The fourth bedroom, the shrouded chamber she'd glimpsed into on her first night at Cloudmont, was always locked up tight. Was it used to conceal other treasures even more magnificent than the Fabergé egg—works of art, coins of gold, magnificent jewels?

At the moment, she knew Donovan worked with his beloved horses and Nell was happily ensconced in the kitchen. It was the perfect opportunity to take another look at the Fabergé egg, and to study the lock that protected it.

She felt no qualms about walking into Donovan's bedroom. After all, she'd been there twice before, and she glanced through the open doorway nearly every day.

There was evidence of its masculine occupant everywhere. Shaving implements were arranged on the dresser, as well as a pair of gold cufflinks, carelessly discarded, and a silver watch. A pair of trousers had been tossed over the back of the wing chair Donovan had slumbered in the first night she'd set foot into this room.

A huge pair of shiny black boots sat beside the bed; his fine boots, not the ones he wore to work with his horses. The gold harmonica she'd returned on her first day as a resident of

Cloudmont rested exactly as it had when she'd first seen it, atop the case that protected the Fabergé egg. Apparently Donovan wasn't too terribly concerned about the instrument being lifted again.

She could smell a hint of the shaving tonic Donovan used, as if the fragrance had worked its way into the pillows and the clothing and would never quite be spent.

Seeing the object of her desire made her dismiss the signs of Donovan's occupancy. At night, by the light of the moon, the egg had been beautiful. By the light of day it was magnificent, wondrous, the most breathtaking sight she'd ever beheld. Gems sparkled, gold shimmered, and the workmanship was perfection. Oh, to own such a thing of beauty, to possess it, to hold it with caressing hands and know that it belonged to you and you alone.

She wondered if Donovan ever took the egg from its case and held it, if he turned it this way and that and admired the workmanship and the exquisite beauty. Did he even appreciate what he had here? She leaned forward slightly, bringing her face closer to the glass covering and the egg. Just the sight of it made her heart beat faster, and she unconsciously licked her lips.

Her eyes fell to the base of the case. The lock appeared to be sturdy. If worse came to worst she could always carefully break the glass and remove the egg, but there was no sport, no honor, no finesse in such a method.

It was the clearing of a throat, a deep rumbling, that grabbed her attention and caused her to spin around. Rory Donovan stood in the doorway, with his arms crossed over his chest and a perfectly satisfied gleam in his eyes, as if he'd expected to catch her and was pleased to be proven right.

"I was just looking," she said, motioning with one gentle hand while she kept her eyes on Donovan. Dammit, she sounded guilty even to her own ears. She tried a smile; it usually worked wonders on men.

It obviously didn't do a thing for this one. Donovan didn't move, didn't smile, didn't appear to relax at all. She reminded herself that she had nothing to be afraid of. He was tall and wide and strong, but since bringing her into his household he had never threatened her. He'd been nothing but a gentleman.

"Want to know where I keep the key?" he asked, his voice a gruff whisper.

More than anything, she wanted to know . . . but of course she couldn't let him know that. "Whyever would I care?"

He did give in to a wicked smile, then, deepening dimples on an otherwise harsh face, as if he knew something she didn't, as if he saw right through her lies. "I used to keep it here." He reached out and slid open a drawer of the bedside table. "But recently I've decided to keep the key close." He flicked open one button of his white shirt, one of the rather plain and coarse shirts he wore when working at the stables, folded back a bit of heavy cotton, and there it was; a brass key suspended from a satin cord and hanging around his neck so that it rested high on his chest.

"Surely you don't think that I—"

"I think you like the egg too much," he interrupted. "And to be honest, your clumsy attempt at pilfering made me realize what a tempting prize it would be to any thief."

Clumsy! How dare he? "Word will get around, I imagine," she said serenely, ignoring the insult. She'd show him clumsy soon enough. She'd steal the egg right out from under his nose and be long gone before he even knew it was missing. This challenge only added spice. When he least expected it, she'd be ready.

She should be terrified to be alone with a man like this one. Too big, too smart, and very, very dangerous. She had avoided men with his reputation for all of her life.

But for some reason she wasn't scared of him at all. Since she'd come to Cloudmont he had been a perfect gentleman, and in truth she'd seen not an inkling of the notorious ladies' man Sally had proclaimed him to be. She'd even decided that she must have been mistaken when she thought he was going to try to kiss her on the night of the foiled burglary. The episode was no doubt a result of a brain addled by the fall, and her active imagination.

He certainly hadn't tried to kiss her since. Not even when she'd fallen from the fence and he'd caught her. Either Sally had been wrong in her assessment of Donovan's character, or else he didn't find Jackie at all attractive. She should have been relieved—and she was, she told herself, she was! But something within her was disappointed, too. No woman wanted to be so easily dismissed.

"Where's Kevin?" he asked.

"Asleep." She smiled, and this time it wasn't planned, but bloomed instinctively. "He was so exhausted after our picnic he needed a nap."

Donovan nodded.

"He's a wonderful boy," she went on, unable to help herself. "You must be very proud."

He nodded again, smaller this time, and looked away, glancing out the open French doors. "He's a good kid."

As much as she cared for Kevin, she knew she couldn't stay and watch over him for much longer. Who would Donovan bring in next, another of the horrible governesses Kevin had told her about? "When my time here is done," she said, "and you bring in another governess for Kevin, I think you should be very cautious in making your choice. He doesn't need a nursemaid, he needs a teacher, perhaps a brilliant tutor who will challenge and excite him. The others bored him, and I can only teach him so much. . . ."

"There won't be any more governesses after you, Miss Beresford." Donovan looked at her again, pinning those eyes on her as he spoke.

"In a few months I'm sending Kevin to a military academy in south Alabama."

"No," she said softly, and then louder. "No. He's much too young to be sent from home."

"I made the decision just a few days ago. It's the perfect solution—"

"No," Jackie said again. "How can you even think of sending him away?" If she had a family she would keep them together through thick and thin. She would treasure every moment. Rory Donovan had everything a man could ask for, and he would carelessly put his only son aside? It wasn't fair, and it wasn't right. Parents shouldn't discard their children so easily, so heartlessly. She knew that it happened, she knew that too well, but still, it wasn't fair. "You'll break his heart."

Donovan didn't deny it. "Broken hearts aren't fatal, Miss Beresford. He'll recover. We all do, don't we?"

She wondered who had broken Donovan's heart. His late wife? One of his many paramours? A young love, perhaps? "He's too young," she insisted, and Donovan actually grinned, a cold, harsh smile that revealed strong, white teeth that looked quite dangerous even from this distance.

"It's none of your concern."

That was the truth, wasn't it? She was simply playing a role, pretending to be lost and alone, pretending to care for Kevin. Why did it feel so damned real at the moment? "I never had any family, to speak of," she said softly. "I never really had a home." Donovan's smile faded, and she was left with the hard, unreadable man she was accustomed to. What difference did it make if she mixed a little of the truth in with her lies? He would never know one from the other. "If I had a home and a family I'd hold on to them for dear life. I'd make time for fishing and playing games, for listening to stories and laughter and tears at the end of the day. I would most certainly not send any member of my family away, no matter how convenient it might be."

Donovan raised his eyebrows in smug surprise. "Miss Beresford, are you criticizing my paternal ability?"

"Yes," she answered without hesitation. "Perhaps if you could make time in your busy schedule for your son he wouldn't be so unruly. Sending him away is hardly the answer," she said with conviction. "Loving him might be a better course of action." And with that, she stalked from the room.

Nell was right, Rory thought as Jackie brushed haughtily past him and headed for her own bedroom. No way was this confident, outspoken woman seventeen years old. She should have hung her head and slunk from the room, caught as she'd been. But had she seemed at all contrite? No. Not only that, she'd turned the tables and made him feel guilty about his decision to send Kevin to Marion.

It was a fine school, and a fine decision. This constantly changing procession of governesses

was not good for anyone, and the only other solution, marriage, was out of the question. He'd
decided on Marion after pondering Nell's
ridiculous suggestion two days earlier.

He stripped off his dirty shirt and fingered
the key that hung from his neck. Had she come
here to admire the Fabergé egg or to figure out
how to steal it?

When he'd cleaned up and changed into
fresh clothes, he headed not for the staircase
but silently toward Kevin's room. As he'd expected, Kevin slept soundly, curled up on the
bed with his favorite blanket clutched in both
hands. What he hadn't expected to see was
Miss Jacqueline Beresford in a rocking chair
near the bed, her eyes on her charge as he
slept.

She evidently didn't see or hear him, because
her expression didn't change. He wished he
could put a name to the enchanting facial cast
that was a mixture of serenity and pain.

Jacqueline Beresford, more than adequate
governess and rather inept thief, was an odd
marriage of frailty and strength, of daring and
softness. He could see all that on her face at
this moment, all that and more. What was she
thinking? On her face, there was a look that
seemed to him as if it held all the longing in the
world.

As he backed silently away from the door he
wondered if anyone had ever looked at him
that way.

Chapter Six

The small dinner party hadn't been planned, but had come together easily. Sally had called in the afternoon, as Jackie had sat with a sleeping Kevin, and Clint Marsh had arrived soon after. The three of them had been visiting in the parlor while Kevin slept the afternoon away, when Nell had poked her head in the doorway and insisted that they stay for supper, promising to serve the meal early so that they could return home before it became truly dark.

Jackie was somewhat relieved. After her encounter with Donovan that afternoon, she wasn't anxious to be alone with him again so soon, not even over supper. Had she said more than was wise? Had she given too much of herself away?

After a pleasant meal, they all retired to the parlor. Jackie liked everything in the big house, but this was her favorite room. It was not as formal as the Clarks' parlor, but it was every bit as fine. A serpentine-back sofa, covered in a brocade of blue and gold, sat against one wall, and there were several comfortable upholstered chairs that would accommodate a man of even Donovan's size. A gaming table was placed against one wall, and on many evenings Kevin had dragged it out on its hidden casters and folded the top back, pulled up a chair and sat there to draw. Once or twice she'd even played him a game of checkers on that table.

Tonight, Donovan was sociable and charming, making Sally and Clint laugh more than once. Clint teased Sally about her new hairstyle, and she answered by smacking him soundly on the wrist with her folded fan and telling him that he was hopelessly impeded where fashion was concerned. The two of them seemed closer than before, as if they were becoming friends. Of course, Sally made friends so easily.

Kevin was present. He sat at Jackie's feet with a wooden train and entertained himself with imaginary cowboys and Indians while the adults gossiped and talked of thoroughbreds and cotton.

Jackie had little to add to the conversation, but she listened intently.

These people were her friends. The very

thought gave Jackie a chill. She'd never had friends before, had never wanted them, had silently laughed at people who trusted others so easily. Jacqueline Beresford relied on herself and no one else, and she liked it that way.

She knew, deep down, that she couldn't live a life like hers and have friends, other than fellow thieves like Mina. She had to be able to move on at a moment's notice, to always think of herself first, to know when to smile and when to run like hell.

Something told her it was time to run now, before she found herself in too deep, before she started to like it here too much.

"Mama wants the two of you to come to dinner Sunday," Sally said brightly, completely unaware of the thoughts that were running through her friend's mind. "You too, Clint, of course," she added coyly.

"That reminds me," Jackie said softly. "I found a pair of your mother's earrings last evening, mixed in with my own jewelry. She loaned them to me to wear with my blue gown, if you'll remember, and I'm embarrassed to say I forgot all about them."

Donovan looked at her then, square on, eye to eye, and Jackie could almost swear that he knew exactly what was going on. That he knew she'd stolen the earrings, that she stole for a living, that for the first time in her life she was going to return something she'd taken.

Kevin chose that moment to put aside his

train and invisible cowboys and Indians to climb into her lap. Did he know she needed to hold him right now? Perhaps he did, bless his little heart. She welcomed him with open arms, as he laid a tired head against her shoulder and made himself comfortable.

"I'm sure she hasn't even missed them," Sally said with a dismissive wave of her hand. "She has more jewelry than any one woman should own."

Jackie would have agreed a few weeks ago, perhaps even a few days ago. It was the greatest justification she knew. Was it fair for some to have so much while others had so little? Of course not. And yet . . . "Let me get them for you," she said, making ready to lift Kevin from her lap and place him back on the floor.

"Don't worry about it now," Sally said sweetly. "If you think of it, bring them Sunday when you come to dinner."

Jackie melted back into the chair, and Kevin came with her, his thin arms winding around her neck. She wondered if the others in the room could tell that she was holding on to the little boy as desperately as he was holding on to her. "I will," she promised.

He did his best not to look at Jackie as she said a whispered good night to Sally and an adoring Marsh. She looked so damned comfortable, so cozy, with a sleeping Kevin curled up in her lap. Even though the child was barely six years old, he didn't look much smaller than the petite woman who cradled him.

He saw Sally and Marsh to the door, doing his duty as host. They had, at best, three-quarters of an hour before dark, but since they both lived so close by they should be home well before then.

Sally had obviously set her sights on Clint as a potential husband for Jackie, and the man didn't seem at all put off by the idea. For some reason he was loath to explore, Rory didn't like the idea at all.

Would Jackie accept if—*when* Clint Marsh asked her to marry him? Rory had an oddly sinking suspicion that she would. After all, she admired his damned nose.

She had no family, no ties, no home, and she obviously wanted them all. There were moments when he saw the craving for them so clearly in her face that he felt it himself. She apparently didn't know how vulnerable commitments like those would make her, how they would change her life so irrevocably.

Perhaps he should simply give her the cash necessary to get her back to England. He'd had problems before she came here, problems she'd been supposed to solve; but Jackie Beresford had brought with her a whole new set of problems, and they were turning out to be more troublesome than the original difficulties.

He stood in the parlor doorway and watched her for a moment. She cradled Kevin as if he were her own, as if she could protect him from anything, everything. Rory's heart caught in his throat. No matter how much you loved your children you couldn't protect them from everything; he knew that all too well.

Maybe he breathed too loudly, and maybe he shuffled his feet. Whatever the reason, Jackie turned her head suddenly and locked her eyes to his. She looked as guilty as she had when he'd found her leaning over his Fabergé egg.

"Why don't you carry him up to bed?" she suggested softly. "He's sound asleep."

Rory stepped into the room and walked toward the chair where Kevin and his alluring governess made the perfect domestic image, trying to act as if he himself hadn't been caught in the act of admiring that picture.

"I know it's a little early, but he's had a long day," she whispered. "Goodness, he'll be up tomorrow at the crack of dawn."

"He's a little big to carry up to bed. Wake him—"

"No." A mere second later she smiled, tilting her head back and looking up at him. "While he might be too big for me to carry up the stairs, I doubt that he's too heavy for you."

Refusing would be ungentlemanly, wouldn't it? Rory took a deep breath and leaned forward, scooping his arms under the limp child. The back of his hand brushed against Jackie's thighs, and again across her midsection. She tensed slightly, and did her best to draw backwards and into the chair until Rory had Kevin in his arms and was moving away from her. Only then did she relax.

Rory headed from the parlor with a sleeping Kevin in his arms, and a silent Jackie a safe distance behind. She didn't say a word but he heard her, heard her soft footfall on the floor and her skirts swishing softly with every step.

He walked up the stairs quickly, listening to Jackie behind him and trying very hard not to look into the face of the sleeping boy he held. When had he last held Kevin like this? He knew the answer to that question: never. There had been a time when he'd made it a point to keep his distance from the boy, and by now it was so natural that the barrier was a part of them both.

Miss Jacqueline Beresford apparently knew nothing of safe distances. She held and hugged and snuggled, giving more of herself to Kevin than Rory had been able to offer. As a result, Kevin had become more manageable almost overnight. There had been a time when it would have been impossible to have Kevin in the same room with company. He ran around and knocked over glasses and vases and shoved his latest pond discovery—usually a frog or a green snake—in some lady's face. Screams and disaster usually followed.

Tonight the boy had been quiet and calm and happy.

He placed Kevin on his bed, and Jackie was there to remove his shoes and socks. Rory backed away and watched from the doorway as she gathered Kevin's nightshirt from the dresser and set about preparing the child for the night. Kevin didn't wake, even as she slipped off his shirt and short pants. She lifted her head as she was sliding a limp arm into its sleeve.

"Thank you," she whispered. "I can take it from here."

He was dismissed, with a smile and a whisper, but he didn't move from his position in the doorway. Watching had become too important.

Yes, he should definitely give Miss Jacqueline Beresford a small fortune and send her on her way. He'd brought her here against her will to relieve him of the problem of caring for Kevin, but in the past few weeks something terrible had happened.

She belonged here, more than he did perhaps. She'd moved in and made this her home, fitting in and making herself a vital part of Cloudmont without even knowing it. Even more, Kevin needed her. Perhaps he even loved her, and God knew the child needed someone to love.

Jackie finished with Kevin, tucking him in and kissing his forehead gently. When she lifted her head and started toward the doorway, she was obviously surprised to see that Rory still stood there.

She was little more than a child herself, in many ways; small, naive, vulnerable. Oh, she pretended to be tough, but when she thought no one was watching there was too much of the dreamer in her eyes. She was everything he'd vowed to stay away from, and he recognized the trouble and heartache she unknowingly offered. So why the hell did the sight of her at certain moments take his breath away?

"Miss Beresford," he whispered. She still hadn't given him permission to call her Jackie. He should get rid of her, before he became as entranced as Kevin was. It would be an easy transition, to go from finding pleasure in watching Jackie to needing her every bit as much as Kevin did. "May I see you in the parlor?"

He was going to send her to jail, since he'd found her in his bedroom just that afternoon. He knew she was still planning to steal the egg, that she was just biding her time until the moment was right. Jackie found she was nervously twisting her hands before her, like an anxious schoolgirl.

Donovan didn't light into her right away. He poured himself a bourbon first, and then he stared into the liquid in the fine crystal, frowning as if he saw something unexpected there. "Kevin likes you," he said, his eyes remaining on the bourbon.

"And I like him," she confessed.

Donovan pulled his eyes from his liquor and stared her down. It was a sudden and unexpected challenge, a contest of wills as he fastened his eyes on hers. Jackie, being Jackie, didn't look down or away.

"I had originally thought a couple of months of service would suffice," he said darkly. "You'd care for my son, I'd pay you, and you'd be on your way."

"That was the agreement."

Donovan broke his stare first, bringing the glass to his lips and tossing back his bourbon. When he was finished, he resumed the contest, locking his eyes to hers. "I've changed my mind."

He was going to send her to jail. Worse, he was going to make her leave Kevin much too soon. She wasn't ready! Just a while longer, that's all she wanted. Just a little while longer. "Have I done something wrong?" Her voice was too small, too weak, too damn needy.

Donovan shook his head slowly. "Not at all. You've far exceeded my expectations."

"Then why—"

"So I think you should stay," he interrupted.

He'd managed to take her by surprise. Good heavens, no one ever took Jackie by surprise! "For how long?" she asked calmly.

"Indefinitely."

Jackie made her way to the fat blue chair where she'd spent most of the evening, and sat down hard. "Stay?" she repeated. Her head snapped up. "But you said just this afternoon that you were planning to send Kevin to a military academy."

Donovan shrugged his massive shoulders. "If you agree to stay that won't be necessary."

She shot out of the chair. "How dare you?" Forgetting that Donovan was twice her size, that he could have her thrown in jail, that he was a man, she advanced on him angrily. "That's blackmail. If I stay, Kevin can stay? If I go, he's sent away to school? You know how strongly I feel that sending him away from home would be a mistake."

"I do," he agreed calmly, even as she poked him once in the chest. She was, this close, eye level with that wide chest, and she'd never felt so small, so insignificant.

That feeling of insignificance didn't stop her from poking him in the chest once again. "It isn't fair."

"Why not?" he asked softly. "You said yourself that you have no family, no home to return to. Nothing to keep you from staying here."

"It isn't fair to ask me to choose between my freedom and Kevin's happiness." She poked him in the chest again, and this time he snagged her wrist in his large tanned hand and stilled her puny attack. She was effectively trapped there, staring at his linen shirt and fine buttons, taking deep, even breaths to keep from screaming.

She'd always known that if Rory Donovan ever caught her she would be defeated. He was too strong for her to fight, too fast for her to flee. A bubble of hysteria rose within her, but she fought back stoically. He would let her go immediately, she told herself.

He didn't. His fingers were firm against her skin, folded over the point on her wrist where her pulse thrummed. He held on so tight that he surely felt her heart pounding. "Who truly has freedom?" he asked. "Seems to me you're as free here as you would be anywhere else in the world."

But she wasn't free here, not at all. The more Kevin relied on her, the more she cared about him, the more trapped she was. The more comfortable she became here the harder it would be to leave.

Bravely, she lifted her head to stare at the man who effectively held her prisoner. She couldn't move away, he was big enough to stop any thought of running she might have, but when she looked into those honey-brown eyes she felt no fear. There was a gentleness in this big man that he usually kept well hidden, and at this moment she could see it too clearly.

"I'll think about it," Jackie whispered. She expected that he would release her, once she'd given him her answer, but he didn't. His grip was gentle but certain at her wrist. She was staring into those honeyed eyes when he began to lower his head, bringing his face closer to hers so slowly that the movement was all but imperceptible. There was a hesitancy in his small movements, an uncertainty.

She held her breath. Did Donovan think that if she stayed in his house he had the right to touch her? Wouldn't it be convenient, to have a willing woman right down the hall; a woman to care for your child and come to your bed when the urge was strong and there was no other compliant partner at hand? She'd show him. When he kissed her, as he obviously intended, she'd bite that full and dangerously soft lower lip of his. She'd draw blood, if she had to, to show him that she was not the kind of woman who'd be willing *or* convenient.

She was prepared to bite down on that intrusive mouth, but she never got the chance. He didn't try to kiss her after all, but tilted his head to one side and took a deep, slow breath. She'd never been this close to a man for this long. If she leaned forward just a fraction her nose would be in his dark golden hair, if she swayed forward she would touch him much too intimately.

Seconds passed slowly. She could feel too much: his fingers against her wrist, his breath against her shoulder, the heat from his body enveloping her. She should be terrified, but she had a sinking feeling the quick beating of her heart and the anxious knot in her stomach had nothing to do with fear.

"You always wear lavender," Donovan said almost longingly.

"Yes," she said. "Do you find it offensive?" If he said yes, maybe she'd start bathing in the stuff!

He drew away and released her wrist, breaking the contact completely. "Not at all. I find it rather intoxicating." He sounded as if the admission annoyed him. It certainly annoyed her!

Jackie took a step back, grateful for the distance, missing the closeness at the same time. An inexplicable want filled her, and she found it truly disturbing. "Perhaps I should stop wearing it," she suggested, somehow certain, as she looked into the confused eyes before her, that Donovan didn't like this new and unexpected element of their relationship any more than she did.

He turned away to pour himself another glass of bourbon. "Perhaps you should." She turned and fled.

The next day, Rory looked forward to a quiet afternoon, but it was not to be. He heard the wheels of a carriage in the drive, and wondered with an unexpected bitterness who was calling this time. It was a little early for Sally, and Clint usually came by horse, not carriage. Perhaps Jackie had another suitor, or a new friend.

He was surprised and a little dismayed when Corinne led Ruth Daniels into his study.

"Rory Donovan," she said with a sweet smile. "Oh, I do so hope I'm not disturbing you."

He put his correspondence aside and stood. Ever the gentleman, he returned her smile. "Never too busy to visit with a beautiful woman."

Ruth blushed. She was his age, perhaps a year older, and just out of her mourning black. To Rory's thinking, she was a little old to be blushing at a simple—and more courteous than honest—compliment.

Corinne lingered in the doorway.

"Would you like a glass of lemonade or a cup of tea?" Rory asked Ruth, motioning for Corinne to attend to her.

His guest raised a hand in refusal. "Nothing for me," she said, nodding to the girl in obvious dismissal.

Ruth came closer to the desk when they were alone, and she glanced over her shoulder once. "I need your advice, Rory," she said in a lowered voice.

"Certainly."

He offered her one of the oversized leather chairs near the window, and even though he was tempted to sit safely behind his desk he lowered himself instead into the matching chair beside her.

"My Henry's been gone thirteen months now," she said, lifting her eyes to him in a way that was much too girlish as she reminded Rory, not very subtly, that she was back on the marriage market. "While he left me in a very comfortable financial situation, I must confess investments puzzle me. Why, I swear I get a headache every time I sit down to peruse those papers and numbers."

"Would you like for me to look over those investments for you?" he offered, hoping to save time.

"Oh, would you? I would be ever so grateful."

Oddly enough, Rory didn't want to know just how grateful. Normally a widow made a great lover. There would be no virginal tears, no expectations, no girlish notions of love and forever after.

Somehow, though, he knew Ruth Daniels wanted more. She was looking for a husband as surely and diligently as Sally was looking for a husband for her good friend Jackie. Given a choice . . .

Oh, no. He refused to allow his mind to wander in *that* direction.

He assured Ruth that he would be glad to look over the investments her late husband had made, and invited her to send the papers over at any time. Their business done, he expected her to rise and leave, but she had made herself quite comfortable in his leather chair and showed no indication that she planned to leave anytime soon.

"You know," she said as the conversation lagged. "I am a bit parched."

Rory rose, grateful for the excuse to leave the room, but he didn't get far before Ruth stopped him. "A splash of that bourbon would hit the spot, I think," she said, nodding to the bar where three crystal decanters and a number of clean drinking glasses were lined up neatly.

He poured a drink for her, and one for himself as well, while she demurred to his back. "I don't usually drink at all, but I feel a cold coming on, and there's nothing like a little bourbon to scare a cold away."

"For medicinal purposes," Rory said as he handed Ruth a heavy glass with more than a splash of his best bourbon in it.

She tossed the liquor back easily, and Rory wondered, as he took his seat and sipped at his own bourbon, if she was looking for courage in that glass.

"Oh, Rory," she said softly, "Aren't you just terribly lonely?"

Before he could answer, she continued.

"I am. I'm just so terribly lonely without Henry, and it doesn't get better, it only gets worse. If we'd had children it would be different, but we were never blessed."

He felt sorry for her, he really did. Loneliness was a terrible curse, and Ruth wasn't handling it well.

"Aren't you?" she asked again, her voice even softer than before as she reached out and placed a hand on his arm. "Lonely?"

He didn't have to answer. Laughter from a short distance away drifted through the open French doors. Kevin's giggle, and a throaty, appealing laugh that he could feel to his bones. The laughter came closer quickly, and soon it echoed on the veranda. Rather than passing by and entering the house through one of the many other doors, Kevin ran into the study with Jackie on his tail.

Rory couldn't help but smile. A moment before, this room had been a prison; it had been heavy and dark and awkward. Suddenly, everything had changed.

Jackie realized right away that he was not alone, and she tried to usher Kevin quickly out of the room. Rory didn't want them to go.

"Kevin," he called before they could escape. "Come say hello to Mrs. Daniels."

Reluctantly, Kevin came back into the room and slunk to Ruth's side. Jackie waited in the doorway, her face flushed, her eyes bright, her plain blouse and full skirt slightly askew and dotted here and there with bits of grass. She'd been running, and her breath came so hard that he could hear it. Dammit, he could *feel* it.

"Hello, Mrs. Daniels," Kevin said obediently.

"Hello, Kevin." Ruth was much too enthusiastic. She reached out and pinched his cheek. "Aren't you just adorable! And growing so fast. Why, the last time I saw you, you were no bigger than this." She held a hand no more than three feet off the floor.

Kevin grimaced as Ruth continued to tweak his freckled cheek. "Yes, ma'am."

Jackie stepped into the room as reluctantly as Kevin had. "Come along, Kevin, it's time to get cleaned up and take your nap."

Ruth's hand fell and she turned her eyes on Jackie. The smile didn't fade, but it hardened. "And who is this young lady, Rory?"

Kevin took Jackie's hand protectively. "This is Miss Jackie," he said. "She's my teacher and my nanny and my friend."

"How nice," Ruth said with a decidedly glacial undertone. She turned her head, and Rory realized that he'd been staring, rapt, at his son and the woman he called his teacher, nanny, and friend. "But really, Rory," she added in a lowered voice. "Do you think it's appropriate to have such a . . . " she cast another hard glance in Jackie's direction, and lowered her voice as if no one but the two of them could hear her whisper, as if Jackie and Kevin would ignore the soft insult, ". . . such a *young* woman living here?"

Young *and* beautiful, she meant. Rory was tempted to say "probably not" and then toss the woman out on her ear. What business was it of hers?

"Most appropriate, I assure you," he said calmly. "I have many servants, and Miss Beresford is simply the newest addition to my household staff." He was tempted to look at Jackie to see how she was reacting, but he kept his eyes on Ruth, to be safe, and discussed her as if she weren't in the room.

"I see," Ruth said skeptically.

"Excuse me, sir," Jackie said in a Cockney accent so ridiculous he was tempted to laugh. "But if you'll release me I need to get the tyke to bed so's I can finish scrubbing the dining room floor and polish the rest o' the silver before I set to milking the cows again."

She didn't wait for an answer, but took her skirt in hand and curtseyed before turning and leaving the room. Kevin's hand was still grasped in hers.

Rory contained his laughter, but he couldn't stop the smile that spread across his face.

"She seems very efficient," Ruth said, apparently fooled and pleased by the ridiculous display Jackie had put on. "Goodness, Rory, I didn't even know you had cows."

He stifled the urge to laugh again, until Ruth placed her hand on his arm again. "Now, where were we?"

Rory stood swiftly. "Good heavens, look at the time," he said glancing at the clock on the mantle. "I have a trainer coming in this afternoon to look at my new stallion, and I just know Alvin won't have everything at the stables in order. It seems I must see to everything myself," he said with a despairing sigh as he offered Ruth his hand. "I'm sure you understand."

Ruth had no choice but to take her leave. "We'll finish this conversation at another time," she said as he walked her to the door. "And I'll have those investment papers delivered to you within the week."

"I'll be looking for them."

Rory threw open the front door, relieved to see that Ruth's driver waited patiently in the circular drive, leaning against the carriage with a casual air. He straightened quickly when he saw his mistress stepping onto the front veranda.

Rory was anxious to get rid of this woman, and more than anything he wanted to rush upstairs and see what Jackie and Kevin were up to. How strange.

Ruth smiled up at him as she took her leave, and it was a sad, almost desolate smile. "You're not lonely at all, are you, Rory?"

He owed her his honesty, at least. "No." He

knew, deep down, that a few weeks ago the answer would have been different, and he was not anxious to explore the reasons for this change.

Chapter Seven

This was the most comfortable bed she'd ever slept in, Jackie decided as she woke slowly. Soft and welcoming, she looked forward to falling into it every night, and on many of these hot afternoons. Today Kevin had exhausted her, and in the hottest part of the day she couldn't imagine attempting anything more physically demanding than sleep. Not long after lunch she'd put Kevin down for a nap, and then she'd come to her own room for just a moment of rest. She'd slipped off her dress, and wearing her chemise and stockings she'd climbed into bed. Minutes later she'd been fast asleep.

Jackie smiled as she rolled into a sitting position. She'd never been so lazy.

At the dresser, she straightened her hair before the mirror. Her lavender water sat there, untouched for these two days. If Rory Donovan found it attractive, she most certainly would not wear it again until she left this house. There was no reason to tempt him or herself with another awkward encounter.

Jackie wondered, with a sharp and unexpected jolt of anger, if that pale and uppity Ruth Daniels wore lavender. She was quite sure that if the woman knew of Rory's obsession with the fragrance, she most certainly would douse herself in it.

She still hadn't given him her answer to his invitation to stay, and he hadn't asked again. In fact, he hadn't said a half-dozen words to her in the past two days. Perhaps he was giving her time to think over his offer, and then again perhaps he was as embarrassed and confused by their last meeting as she continued to be.

Though she would have been more comfortable without them, Jackie slipped into a simple sea-green afternoon dress and stepped into her shoes. She couldn't possibly feel anything for Rory Donovan! For years, she'd made a practice of never feeling anything for anyone, particularly men. Kevin was different; he was a child and he needed her. But Rory Donovan was a man, and a large, domineering, reputedly womanizing man at that.

It would be incredibly foolish for her to stay here for any longer than was absolutely necessary. She liked it here too much, she was beginning to care for Kevin more than was wise, and Rory Donovan . . . Rory Donovan teased and tempted her senses, and no good could come of that!

Jackie loved this room that was, for the moment, hers. She had a feeling that no matter what happened outside the walls, it would be spring here all year round. The pale peach walls and white trim were soft, and the quilt that covered her high bed repeated those colors, as well as other pale shades of the season. Upholstered in silk a darker shade of peach than the walls, the chaise near one of the French doors was perfect for an afternoon of daydreaming, and the lace curtains nearby were almost always dancing with the breeze that wafted through the house. Vases of freshly cut flowers brought spring inside this room. Remarkably, she found peace here.

She had every intention of looking in on Kevin before heading downstairs for a cup of tea, but to her surprise his rumpled bed was empty. His afternoon naps were usually long and deep. Some afternoons she'd sit for a while and watch him, marveling at the complete and total sleep that claimed the child.

Kevin was probably in the kitchen, getting in Nell's way and hounding her for cookies that would spoil his dinner, Jackie decided as she descended the stairs. Goodness, he would be cranky this evening with no more of a nap than this!

At the long table on the brick walkway, Corinne was laying out a pie to cool. She nodded and smiled shyly as Jackie walked past.

She stepped into the kitchen expecting to see Kevin there, at the small oak table or at Nell's side. But all was orderly and silent, and Kevin was nowhere to be found. Nell looked toward the doorway with a smile.

"Would you like a cup of tea?" It had become an afternoon ritual, and Nell was already headed for the pantry.

"No," Jackie said with a frown. "Have you seen Kevin?"

Nell didn't slow her progress. "No. I take it he isn't still napping?"

"I fell asleep," Jackie said, experiencing a surge of guilt for her laziness. "And when I woke up he was gone."

"He's probably down by the pond," Nell said, apparently unconcerned.

"By himself?" There was a knot in Jackie's stomach, a sickening, gut-wrenching knot.

Nell just smiled. "He knows better than to go into the water, and Mister Rory taught him long ago which snakes were poisonous and which were not, and—"

"Snakes!" Jackie shouted. She didn't listen to the rest of Nell's calm response, but took off running, bursting through the door and almost knocking Corinne down as the young girl tried to reenter the kitchen.

If anything happened to Kevin she'd never forgive herself. He could fall in the pond and drown, or come across one of those poisonous

snakes Nell spoke so blithely about, or . . . or
. . . Oh, how would she tell Donovan that she'd
failed miserably in her duties? He would never
forgive her, either.

She'd never run so hard and fast, not even on
the night she'd fallen from Donovan's gallery
and he'd come after her.

When she rounded that last big oak tree and
saw Kevin, sitting on the ground a good distance from the pond and apparently safe and
sound, she didn't know whether to cry or
laugh, whether to hug the kid or shake him till
his teeth rattled. She slowed down considerably, but her walk was brisk as she approached
the pond and the child who sat on the ground
with his head hanging low. She heard the first
big sniffle as she opened her mouth to chastise
him for making her worry so.

"What's wrong?" Tired from running and
worrying, she dropped to the ground to sit beside Kevin, and cocked her head so she could
see his face. His freckled cheeks were damp
with tears, and his lower lip was stuck so far
out it was almost comical. Almost.

He sniffled again, and then he threw himself
into her lap and sobbed miserably, great, gasp-
ing, heartbreaking sobs. She began to worry all
over again.

"Are you hurt? Has something happened?"

Kevin shook his head against her now damp
skirt. "No."

She felt such relief she surprised herself

again. "Then what's wrong?" He continued to sob. "You must tell me," she added gently.

His tears ended, and he sniffled loudly as he lifted his head and repositioned himself so he was sitting in her lap, facing her. "You were asleep when I got up," he said thickly, "and I didn't want to wake you up so I came here with my harmonica, to practice. Pa taught me to play "Pop Goes the Weasel." He always says I should practice outside, 'cause the music sounds better in the open air, and sometimes I practice here."

"I didn't know you played the harmonica." Her arms wound and locked around Kevin, and he seemed to find some comfort in her embrace. It was a peculiar feeling, to offer comfort, but a warming one.

"Pa gave it to me," Kevin said with just one small sniffle, " 'cause I kept borrowing his and forgetting where I put it, and his is a fancy one."

The gold harmonica. "So you came out here to practice," she said softly.

"Billy Ray was here," Kevin said angrily.

"Who's Billy Ray?"

That lower lip stuck out again, but there was not another sob or tear. "He's white trash, just a nasty old cracker."

"Kevin Donovan!" Jackie scolded. "That's not nice."

"Well, he is. His daddy is a sharecropper, and every now and then he tries to fish in my pond."

Jackie could feel sympathy for a kid who came from that kind of background. "I imagine he doesn't have a fine pond of his own," she said softly.

"Well, sometimes I let him fish here," Kevin conceded. "Pa said I have to."

Jackie nodded. "So, Billy Ray was here when you arrived ready to practice."

"He said I scared off all the fish with my playin'."

"So, Billy Ray's a music critic," Jackie observed with a small smile.

Kevin looked up at her, dark brown eyes still filled with tears. "Huh?"

"What happened next?"

The frown was back, as well as more tears in those eyes. Why did the sight make her heart tighten?

"He said he wanted to make a trade, and he offered me some beans for my harmonica. I said no, but then he said they were *magic* beans."

For the first time, Jackie noticed that Kevin's right hand was balled into a tight fist. "Magic beans," she repeated, and Kevin uncurled little fingers to reveal three dried beans in the palm of his hand.

"I gave him my harmonica and he gave me these beans, and when he walked off he laughed at me. He said I was a stupid kid, and there was no such thing as magic. They're just beans. Just regular, not magic beans, and it was too late to take the trade back." He drew back his hand as if to toss the beans aside, but Jackie stopped him with a gentle hand over his.

She'd never believed in magic. Never. There had been no fairy tales for her, no Santa Claus, no dreams of knights and princesses. If she had been able to believe in magic her entire life might have been different.

Every kid should have some magic in his life. Maybe she'd never known magic herself, but that didn't mean she couldn't give it to Kevin. "Maybe Billy Ray's wrong, and these really are magic beans. May I see them?"

Skeptically, he dropped the three very ordinary dried beans into Jackie's waiting palm. She studied the beans carefully, turning them this way and that in the light. Looking up after a thorough inspection, she saw that Kevin's eyes were wide and dry.

"I think you may have some magic beans, here," she whispered.

"Really?" a smile bloomed on his face, a freckled visage that was red from crying.

Jackie nodded. "There are rules, of course, as there always are with magic objects of any kind."

"What rules?"

Jackie took a deep breath. "You must hold a bean tightly in your hand," she whispered, sharing the secrets of the universe, "and wish with all your heart. It cannot be a silly wish, for something impossible, but must be for your heart's truest desire. And then, when the wish has been properly made, you must tell someone you love what you wished for." She looked down at the ordinary beans. "You have only three. I'd suggest you save them and use your wishes wisely."

Ignoring her advice, Kevin plucked one bean from her hand and made a fist around it. He closed his eyes and held them tightly closed for a moment, and then he smiled. Jackie could only hope that he would tell his father what he wished for, so the wish would someday come true.

His eyes flew open, and he grinned widely as he threw his arms around Jackie's neck. "I wished for my harmonica back," he whispered.

Rory walked toward the house quickly, for the first time in a long while actually looking forward to stepping into his house at the end of the day. It was a dangerous and unwanted feeling, but one he couldn't deny.

He'd exhausted himself, working the new stallion and then throwing himself into the menial chores at the stables, chores he had hired hands to see to. There was nothing like an afternoon of physical labor to make a man forget his troubles, and perhaps to forget a certain blue-eyed girl who had wormed her way completely into his household.

But he hadn't really forgotten Miss Beresford, had he? She kept popping into his mind unwanted, lavender water and haunting laugh and rare smile, cautious eyes and tempting mouth and fearless glare.

Rory shook his head as he came into the house through the open doors to his study. What had happened to him?

The house was quiet, which meant Kevin and his governess were not yet back from their afternoon excursion. He walked through the house, headed for the kitchen and a cup of strong coffee, telling himself with every step that he was grateful for the moment of silence.

Nell and her girls were busy with the preparation of supper. Pork chops were frying, and green beans with fatback were simmering. Potatoes were boiling, and he could detect the smell of cinnamon from the oven. Nell's spice cake, if he wasn't mistaken.

Nell poured his coffee, which by this time of day was a thick, almost undrinkable brew, and with a stern hand led him from her kitchen and onto the brick porch.

"You'll just get in the way," she said as she ushered him beyond the long table where pies were cooling.

Nell wanted more than to get him out of her kitchen, he knew. She followed him to his favorite chair, and when he sat down she took the smaller chair beside him.

"It's something, isn't it?" she said in a low voice.

"What's something?" He took a sip of the hot, black coffee and leaned back, wary. It was wonderfully cool here in the shade, and he wanted to close his eyes and savor the moment.

Nell gave him a wide smile. "Miss Jackie and Kevin, of course. Have you ever seen such a pair? She's known the child but a short while, and yet there's a bond between them you can't deny. He's come to depend on her, and I think she needs to be needed."

"What are you getting at?" he asked suspiciously. If she was going to bring up that ridiculous suggestion that he marry Miss Beresford . . .

"Nothing," Nell said, making it very clear it wasn't *nothing* at all. "I just find it rather remarkable that they get along so well, that's all. Why, they came in this afternoon whispering and giggling and carrying on. . . ."

"They're here?" he looked toward the dining room door. "The house is so quiet I thought they were still far afield." Why did he feel a surge of his heart that could only be anticipation?

"They're getting cleaned up for supper." She leaned forward and wrinkled her nose. "I suggest you do the same."

Rory finished his coffee and stepped into the house by way of the dining room door. Silent, even on his big feet, he crept through the dining room and into the entry hall. When he was at the foot of the stairway he heard them at last; soft laughter, a drawer being closed, a muffled voice and a childish giggle.

He listened for a long moment, a foot on the bottom step and his head lifted to peer at the empty stairway. Why was it so easy for Jackie to give Kevin everything he himself could not?

Jackie looked over her shoulder, even though she knew Cloudmont was well behind them. Donovan, seated beside her and dressed in his very best, drove the horse and phaeton expertly, his eyes on the road, his hair turned paler than usual by the sun.

"We should have brought Kevin with us," she said, not for the first time. "Are you sure he'll be all right?"

Donovan turned a wide smile to her. Oh, she wished he wouldn't do that! It made her heart do a strange little flip in her chest.

"He'll be fine. Believe it or not, Nell has spent many hours with Kevin, and they've both survived so far."

She didn't know if she was distressed because Kevin had been left behind, or because she would be spending the entire day in Donovan's company without the buffer of his child between them. This ride to the Clarks' house was bad enough, situated closely beside Donovan on the seat of his fine buggy, and ahead there was the dinner and the visiting to endure, and then the ride home.

It wasn't that she didn't enjoy the company of the Clarks; she did. But she was tired of lying to them. For the first time in her life she was tired of playing a part. She had no choice, and this promised to be a long day.

"Have you thought over my offer?" Donovan asked out of the blue. "About staying," he clar-

ified, even though there had been only the one
offer.

"I've been considering it." In truth, she had-
n't been able to think of anything else. She
liked it here, she was comfortable and safe, and
she loved Kevin. There, she'd finally admitted
it to herself. She loved that funny-looking kid
with his freckles and his red hair and his bright
laughter. Why shouldn't she stay?

Because staying here was changing her,
that's why. She became softer, more vulnerable
every day, and that couldn't be good. It could-
n't be.

"I'm not qualified to teach Kevin for much
longer. My own formal education was"—*nonexistent*—"lacking in mathematics and science."

Donovan nodded, as if he were giving the
problem serious thought. "I've been thinking of
enrolling Kevin in a private school in Florence,
in the fall. It's a good school, and the trip's not
so far that he couldn't attend classes and be
home every night."

Jackie smiled. "I like that idea much better
than sending him to a boarding school."

"I'd still need you to stay on, of course," he
added soberly. "He's too much for Nell to handle full time, and I make occasional out-of-
town trips that keep me away for days at a
time."

Jackie wished Donovan would make one of
those out-of-town trips soon, but she had a
feeling he still didn't quite trust her. Oh, he
trusted her with his child, but he didn't trust

her with his Fabergé egg, she supposed.

"So?" he prompted impatiently when she said nothing. "Have you made your decision?"

She stared at his stern profile. Drenched in sunlight he was golden and beautiful, a fair-haired giant with honey eyes and a sensual drawl. Harsh and handsome, hard and yet surprisingly tender, he touched her deep inside, in places that she knew with all her heart were best left unexplored. Staying would be foolhardy, the most dangerous thing she'd ever done.

But she wanted to stay; with all her heart she wanted to stay. "No," she said softly, "I haven't decided yet."

Donovan grumbled, but he didn't press her. They were almost at the Clarks' house when he leaned slightly to the side and took a deep breath.

"I thought you were going to stop wearing that damned lavender water."

Her heart skipped a beat. "I did."

He turned piercing pale brown eyes to her. "Then why the hell can I still smell it?"

This was an unexpected and disturbing turn of events. Rory sat back and watched sullenly as Clint Marsh turned on the full force of his negligible charms. Marsh smiled and complimented Jackie on the blue gown she wore, though he was inept and merely mumbled something about how "downright purty" she was in that dress. Moron.

He should've mentioned how the blue brought out the exceptional color of her eyes, and perhaps he could mention how extraordinary her perfect skin was even by the harsh light of day. If Marsh had a lick of sense he'd tell Jackie that she was elegant and beautiful and much too delicate for the likes of a simple farmer like himself. Still, all he managed was "downright purty." Moron.

Dinner had been pleasant enough, but then Jackie had been seated by him, while Marsh was seated across the table next to Sally. But once they'd retired to the veranda, Clint had staked his claim in the chair next to Kevin's governess.

She didn't seem to mind. In fact, she smiled brilliantly, and laughed at Clint's lame attempts at exercising his wit, and did damn near everything but bat her eyelashes at the smitten man.

Rory narrowed his eyes as he watched. If he didn't know better, he'd think he was jealous. Jealous of a supposed seventeen-year-old who always smelled of lavender. Jealous of a would-be thief who allowed everyone but him to call her Jackie. Jealous because she had a smile for everyone but him. Ridiculous.

Finally, thankfully, Clint ran out of conversation, and Jackie turned to Mavis.

"Mrs. Clark," she said, standing and reaching into the deep pocket of her skirt to withdraw a carefully folded handkerchief. "Did Sally tell you how I found these earrings in with my jewelry? You can't imagine how sorry I am about the mistake." She unfolded the handkerchief to reveal two small diamond earrings. "Please forgive me."

Rory's eyes were on Jackie's tense face. She truly was asking for forgiveness, it seemed. There was a touching sorrow in her eyes, a tenseness about her mouth as she waited for Mavis's response.

Mavis barely glanced at the earrings resting on a bed of linen. "I hadn't even missed those," she declared airily. Her eyes lit up as an idea came to her. "Why don't you keep them?"

Jackie went pale. "I can't," she whispered. "They're not mine, they're yours."

Mavis waved an indolent hand in a dismissive gesture. "I haven't worn them in ages, and diamonds don't suit Sally at all. With her fair hair and skin she needs color in her gems. Sapphires and rubies suit her best. But my dear," she dipped her chin and studied Jackie with a smile, "if I remember correctly those diamonds suit you quite well."

The earrings remained offered on Jackie's palm. She didn't look elegant at the moment. She looked more like a little girl playing dress-up, and she'd just been caught trying on her mother's best dress. "I can't accept these. They're not . . . they're not *mine*."

"I want you to have them. Good heavens, child, has no one ever given you a gift before?" Mavis asked dismissively, and then she turned to Sally with a sudden and brilliant thought about the barbecue they were planning for next month. Sally asked Clint for his opinion of the menu, and he seemed more than pleased to move closer to her to discuss punch and pies, barbecue beef and pork.

Rory was the only one who watched as Jackie stared at the earrings with what might have been tears in her eyes. Perhaps no one *had* ever given her a gift before. It was hard to believe; she was such a beautiful girl. But as the plans for the barbecue continued, Jackie took her seat and folded the handkerchief carefully over the diamonds.

He decided then and there that one day he would give her a gift, something that would make her smile and cry, something that she would cherish the way she cherished those earrings.

Rory was actually beginning to feel content, until Clint Marsh left Sally's side—at the blonde's obvious urging—took Jackie's hand in his, and asked her to go for a walk in the garden.

The earrings weighed nothing, but they were heavy in her pocket. She could feel them there, with every step she took. Why had Mrs. Clark given them away so easily? In Jackie's world you fought for everything you claimed as your own, but in the Clarks she saw a lack of selfishness that stunned her.

Clint was chattering on about his farm and the plans he had for it, as he often did, repeating himself nervously, so she didn't feel obligated to listen attentively as they strolled through the paths of the Clarks' flower garden.

She did hear his frustrated cry of, "I'm no good at this!"

"No good at what?" she asked absently, coming to a halt near a well-tended row of red rosebushes. She should have known the moment she looked into his face and saw those moony dark eyes that he was up to no good. If she hadn't been so distracted by the weight of the diamond earrings in her pocket she would have known what was coming and defused the situation long before it had gotten this far.

He grabbed her hand and brought it to his lips for a kiss. "Marry me, Jackie," he said as he took his mouth from her knuckles.

"What?" she whispered, stunned by the sudden question, just as stunned that she hadn't seen it coming.

He smiled, evidently interpreting her breathless confusion as a good response, then tilted and lowered his head in an obvious effort to kiss her on the mouth.

She did have the sense to step back and out of harm's way before his lips could find hers. "Oh, Clint," she whispered, and his smile disappeared.

It would serve her purposes to say she would consider the proposal. She could string the adoring Clint along for a few weeks, perhaps even a few months more. Like Kevin, Clint's attentions served as a needed buffer between

herself and Donovan. Perhaps the man would-
n't sniff at her if he thought her to be a
promised woman.

"Oh, Clint," she said again. "I can't marry
you."

His face fell. "I did it wrong, didn't I?"

Jackie wound her arm through his and took
a step toward the house. "It was a beautiful
proposal," she said brightly, and she leaned a
bit closer to her admirer. "My first, I might
add."

"Really?" The thought seemed to cheer him
considerably.

"Yes," she said brightly. "A woman's first proposal of marriage is always special."

He actually smiled. "I wish you would say
yes. Sally thinks we're well-suited, she told me
so a dozen times. As a matter of fact, she said
the garden was a perfect place for a romantic
proposal. Maybe I shoulda waited a while
longer."

They continued toward the house. Jackie
didn't want to give him another opportunity to
try to kiss her.

"You're a very nice man, and a good friend,"
she said. "But I don't love you." Strange words
from a woman who had never believed in love.
Still, she couldn't tell Clint that she was terrified of the very thought of sharing a bed with a
man, that she had decided long ago never to
marry. Now it seemed she was just as terrified
of giving her heart away.

"You could grow to love me, perhaps."

Linda Jones

Jackie shook her head slowly. The veranda was in view, and she could feel Rory Donovan's eyes on her. When she was a little bit closer she could see that she was right. He sat in a chair that was dwarfed by his size, but he seemed comfortable enough with his legs stretched out and a glass of bourbon in one hand.

She had almost reached the veranda when she saw the absolute vexation on his face, the fury in those eyes that remained fastened on her. What on earth had they been talking about to get him in such a state?

Clint knew no shame. As they joined the others he sighed deeply, and placed a hand over his heart. "I just asked Miss Jackie to be my wife."

Before he could finish Sally squealed and jumped from her seat to clasp her hands and jump up and down. "I knew it," she shrieked. "I just knew it."

Donovan stood slowly, unfolding himself from the chair that was too small for him. His eyes remained locked to hers, and if anything the anger there was stronger than before. There was a tic in his cheek, where he clenched his jaw, and his hands were folded into tight fists, as if he held Kevin's magic beans.

No one else seemed to notice.

"She refused me," Clint finished with a mildly dejected sigh.

Sally's smile faded and she reclaimed her seat. Mrs. Clark gave Jackie a sympathetic and questioning look, and Mr. Clark, bless him, tried to change the subject, asking Donovan again about the new stallion he'd bought.

Donovan didn't answer right away, but stared at Jackie a moment longer. Why did he look at her that way, with intense honey-brown eyes that flashed like hard amber? Those eyes bored into her, cutting at her, and they were somehow as intimate as any hand at her wrist or kiss on her lips.

The fury faded from Rory's face, and he retook his seat and answered Mr. Clark's question. He remained restless, though, as if thunder lurked beneath his calm surface, and before ten minutes had passed he stood again, offered Jackie his hand, and said, "Miss Beresford, I believe it's time to go home."

Chapter Eight

Rory kept his eyes on the road ahead, but he was very well aware of every move Jackie made. Her head was turned away from him as she watched the side of the road, taking in the lush green of the trees and grass, and the bright colors of wildflowers that sped past, and every now and then she sighed deeply. It was unlike her to be so pensive.

Once they got home Kevin would be there with his questions and his adoration, and Nell would expect all the details about the meal they'd been served and the gossip that was shared, and Jackie would eventually excuse herself and be off to bed before he ever had a chance to question her about the afternoon's events.

141

A foolhardy instinct made him pull the phaeton to the side of the road.

Now he had Jackie's undivided attention. Her head snapped around, and she practically mowed him down with that glacial stare of hers. Good; she was almost her old self again. He had to admit, for a little bit of a thing she had the most audacious glare.

"What are you grinning at, you fool?" she snapped.

"Nothing." He leapt from his seat and circled the conveyance, striding quickly around the rear of the phaeton until he stood beside Jackie and offered her his hand. She was resistant, and she kept her seat.

"Why have we stopped?"

Rory didn't drop his hand. "I want to talk to you privately," he said truthfully, "and I don't know when I'll have another chance."

Still, she didn't take his hand. "I don't know why we can't talk as we ride," she said stiffly. "Surely you and I don't have so much to discuss that we can't finish the discussion long before we get home."

"Jackie—" he began, and was silenced by a censuring lift of her eyebrows. "Miss Beresford," he said through clenched teeth, and she responded with a barely restrained smile. "A moment of your time, that's all I ask."

Finally, after more reflection on her part than Rory thought was necessary, Jackie put her hand in his and he helped her to the ground. Dammit, he knew she wasn't wearing that lavender water anymore, so why could he still smell it? It was in her pores, in every piece of clothing she owned, perhaps. And then again, maybe he just wanted to smell it.

Where to begin? He didn't want to scare her off, and no matter how invincible she sometimes seemed, he had a feeling she was easily unsettled.

"Is anything wrong?" Rory asked as he released Jackie's hand.

"No, not at all," she insisted. He didn't believe her. Her eyes were too wide, her voice much too calm.

"I guess I'm just rather surprised that you refused Marsh's offer," he admitted. Surprised and grateful. He'd never find another governess like this one. It was for Kevin's sake he was relieved, of course. He'd never entered into this arrangement with any illusions, so why had he felt something akin to a loss when Marsh had said he'd asked Jackie to marry him? He didn't *have* her, so he certainly couldn't *lose* her.

"Are you?" She glanced up and to the side, studying his face for a reaction, he supposed.

"I thought you liked him."

Jackie stepped away from him and away from the road, heading for the narrow stream that was just over a small rise. He followed closely behind her, waiting for the answer he knew would eventually come.

"I do like Clint," she said softly as she stood near the rushing water, her shoes and the hem of her gown lost in tall grass and yellow wild-flowers. "But I don't love him." She sighed, as if that admission pained her. "In truth, Mr. Donovan, I will never marry."

She sounded so certain, and not particularly happy about the decision.

"Why not?"

She looked at him hard, as if judging whether or not he was worthy of an answer to such a personal question. He stood on the slope, and she, a foot or more shorter than he, stood on lower ground. The distance between them was too great for his liking, so he lowered himself to sit on the hillside. From here, he could see her face much more clearly.

"Several reasons," she answered. He could see the inner struggle as she decided if she should say more. He didn't press her, but waited patiently. She turned to face the stream before she continued. "Family history is very important to you Southerners, isn't it?"

"I suppose," he conceded.

She glanced over her shoulder to him, a small and rather sad smile on her face. "Sally says your father was a scalawag."

Rory broke into a wide grin. "He was that. My father sided with the Yankees during the war, and bought Cloudmont from the Greenes shortly after it was over. The Greenes were one of the area's fine old families, and they had not fared well. No one has ever forgiven my father, and there are many who have never forgiven me. Some will never forgive Kevin or his children, either."

He leaned back and turned his face to the sun. "Well, maybe they'll forgive Kevin, since his mother was a Greene." He hadn't meant to sound bitter, but was certain he had. So much time wasted, so many bad decisions he'd have to live with forever. "My marriage to Margaret was supposed to bring an end to the bitter feelings. The Donovans would be forgiven, and a Greene would be at Cloudmont where they belonged. It was supposed to be the perfect solution." He had never talked about it with anyone, had never had the urge.

"Was it?" Jackie asked softly.

"No."

When he looked up she had her back to him once again. "At least you know who your father is," she said so quietly he barely heard her. "I don't. I don't know who my mother is, either."

She turned to face him, then, and he could see that she was prepared for anything: horror, contempt, pity. Perhaps she expected all three. "I'm not seventeen, Mr. Donovan," she said sharply.

"I know," he whispered.

He could see the surprise in her eyes, then a flicker of something he couldn't quite read. Both were gone so suddenly that he might have been mistaken about them in the first place. She didn't ask him how he knew, but continued. "I don't know how old I am, though I imagine I'm somewhere between twenty-four and twenty-six. I don't know when my birthday is, when or where I was born, or who my parents are. They . . . gave me away or sold me when I was not much more than a baby. Beresford is just a name I took. I don't even know what my real last name is."

He wanted to take her in his lap and hold her the way she always held Kevin, with soothing hands and whispered words that somehow made everything right with the world. Foolish thoughts. "This is why you refused Marsh?"

"This is why I'll always refuse marriage, if any other man is ever foolish enough to ask me. If you don't want me to remain at Cloudmont, now that you know the truth, I'll understand." Her back stiffened, and she looked like she was prepared for a nasty rebuff.

"Miss Beresford," he said formally, "I can assure you your lineage had nothing to do with my offer of a permanent position in my household. Good God, you're not a horse."

She blinked once, twice, and this time her surprised expression didn't fade so quickly. "You're sure?"

Heaven help him, he'd never been more sure. "Most positive."

Jackie left the bank and came partway up the hill before she sat carefully beside him. She left a couple of good feet between them, and he made no move to close the gap. "What will happen if you decide to remarry, and your wife decides she doesn't want another woman in the house? She might prefer to care for Kevin herself."

"You're not the only one who's decided not to marry."

"Ah, yes," she said softly. "I keep hearing that you're quite the ladies' man. It would be a shame to tie yourself down to one woman."

How much could he tell her? She'd shared her deepest secrets with him, maybe he could open up to her—a little bit. "The truth is, I'm not very good at marriage. I tried to be a decent husband to Margaret, but nothing I did was ever good enough." He tried a crooked smile. "There's no reason to put another poor unsuspecting woman through that ordeal."

"Did you love her?"

His poor attempt at a smile failed him miserably. God, she cut right to the heart of the matter, didn't she? No mercy, no dancing around the issue. "No," he finally answered, telling the truth for the first time. "We were very young, and we got married because it was what our fathers wanted. I don't recall that anyone asked me if I wanted to marry her or not. It just . . . happened. I tried to love her, I think."

She didn't ask him to clarify, but nodded her head as if she understood.

"So," he continued, "You won't have to worry about a Donovan bride coming into the house and tossing you out."

She contemplated the water and the sky and the wind, perhaps. He wondered, for a moment, if she'd even heard.

"Then I've made my decision," she said without looking directly at him. "I'll stay."

"Very good, Miss Beresford."

She turned her head to look at him then, all wide blue eyes and tempting lips—and Heaven help him he was not a man to be tempted, not any more. "Perhaps you should call me Jackie."

She shouldn't be so ridiculously happy that she wore a silly grin for no reason. But the sun was shining and a soft breeze kept it from being too hot, Kevin skipped by her side as he rambled on about plans to collect frogs as pets, and Jackie had a home for the first time in her life.

Donovan wanted her to stay. Even knowing that she had lied, even knowing that she didn't know who her family was, he wanted her to stay. Perhaps he would become her friend after all.

He still didn't know the worst of it, of course, that she had made her living as a thief all her life and that she had lived on the streets at times not knowing where her next meal was coming from. But still, he'd offered her his home indefinitely.

They were rounding that last oak tree when she saw the young man sitting on the bank of the pond—facing away from them—tunelessly playing a harmonica. Kevin quit rambling, and his smile disappeared.

"Is that Billy Ray?" Jackie whispered.

"Yes," Kevin said sullenly.

Good heavens, this was no child! Billy Ray

had to be sixteen or seventeen years old. Jackie felt a sense of rage well up inside her. How dare this young man take advantage of a little boy?

"He still has my harmonica," Kevin took a step forward, but Jackie pulled him back with a hand at the collar of his shirt. "My wish didn't come true after all."

"You have to give wishes time, Kevin. Patience," Jackie whispered. "Magic takes a lot of work."

He was losing his faith, she could tell as he looked up at her skeptically.

She gave him a brilliant smile. "I just had a thought. If I'm going to sit here while you hunt for those frogs of yours, I'll need something to drink. Goodness," she moved a hand to her throat. "I'm already feeling parched."

Kevin wrinkled his freckled nose at her.

"Would you be a dear and go back to the house and have Nell fix me up a glass of lemonade? And some cookies, too," she added when he didn't move.

"Do I have to?" he whined.

"Yes," she said, her smile never fading. "You have to."

Jackie waited until Kevin was well on his way before she started walking toward Billy Ray. She hid her anger at his deception behind the sweetest smile she could muster.

"Well," she said when she was just a few feet away. "Good afternoon, sir."

He looked over his shoulder, and upon seeing

Linda Jones

her he jumped to his feet and dropped the harmonica in his shirt pocket. "Good afternoon," he returned, his eyes lighting up as he looked her up and down. "You must be that new woman what's livin' at the big house."

His accent held none of the charm Donovan's did, but was coarse and unrefined. "Yes," she answered, taking a step closer and offering her hand. "Miss Beresford. I'm Kevin's governess."

He took her hand and shook it vigorously. "I'm Billy Ray," he said with a nefarious grin.

"My goodness," she said when he finally released her hand. "You Americans are a strong and hearty lot of men, and I've found that to be particularly true here in the South. Why, I do believe there must be something in the air."

He beamed and puffed out his chest, and Jackie did her best imitation of Sally's coy smile. She lifted one hand toward his puny chest and wiggled hesitant fingers. "I don't suppose I might . . . oh, it's too much to ask."

"What, what?" he asked anxiously. He was all but salivating, and Jackie decided she could get this boy to do her bidding at this moment. Anything at all.

"I've never seen a chest quite like this one," she said, wiggling her fingers toward his narrow chest and the pocket that held Kevin's harmonica. "Might I touch it?"

He swallowed hard, and a prominent Adam's apple bobbed up and down. "Uh, sure."

She reached out and feathered the fingers of both hands over his shirt, while he turned red-

150

der and redder, and that Adam's apple went up and down and up and down. . . .

Jackie took a step that would bring her closer to Billy Ray, purposefully twisting her ankle in the process. She cried out and fell against his chest, shoving hard and regaining her footing just as he flew backwards and into the pond, where he landed with a splash.

Jackie stood on the bank, calm as could be, while Billy Ray splashed and found his footing in the murky water.

"Dag nabbit," he sputtered.

"Oh, I'm so sorry," Jackie said insincerely.

Billy Ray stepped slowly out of the pond, dripping with water and mud. Soaked clothing clung to a scraggly-thin body, and longish wet hair was slicked back to his skull and plastered to his neck. A pond weed of some sort, long and green and slimy, hung from his shoulder. He looked at her through narrowed eyes, obviously wondering if the accident had indeed been anything of the sort.

Jackie would never tell the truth. She giggled and pointed as she backed away. "My goodness, don't you look a silly fright?"

His manly ego deflated, he looked like exactly what he was, a bad-tempered bully. "You pushed me," he accused.

"It was purely an accident, I assure you."

He sniffled loudly, shook off much of the water, and patted his soaking wet shirt. He patted it again. "My harmonica!" he groaned, looking back into the pond.

"Oh, dear," she said, backing away another two steps. "It fell out of your pocket while you floundered?"

"I reckon it did." He faced the pond with hands on his hips, and after a moment's consideration he walked back in and fell to his knees to search the mucky bottom. "It ought to be right about here."

"Yes, it should," Jackie encouraged. "I do hope you find it."

She left Billy Ray searching for a harmonica he would never find. Halfway back to the house, she met Kevin, who was cautiously bearing a glass of lemonade and several cookies wrapped in a linen napkin.

"Let's not go to the pond this afternoon," she said as she met him. "That odious Billy Ray person is still there, and I have no wish to spend the afternoon in his company." She looked to the west and the gray clouds that would soon threaten their sunny day. "Besides, it looks like rain."

Kevin grumbled, but he joined her as she trekked back toward the house. "Perhaps we can work on our drawing this afternoon. Can you draw a frog?"

"Yes!" he said, excited at the prospect. "I can draw snakes and fish, too."

"Wonderful," she said softly, fingering the harmonica in her deep skirt pocket.

Rory glanced up from the book he held, peeking over the top to watch Kevin and Jackie playing a game of checkers. Kevin had pulled the gaming table to the serpentine-back settee where Jackie sat, and had placed his own chair on the opposite side.

This was new to him, the nightly gathering in the front room after supper, but he found he looked forward to it every night. There was something comforting about the companionship, even if he did nothing but watch.

And Jackie was very easy to watch. Every move she made was graceful, every smile was heartfelt and warm, every word she spoke was melodious.

He couldn't remember a word of the chapter he'd just read, not a single word. This was bad, very, very bad.

Jackie glanced up, and he raised the book to conceal his face, just in time.

Kevin had fallen asleep almost immediately after another busy day. The rain the gray skies had promised had arrived during supper, with wind that rattled the windows and the leaves in the trees, and rain that beat against the house furiously. There was no lightning, though, no thunder to break the night.

Jackie had slipped into her nightdress hours ago, but she couldn't sleep. She'd finally given up and left the bed, slipping into a muslin wrapper against the chill before stepping through the French doors and onto the gallery. The overhang had protected the flooring from most of the rain on this side of the house, but half the floorboards were damp. The rain continued, softer now, and the wind had died down to a gentle breeze.

After Kevin had fallen asleep, she'd placed the harmonica she'd lifted from Billy Ray's pocket beneath the pillow. It was the first time she'd ever *returned* something in the dead of night. Usually she was taking, not giving. Oh, she couldn't wait to see Kevin's face in the morning, when he discovered that magic was real and wishes could come true.

She leaned against the wall beside the French doors and looked out on the night. The night had always been her time, before coming here. A time to slip into rooms where people slept and take the prizes she desired. When she stole from people who had what she'd never known—money, families, security—she felt equal to them, perhaps even better than them. It had been a game as much as a way of surviving. *I'm smarter than you. Anything you have I can take away.*

She didn't miss it.

Donovan didn't make a noise as he stepped from his own room to the gallery. His torso was exposed, his feet were bare, but he was, at least, wearing trousers. She couldn't help but smile. Perhaps he couldn't sleep, either.

He apparently didn't see her as he stepped to the railing, his feet on the wet floorboards. Her smile faded slowly. He looked out over this land with such tenderness, but there was sadness, too. She'd thought, once, that Rory Donovan had everything a man could ask for. Why wasn't he happy?

"Sometimes I just can't sleep," he said softly, disproving her theory that he believed himself to be alone. "No matter how tired I am, no matter how much I want to sleep . . . sometimes I can't."

"Me, too," she whispered.

Donovan glanced over his shoulder to the shadow where she hid. "What keeps you awake?" he smiled, and her heart did that strange little flip again. "Guilty conscience?"

Her heart caught in her throat and an unexpected quiver racked her bones. He knew! He knew everything . . .

"After all," he teased, "you fooled half the county into believing you were seventeen, and you damn near made off with my mouth harp."

Small sins; if only he knew the rest. . . . "I'm just restless. I haven't stayed in one place this long since I truly was seventeen, or thereabouts."

As he turned away from the railing and came toward her she reminded herself that he was her employer, nothing more. Well, perhaps she could call him a friend. His intentions were honorable, always, even if he did occasionally sniff at her longingly.

"I have to tell you," he said when he stood so close that she could see the pale hairs on his chest. Jackie held her breath, afraid that if she inhaled too deeply she would find the scent of him too tempting to bear. "I've never seen

Kevin so happy and well behaved," he continued, unaware of her inner struggle. "Why, he hasn't once prowled into Nell's kitchen with a snake or a toad since you came here."

"He did that?"

"Several times." His smile faded. "Then there was the worm incident, and the pen-and-ink drawing on one poor governess's best dress, and the unfortunate woman who woke early one morning to find a frog perched on her chest. . . . "

"Kevin did all that?"

"And more." Donovan reached out and touched her cheek with one large hand. "Thank you."

No one had ever touched her like this, gentle and undemanding, so softly that the sensation was no more substantial than the night breeze on her skin. She'd avoided being touched by men at all, and when she was forced to touch a man, she'd made sure she was always in control.

She wasn't in control now, Donovan was. He was the one who had reached out to her, he was the one who could alter the easy caress at any moment by moving closer or lifting his other hand. She should have been afraid, but she wasn't. She should have backed away, brushed his hand from her face, made it clear that she did not want to be touched by him, not in any way. She couldn't.

"All I did was love him," she whispered. "It was very easy."

With an obvious reluctance, the hand fell away from her face. As the man who had touched her so gently took a step back, Jackie was assaulted by a fierce realization. It would be just as easy to fall in love with Donovan.

Chapter Nine

Jackie was sleeping so soundly that she had no warning. Her bed shook and bounced and a body was thrown atop hers. She woke with a start, a touch of panic in her racing blood. The panic disappeared when she heard a trill of laughter and saw Kevin's freckled face near hers.

"You were right!" he shouted as he bounced beside her. "There is such a thing as magic!" He held the harmonica high for her to see.

"It appeared as you slept, I see," she said calmly. "I should have known." She yawned as she sat up slowly. "Night is the time for magic."

Kevin sat cross-legged beside her and began to play. His tune was vivacious but unrecognizable. No wonder Donovan made him practice outside. Jackie leaned back against the headboard and listened. The notes were harsh and loud and discordant—and music to her ears. How could she not smile?

By the light of the morning sun, Kevin played his harmonica and bounced in time atop the quilt. Jackie watched and listened with a steady smile on her face, and more serenity in her heart than she'd ever known.

"What the hell—" Donovan's deep voice intruded, and he appeared in the doorway with one boot on and the other in his hand, his hair still mussed from a restless night on his pillow and his shirt buttoned halfway up his chest. His complaint died away when he looked in at the scene on the soft feather bed.

Kevin didn't stop playing, but only tried harder—and louder—for his father's benefit.

Donovan leaned against the doorjamb and relaxed, and a smile actually crossed his face. Jackie laughed as Kevin hit a high, piercing note and Donovan flinched. He didn't leave, though, but stayed and listened and watched. She lifted her gaze from Kevin to find that Donovan wasn't watching his son, but was staring at her—and much too intently.

Kevin finally put the harmonica down on the bed and leapt from the mattress to go to his father. "It's magic, Pa," he said, his excitement and energy boundless. "I got my harmonica back!"

Jackie did not want to explain all that had

happened; how the harmonica had disappeared in the first place or how she had gotten it back. "Kevin, you finish getting dressed and I'll meet you downstairs for breakfast. Aren't you hungry?" He always was.

"I'm starving!" he said as he came to retrieve his harmonica.

Donovan stopped his escaping son with a gigantic hand on a narrow shoulder. "How about a little fishing this afternoon?" he asked softly, almost as if he were afraid Kevin would refuse him.

"Sure!" Kevin's grin could light up any room.

Donovan cast a quick glance toward the bed. "I'll ask Nell to pack the three of us a picnic, and after I'm finished with the horses and you're done with your reading, we can go down to the river."

Kevin jumped up and down, and Donovan turned his gaze back to Jackie. He didn't look away so quickly this time. "What do you say, Miss Beresford?"

"Excellent idea, Mr. Donovan."

As he backed out of her room, he closed the door silently behind him.

He still didn't know what had possessed him to suggest this outing. The sight of Kevin and Jackie on the bed, a heart-tugging domestic sight if ever he'd seen one, had likely muddled his brain. Then again, perhaps it had been the way she'd whispered to him last night when they should have been asleep, or the way her skin had felt beneath his fingers, or the way her eyes got so big when he barely touched her. . . .

Hadn't he promised himself that he wouldn't fall into this trap again? For years he'd managed to keep women like this one at a distance, with a practiced wandering eye and the assurance that holding anything dear wasn't worth the suffering that was inevitably involved. One woman was as good as another, in the dark.

He'd laid his soul bare once before, and had been punished for the folly. How many nights had he assured himself that if he could harden his heart it wouldn't break again?

But somehow Jackie had crept in, just as surely as she'd crept into his house with the intention of stealing his Fabergé egg.

They could have loaded up the wagon and ridden to the river, but it was such a pretty day a walk seemed a better idea. Besides, the picnic basket Rory carried wasn't all that heavy.

When the river was in sight Kevin headed for it at full speed, his little legs working as hard as they could, his fishing pole wobbling this way and that as he ran. Jackie chose a spot that was high and dry, and she began laying out the picnic Nell had packed for them. A large blanket went down first, and then she placed the basket smack dab in the center and began to unpack.

When their lines were in the water, Rory looked sideways at Kevin. Perhaps he was easy to love, as Jackie said, but he had to admit he'd had a hard time of it. Still, nothing in the past was Kevin's fault. He was a child, innocent, so giving and open.

"Looks like a good spot," he said softly.

Kevin glanced up, perhaps surprised that he'd been spoken to. "Yep," he said. "I'll bet there's some big ol' catfish out there."

Rory nodded. "I sure would like to catch one or two."

Kevin nodded this time, solemnly as he turned his face and his attention to the river. He had such fair skin, like his mother, pale and freckled. The sun would be harsh to such skin, wouldn't it?

"Where's your hat?" he asked.

Kevin wrinkled his nose as he looked up. "I forgot it. Miss Jackie says I'll burn up if I'm not careful." His eyes got big. "We don't have to go back, do we?"

And give this up? Not that easily. "Nope," Rory said certainly, and then he took the wide-brimmed hat off his own head and dropped it on Kevin's. The kid looked so funny in the over-sized hat he had to laugh, and as the brim fell over his eyes Kevin laughed as well.

After several quiet minutes of fishing with no results, he convinced Kevin that it was unwise to fish on an empty stomach, and they headed for the feast. Jackie was waiting, sitting on the blanket with the sun in her hair and a soft breeze whipping a few unruly strands this way and that. She wasn't dressed seductively or even beautifully, but somehow the plain yellow muslin she wore suited her. There was something so distinctly feminine in the ordinary pastel dress, something positively enchanting in the strands of hair that blew across her face.

Damn, he was getting in way too deep, and he didn't know how to fight his way out. Worse, he didn't know if he wanted to find his way out or not.

Well, this was a fine mess. Jackie faced Rory's visitor, the offensive and pasty-faced Ruth Daniels, and offered her a cup of tea while she waited.

They were in the small parlor, where Eleanor had escorted Mrs. Daniels upon her arrival. It was a rarely used room kept for company, and was formal and austere, with its red velvet chairs and gold-framed portraits and marble-topped tables.

Mrs. Daniels, from her perch on the edge of a chair near the window, icily declined tea.

Jackie was headed for the doorway, making her escape, when Mrs. Daniels' chilling voice stopped her.

"Your accent has changed," she observed, sounding not at all surprised. Of course, there were any number of people she could have spoken to since her last visit, people who would have challenged the notion that Jackie Beresford was a Cockney serving girl. "You played a bit of a joke on me on my last visit, didn't you, Miss Beresford?"

Jackie stopped in the doorway, and gathering all her strength she turned to face the intimidating woman. She kept her chin high and her shoulders squared. "You must forgive me. I was poking a bit of fun at Mr. Donovan, not at you." She managed a smile. Oh, she did *not* like this woman! "It was all his talk of servants, I suppose."

"But you are a servant," Mrs. Daniels reminded her. "Come," she said, "and sit with me while I wait for Rory." It was a command, and Jackie absolutely hated commands. Why should this woman have the right to tell her what to do?

Still her curiosity exceeded her outrage, and Jackie made her way to a chair near the pale and frosty Mrs. Daniels. "I would be most happy to keep you company until Mr. Donovan arrives. It sometimes takes a while to lure him away from the stables."

Jackie sat carefully, very well aware that next to the gray satin and silk Mrs. Daniels wore her own blue dress was plain, less than ordinary. Still, she refused to let this haughty woman make her feel inferior.

"Where's the boy?"

The boy. Couldn't she even remember his name? "Kevin is asleep," Jackie answered.

"Good." There was something hard in Ruth Daniels's eyes, something Jackie didn't like at all. It was calculating and belittling, and she prepared herself for whatever was to come. Suddenly, she wished she'd dismissed her curiosity and escaped when she'd had the chance. "It will give us a moment to chat."

Chat? Jackie had a feeling this woman never chatted. She might lecture, or demand, or whine. Chatting was a friendly term, and there was nothing friendly about Ruth Daniels.

"That would be lovely."

Ruth raked her eyes over Jackie, taking in the dress and the shoes and the simple hairstyle that was already going awry. "You're a pretty enough girl," she said when she was done. "Pretty, and young, and naive enough to believe in fairy tales."

Jackie didn't challenge the woman, even though she considered herself neither young nor naive. *Pretty enough* was correct, perhaps. Jackie knew she wasn't ugly, but there was nothing particularly beautiful about her, either.

"I have a friendly word of warning for you," Ruth continued, and there was nothing friendly about her tone of voice or the sharpness in her eyes. "Rory Donovan is no Prince Charming, and you, my dear, are no princess. You can fool yourself into thinking you're something more than an employee in this house, but in truth you are now and always will be a servant. Rory might gladly sleep with you, but he would never marry you."

Jackie hid the panic that welled up inside her. What Ruth Daniels said might not be friendly, but it was the truth. She knew it too well. Still, she wouldn't give the woman the satisfaction of a denial or an argument or a single tear.

She smiled, quite brightly. "Well," she said, lowering her voice to a level of intimacy. "I appreciate the warning, but there's no need for it, truly."

"Really?" Ruth drawled in disbelief.

"Why, what would Mr. Donovan want with the likes of me when he has all those other women." She sighed deeply. "Women much more beautiful than us, I'm afraid."

Ruth's face hardened, but she didn't respond to the mild insult. "Women?"

Jackie leaned forward and whispered. "Surely you know of his reputation with the ladies."

"I've always thought that Rory's reputation was an exaggerated one." Now she seemed worried.

Jackie shook her head slowly. "Not at all. Nearly every night of the week there's a different woman in this house," she confided. "Sometimes more than one," she added.

Ruth went pale. "More than one?"

"Just last week two ladies arrived quite late in the evening," Jackie whispered. "They were identical twins, redheads named Florida and Georgia. Oh, their gowns were so beautiful," she said dreamily. "One was green silk and the other was blue, and they were so low cut you could see . . . well, you could see nearly everything."

Ruth Daniels fidgeted on her chair. "I'm sure you're mistaken. . . . "

"He brought them right into this parlor,"

Jackie continued. "Kevin had gone to sleep, and I had come downstairs for a cup of tea. I couldn't help but glance into this room as I passed. Why, right in that very chair where you're sitting now he sat, and they—" She snapped her mouth shut. "Oh, I can't say it. Still, you can see why I would never think of Mr. Donovan as a—what did you call him?—Prince Charming."

Ruth was now sitting on the very edge of her chair, and fidgeting uncomfortably. "An unmarried man might stray, but with the right influence—"

"I'll never forget the sight of it," Jackie said as if she didn't hear the woman. "There Mr. Donovan was, basking in the undivided attentions of two women who—well, I can't say it. It was just too shocking."

"I find this hard to believe," Ruth said. "All the rumors of his womanizing, I thought they were nothing but gossip."

Jackie rose slowly from her chair. "Well, perhaps I can tell you, if I whisper in your ear."

Ruth was frozen as she waited, and Jackie had a feeling the woman didn't know if she wanted to hear or not. She bent slowly to bring her mouth close to Ruth Daniels's ear, and she whispered, her words so soft Ruth would have to strain to hear it all, if she wished. As she whispered, she found the clasp on the diamond bracelet at Ruth's right wrist and released it, and without pausing in her sordid tale she slipped the bracelet into her pocket.

When she moved away, standing tall, she felt quite satisfied with herself. Ruth Daniels was red as a beet, from her neck to her hairline. Even her ears were red.

"A lady would never repeat such a story," the woman said haughtily when she found her voice.

"It was just a friendly warning," Jackie said sweetly. "Besides, as you so like to remind me, I am not a lady."

Rory stepped into the parlor, and when he said hello Ruth Daniels jumped from her seat.

"Oh, Rory, thank goodness you're here," she said, and Jackie wondered if she would repeat the story. "I have those papers you said you'd look over."

"I'll be leaving, then," Jackie said with a smile. Rory barely nodded in her direction as she left the small parlor.

She stood in the entry hall for a few moments, listening to their greetings. Ruth Daniels was evidently not going to repeat the secrets she'd been told.

Jackie lifted the bracelet from her pocket. Goodness, the thing would bring a small fortune!

From the parlor, she heard Mrs. Daniels's lowered voice. "There's something very odd about that new governess you hired."

"Jackie?" Rory responded, and she had to smile at the disbelief in his voice. "She's the best governess we've ever had." He continued to defend her, and Jackie leaned against the wall and listened. "Kevin adores her. Fiddle, everybody adores Jackie. What makes you say she's odd?"

"There's just something about her. . . . "

Jackie stepped into the room, and Rory stood. He'd been sitting in the now infamous chair Ruth had vacated, and Ruth had taken Jackie's chair.

"Pardon me for intruding," she said in her most servile tone of voice, "but I found this in the entry hall. Mrs. Daniels, is it yours?" She held forth the diamond bracelet, and watched as Ruth grasped her bare right wrist.

"Yes. Oh, my, I didn't even realize I'd lost it."

Jackie placed the bracelet in a waiting hand.

With every day that passed, this place felt more like home, these people felt more like family. Jackie ignored the inner warnings that told her all would not be well. No one lived like this forever, right? Something was bound to go wrong.

But for now she allowed herself to enjoy the moments of perfection as the days passed.

Almost four weeks had gone by since she'd agreed to stay at Cloudmont. If occasionally her heart beat too fast when she looked at Donovan, if she sometimes thought about sneaking down the gallery at night not for a glimpse of the egg but for a glimpse of *him*, well, those were moments of weakness she was learning to deal with.

This was one of those moments. Donovan and Kevin were on the floor playing with wooden trains. It was rather ridiculous and more than a little heartwarming to see that six-and-a-half-foot body stretched across the rug on its stomach. He made silly *choo-choo* sounds and laughed with Kevin when he did the same.

Jackie mended Kevin's favorite fishing shirt and watched out of the corner of her eye. They were almost a real family. She could swear Donovan and his son were closer than they had been when she'd come here, and she wanted to believe she could take some of the credit for the improvement.

Since she had no interest in marrying, and Donovan didn't plan to wed again, it worked out well to her way of thinking. Kevin needed someone to care for him, and Donovan had been doing a poor job on his own. They needed her. Jackie had to admit that she'd come to need them, too. She needed a roof over her head and a child's laughter, sunshine and rain and the assurance that she'd be here tomorrow and the day after that and the day after that. Even more, she needed these men to need her. Together, the three of them were invincible.

Perhaps this was an unconventional family, but it was all she had; all she could ever have.

When it was bedtime, she chased Kevin off to his room with a promise that she'd be up soon to tuck him in. Donovan removed himself from the floor and collapsed into his favorite chair, and for a moment he closed his eyes.

Jackie gathered together her materials and stuffed everything into a small canvas sewing bag. When she stood she looked at Donovan and saw that he was staring at her again. It had become a habit of his, of late.

"I never knew a six-year-old could be so exhausting," he confessed.

"Well they are. Especially those who never seem content to rest," she added with a smile.

He leaned his head back and closed his eyes once again, and she saw a small tear at the shoulder seam of his shirt. She was getting quite good at sewing, for one who'd taken it up so late in life. "You should give me that shirt to mend," she said, stopping as she passed to poke a finger in the hole. Donovan jumped as if he'd been shot when her finger met his shoulder, and Jackie quickly drew her hand back.

He looked up at her from his easy chair, honey eyes tired and deep and questioning. Somehow she was as close to this man as she'd ever been to anyone. She knew every feature of that face so well she could close her eyes and see him perfectly. She recognized every nuance of his voice, every flicker in his eyes. It was quite disquieting, and just as inescapable.

She reached out and touched his cheek, brushing her fingers softly across the hard planes of his face. The end-of-the-day bristle was rough to her touch, and she allowed the tip of one finger to graze over the softer skin high on his cheek. "You have a fiber from the rug on your cheek," she explained as she brushed it away. He didn't move or take his eyes from her.

Oh, this could be dangerous. She'd never wanted a man to touch her before, so what was this longing she couldn't rid herself of? The memories of Luther, memories of men who'd offered her money to lie with them, usually they were enough to kill any tender feelings that might come to the surface.

But lately she'd found that these feelings for Donovan were stronger than her memories. How could that be?

Her hand fell away, and she headed for her room with a curt "goodnight."

Donovan didn't say a word in response.

Rory glanced at the clock on the mantle. They should have left for the Clarks' barbecue half an hour ago, and still Jackie wasn't ready. It wasn't like her to keep him waiting; she was always so prompt.

When he heard a soft footfall he mumbled "Finally!" and spun around to see Kevin standing in the doorway. The child was still put out at being left behind again, but this was to be an adult barbecue with a dance to follow. They likely wouldn't get home until very late, long past Kevin's bedtime.

Kevin held his hands behind his back, and looked up almost suspiciously. "Miss Jackie says she'll be down in a few minutes."

Rory shook his head. A few minutes! What was taking her so long?

"Can I have a talk with you?" Kevin asked,

his words grown up, his voice that of a child.

"Of course," Rory said seriously, taking a seat and waiting for Kevin to continue.

He expected the boy to stand before him and either complain again about being left behind or ask for a new fishing pole. But Kevin surprised him, climbing into his lap and making himself comfortable. When Kevin was seated comfortably on Rory's thigh, he opened one hand and displayed a bean.

"This is a magic bean," the kid said earnestly. "Do you know about magic beans?"

This was a new one. "No, I'm afraid I don't."

"There are certain rules you have to follow when you have magic beans," Kevin instructed. "Miss Jackie told me all about them. I just have two beans left, so they have to be important wishes, don't you think?"

"Absolutely," Rory agreed.

"These are the rules." Kevin held the bean reverently before him. "The wish has to be for something real, not something silly, you have to wish with all your heart and then tell someone you love what you wished for." He turned dark brown eyes up solemnly. "Then sometimes you have to be patient."

"I see," Rory muttered, suppressing a smile. *What utter nonsense.*

Kevin closed his eyes and made a fist around the bean. His nose wrinkled and his mouth was screwed up tight as he squeezed his eyes shut ever tighter. There was such intense concentration on that freckled face, for a long moment. Then, without warning, he opened his eyes and looked up.

"I don't want Miss Jackie to be my governess anymore," Kevin whispered, and Rory's heart leapt in his chest. What on earth had happened to make Kevin want to wish Jackie away? He had his answer as Kevin continued in a very soft voice. "I want her to be my mother."

It was a ridiculous wish, an outrageous request. . . . So why did it sound so right?

Jackie chose that minute to step into the room, and Rory put aside his shock and decided on the spot that it had been worth the wait. She wore a dress he hadn't seen before, white flocked with blue flowers. It fell off her shoulders, exposing creamy skin he had not seen or touched, the gentle curve of her shoulder and upper arm. Her hair was styled more intricately than usual, soft curls and blue silk flowers. She wore the diamond earrings Mavis Clark had given her, and no other jewelry. Something about her spoke of summer to come, of hot days and warm nights and brilliant blue skies.

She was exquisite. Rory set Kevin on his feet and stood slowly, for some reason certain that to move too quickly would spoil the moment. He took one step closer to Jackie, and the scent hit him; not just the hint of lavender that had so haunted him recently, but the full intoxicating scent he remembered from the first night he'd met her. Evidently she'd ended her ban on the fragrance. He should be distressed, but found that, perversely, he was not. Instead, he viewed her action as a gift, one he couldn't thank her for without revealing more than was wise.

"I'm so sorry I made you wait," she said sincerely.

He answered with a smile. "I hadn't noticed."

She seemed relieved, and that made Rory glad he'd told the small lie.

"I need to have one last word with Kevin," he said, turning about and leaning down to place his mouth close to a waiting ear. "Let's keep this wish our secret," he whispered.

Chapter Ten

Jackie had been to soirees and balls before, when she'd been working her scam on a wealthy family. From Boston to Richmond to Charleston, she'd smiled and flirted and pocketed pieces of jewelry as she moved through the crowd, knowing all the while that she'd soon be leaving these people and this lifestyle. In all her life she'd never been to a grand party as a true guest.

The Clarks' impressive and lush lawn was overflowing with finely dressed folks who laughed and ate and drank. Jackie sat back and watched a group of colorful ladies walk across the green grass, looking for a moment like living, breathing flowers with their bright gowns and silk adornments.

Couples whispered with their heads together, men argued politics and cotton, and women talked of the latest fashions and their adored children. Hopeful gentlemen pursued their favorite ladies, bearing lemonade and compliments.

Jackie had not been lacking in chivalrous attention herself. Clint had stayed at her side most of the day, bringing her lemonade and cake, telling her again and again how lovely she was, whispering into her ear and asking if she wouldn't reconsider his proposal.

There were others as well. Sally was still determined to find her friend Jackie a husband. If Clint wouldn't suit, why, surely one of the other local men would do! She listed their attributes and minor faults as each one walked by, and did her best to introduce each and every one. They were attentive, and at one point Jackie had looked about to see that more than a half-dozen handsome gentlemen were gathered vigilantly around her lawn chaise.

It was flattering, but also a little disturbing.

More than once she looked for Donovan, hoping he would sweep in to rescue her. He was never in the same place for very long. He was deep in conversation with Mr. Clark one time, flirting outrageously with a woman old enough to be his mother the next. This time, when she looked for Donovan, she found him standing all alone, his back to an ancient oak tree as he stared unsmilingly at Jackie and her contingent. She wondered if Donovan knew what it meant to her to be here, and she smiled at him while Clint chattered on about the magnificent color of her hair. She owed him so much for this chance at a new life.

Rory wasn't alone for long. That hag Ruth Daniels came upon him with a coy smile and a fluttering fan. Obviously the woman had not been scared away by Jackie's whispered libidinous tale. Perhaps Ruth thought she was the one who could change Rory's womanizing ways.

Jackie's smile died as Donovan turned his charms on Ruth. He said he had no plans to marry, and she believed him, but there was a calculating gleam in Ruth Daniels's eye. Jackie remembered it from their previous meetings. Rory might not have plans to wed again, but that didn't mean some devious and attractive woman wouldn't swoop in and do her best to change his mind. Oh, another woman in the house would ruin everything!

Sally saved her from the adoring lads, stealing her away for a short rest before the cotillion got underway. There were several requests for promised dances, requests Jackie deftly ignored as Sally led her toward the house. She glanced over her shoulder once, to see Donovan still deep in conversation with Ruth Daniels. He gave the wench that devastating smile of his, and even though she couldn't see from this distance, Jackie knew his eyes were sparkling and he was about to say something brilliantly charming.

Yes, another woman in the house would ruin everything!

As far as Rory could remember, he'd never been jealous before meeting Jackie. Margaret had been young and shy when they'd met and married, and even later . . . since he had never loved his young wife he hadn't been jealous. Angry, yes. Hurt, more than he liked to admit. But jealous? Never.

But he didn't love Jackie, either, so why was he incensed to watch her dance with a succession of other men? Clint, Telford, and every other eligible man in Lauderdale county had claimed at least one dance. Rory had danced several times himself, with Mavis Clark and Sally, and twice with Ruth Daniels, who either had something permanently in her eye or had been attempting to flirt with him by batting her pale lashes in his direction all evening. He had never in his life found a woman's attentions annoying—until today.

When he'd seen Jackie just that afternoon, looking beautiful and bright, he'd been delighted. His heart had leapt, and he'd had this urge to reach out to her with everything he had and everything he was. To tell her how proud he would be to arrive at the Clarks' with her on his arm. What had he been thinking? They weren't a couple, and they couldn't ever be. Could they?

Kevin wanted Jackie to be his mother, and

Rory—well, Rory wasn't sure exactly what he wanted, but it certainly wasn't to stand here and watch Jackie dance with every man in the room but him! If one of them managed to sweep her off her feet, she'd leave Cloudmont in the blink of an eye. Dammit, he didn't want her to leave. The house wouldn't be the same without her. Kevin wouldn't be the same, either, and Rory had to admit he liked the change in the boy. An ardent and adoring man might spoil their cozy arrangement.

As the music ended he made his way across the crowded dance floor. To hell with what everyone would say if they danced together. One dance, and he'd be careful not to hold her too close or smile too wide. To the people in this room, she was his employee. Even a hint that there was anything more would be scandalous.

He managed to claim his dance just a step before Clint made another appearance, and when the music began he swept Jackie away from her most zealous admirer. This close, he was reminded of how very small she was. Her hand in his was tiny and pale by comparison, and he was careful not to hold that warm hand too tightly. She was not much more than five feet tall, certainly, no bigger around than a mite, and in his arms she seemed incredibly delicate, fragile to a fault.

Still, that fall from the gallery hadn't damaged her any, so she must not be too fragile.

"What are you grinning at?" she asked, trying for a sharp tone and falling far short.

"I was remembering the night I caught you admiring my Fabergé egg," he said over the music. "I thought you were a boy, maybe one of the sharecropper kids come to see what he could pilfer from the big house."

She looked suitably insulted.

"You look nothing like a boy tonight," he added, his voice lowered so Jackie could hear him over the music but no one else was likely to make out what he was saying.

"Goodness, Mr. Donovan," she said in a passable Southern accent much like Sally's. "Is that supposed to be a compliment?"

"You're beautiful," he added seriously, and the remembrance of her many admirers stole his momentary happiness. "Surely you've been told several times today."

"Several times," she confirmed seriously, and then she broke into a smile and laughed artlessly.

She was far too lovely and special to remain unmarried and alone all her life. One day some man would come along and steal her heart, and she would leave the Donovan men behind with nothing more than a touch of regret. The very thought made Rory ill.

He looked around the crowded ballroom, searching for a way out. There was a large crowd of partygoers outside, beyond the open doors, and there were men smoking and drinking brandy in Walter's library, the only downstairs room other than the winter kitchen that had not been cleared for dancing. Rory steered his partner toward the entry hall. He was a frequent guest in the Clark household, and he knew the place almost as well as he knew his own home.

Near the entry hall he stopped dancing, but he didn't release Jackie's hand. He pulled her past the stairway, through the dining room where a group of ladies gossiped and munched on cake, into the winter kitchen. It was deserted on this warm night, as the maids and cooks were in the main kitchen, busy preparing dish after dish for the hungry guests. Still, the door was opened to the covered walkway to the separate kitchen and he did not want to take the chance that they might be disturbed. He didn't hesitate to pull Jackie into the pantry and quietly shut the door.

"What on earth are you doing?" she asked. He could hear the humor and wonder in her voice, but it took a couple of minutes before his eyes adjusted to the dark and he could see her face.

"I want to talk to you, and this is the only place I could think of where we won't be interrupted."

"It can't wait until we get home?"

Home. When he heard her speak of Cloudmont as home he knew he wasn't making a mistake. "No," he whispered. "This can't wait." He continued to hold her hand, and she hadn't yet tried to pull it away. He took that as a good sign.

He'd never been in such cramped quarters. There was a shelf behind him, another to his side, and the ceiling in the pantry was rather low. Perhaps the closed quarters were the reason his heart constricted.

"I know I said I'd never marry—"

"Don't say it," Jackie said coldly, jerking her hand from his. "I can't believe this! Let me tell you something, mister." She jabbed at his chest forcefully. "I've known women like that Ruth Daniels all my life. They can pretend to be sweet and adoring, and as soon as they have what they want they hit you with the ugly truth. I thought you were too smart to be fooled by such a transparent display. Oh!" she slapped his chest hard this time. "Men are so incredibly stupid!"

Ruth Daniels? "What are you talking about?"

"You want to marry that pasty-faced wench, I know what's happening. She'll promise you that she doesn't mind having me in the house, but once you're married—" Her strong voice broke, and she actually sounded like she was on the verge of tears. "Once you're married she'll find a reason to be rid of me, you just wait and see."

"Jackie, you have this all wrong," he whispered.

"I knew this would never work." There was a touch of real panic in her voice. "Well, maybe I won't wait around for that whey-faced hag to toss me out. I don't stay where I'm not wanted."

She tried to make her way past him to the pantry door, but he wasn't about to let her pass. A simple shifting of his weight blocked her exit. "Would you just listen to me?" he said, reaching out and taking her hand again. She was still, too still, and he reached down to place a hand under her chin and tilt her face up so he could see it. Even in the dim light that shot through the cracks in the pantry door, he could see the anger and the hurt in her eyes.

"I have no intention of marrying Ruth Daniels," he whispered.

"Then why . . ."

He hadn't kissed a woman in five years. Longer, since he and Margaret had not been close in the year preceding her death. It seemed too much like giving something of himself, and he was not much of a giver these days. He was a taker.

But he wanted to kiss Jackie more than he'd ever wanted anything. It was a compulsion, a need he couldn't fight. She quit speaking as he lowered his mouth toward hers. He half-expected her to move away, but she didn't. She waited, and the hand in his tightened, not in encouragement, he knew, but in apprehension.

A simple, soft, easy kiss, that's all he wanted, he thought as his mouth hovered above hers for an instant, before he gave in to temptation and settled his lips softly over hers.

Jackie didn't respond at first, but stood there motionless and allowed him to kiss her. She didn't even breathe as he brushed his mouth over hers. He didn't place his arms around her, didn't try to clasp her tight, but held her hand and caressed her only with his lips upon hers.

When she at last accepted the kiss he felt it, in a breath that brushed his lips, in the gentle quiver of her mouth. She tilted her head and moved her lips ever so slightly, and in that moment he was overwhelmed with a host of emotions he'd locked away. Jackie no longer simply accepted the kiss; she was tasting and teasing and discovering, just as he was.

Heaven help him, she tasted and smelled so good he didn't ever want to leave this pantry. His planned simple kiss turned to much more, a gentle dance of lips and tongues that he could feel in his blood. He wanted her more than he'd ever wanted anything—and that couldn't be.

Still, he couldn't deny that he was thunderstruck by this simple kiss.

Jackie slipped her hands around his waist and held on tight, and without thinking he lifted her off her feet. She dangled before him, face to face, mouth to mouth, and when he heard the little catch in the back of her throat it almost sent him over the edge.

It was the light that intruded first, a harsh and unwelcome interruption that came just before a familiar voice said, "I'm sure there's another bottle—"

Rory glanced at the open doorway and a shocked Mavis Clark. Sally stood behind her mother, obviously just as aghast at the scene they'd stumbled upon. It was almost funny. Almost.

He lowered Jackie slowly. "Mavis, Sally," he said calmly. "You're just in time."

"Rory Donovan!" Mavis snapped as her senses returned. "This is most inappropriate."

"Just in time for what?" Sally asked, now more confused than shocked.

Rory looked down at Jackie. Poor girl, she was embarrassed, and rightly so. But God, she was beautiful. Her hair was just slightly mussed, her eyes were bright, and her lips were red and swollen, obviously well-kissed. This wasn't a mistake.

"Jackie," he said softly, bringing her hand to his lips. "Will you marry me?"

Her face drained of all color as she looked up at him, and her eyes widened. In fear? In shock? He didn't know, but he didn't like it, anyway. "No," she whispered.

"Jackie!" Sally hissed. "Say *yes!*"

Jackie ignored her friend. "No," she said again. "I can't marry you."

Rory turned to Mavis. "Close the door," he said. "We're not finished."

"This is most unsuitable—"

"Close the door!" he shouted, and without another word, she did.

"Well, I never." She heard the muffled voice from the other side of the door.

As Jackie's eyes adjusted to the darkness that had returned when Mrs. Clark had slammed the pantry door, Donovan kneeled down on one knee before her. It couldn't be comfortable down there, surrounded by dry goods and shelves all around. He was so close, and necessarily so, his face was practically pressed against her midsection.

"Get up!" she hissed.

"Marry me." He said the damnable words again.

"No!"

"It's the logical solution."

"Solution to what? As far as I can determine everything's just fine as it is."

"It came to me this evening," he said, undaunted. "I watched you dancing with all those men, and I thought . . . " he paused. "Eventually people will talk. Maybe not now, but when this arrangement of ours is a few months or a few years old the gossip will turn ugly. Kevin will suffer for it."

"That's a low argument." He knew she would do anything for Kevin.

"That's not the only problem a marriage would solve."

She held her breath. He wanted her in his bed, that's what this was all about. She'd agree to marry him, and maybe she'd even agree to lie with him, and then he'd be done with her. Nothing could be worse. "What problem?"

"Tell me, Jackie, how do you like all those ardent young men clamoring at your feet?"

"I hate it!" she said. "It was flattering at first, but it quickly became annoying. After a while it was as if I couldn't breathe properly for all the attention, as if I would never be able to take a deep breath again if they didn't back away." Goodness, she could hardly breathe now!

"Neither of us would have to worry about such unwanted advances if we were married."

She almost smiled. It sounded as if Ruth Daniels's advances were unwanted! "Rather drastic, don't you think?"

"Perhaps." He still knelt on one knee before her, waiting for an answer.

She could still feel his mouth on hers. Rory Donovan had provided her first kiss, and it had been much more than she'd expected. She'd expected to feel contact only at the point of impact, and while the pleasant sensations had started with her lips, they certainly hadn't ended there. She hadn't known that a kiss could make her tremble to her bones. Goodness, she was still trembling! Yes, she was trembling and tingling and overly warm.

"I'm not ready for marriage," she whispered. "I'm . . . scared."

"Of me?"

Of everything. She was afraid this feeling might be love, and in the long run love would only hurt her. In all her dreams she'd never imagined this for herself. Love, a home, it was almost too much to hope for. Most of all, she was afraid of the marriage bed. Good God, it was just her luck to go and have such strong feelings for a man who was as tall and wide and hard as Rory Donovan! There would be no refusing him, would there? He had the strength and the size to overpower her, to take whatever he wanted. Was she afraid of him?

"Yes," she admitted.

She thought he would be insulted, that he would storm away and leave her there. She'd have to make her way out of Alabama alone, perhaps back to Baltimore to Mina. Maybe Luther was dead, or had moved on, and she could be with her friend without wondering if the man who had raised her was going to be around the next corner.

But Donovan didn't run. Instead, he kissed her hand. "I think I understand," he whispered. "We know one another, but perhaps not well enough to jump headfirst into a marriage. We can take all the time you'd like, before making this a real marriage. Think of it as a marriage of convenience, a business arrangement if you will, and if as time goes by it becomes more, then we can count ourselves lucky."

"What if it doesn't?"

There was a moment of silence. Jackie held her breath as she waited for an answer. "Perhaps we can still count ourselves lucky. I like you, Jackie. I don't know many men who can honestly say that about their wives."

She smiled widely. He *liked* her! "Before I think about saying yes," she said, "there's something else I have to tell you."

"Another deep dark secret?" Amazingly, there was a note of teasing in his voice.

"I'm not English," she said quickly, and then she waited for an explosion that never came.

"I know," he whispered.

"How can you possibly know?"

He kissed the hand he held. "When you're angry the accent leaves you, did you know that?"

"No."

"Well, it does. Honestly, Jackie, I couldn't care less, but"—he sighed, almost melancholy—"if you're going to be completely honest I suppose I should do the same."

Here it comes, she thought, the one qualifier that would spoil everything. He'll keep mistresses, he likes to beat his wives . . .

"I don't want other children," he said quickly.

Thank God! "Neither do I. Frankly, the prospect of childbirth terrifies me. Kevin is plenty."

He nodded once, apparently pleased that she accepted his condition. "If we ever do have a real and complete marriage, there are ways to prevent pregnancy."

She knew all about them from Mina, who had always loved men and the pleasure they gave her, but had never wanted children. "There are?" she asked naively, and immediately she was ashamed. Lying still came too easily.

"Yes," Donovan answered.

Jackie took a deep breath. "Yes," she whispered. "I think it would be an excellent idea if

191

we got married, purely as a business arrangement," she added quickly. "Those suitors are already getting tiresome. I shall be glad to be rid of them."

Donovan stood and kissed her, quickly this time. This meeting of their mouths was nothing like the all-consuming caress they'd shared minutes ago, but it was pleasant just the same. It was familiar and somehow comforting.

"Good," he said, sounding relieved. "I'll make the arrangements and we can be married tomorrow."

"Tomorrow!" So soon? Oh, she wasn't ready!

"I don't think the Clarks are going to allow you to return to Cloudmont with me tonight," he said wistfully. "And I have no wish to wait for weeks while you sew a new dress and send out invitations and whatever else is involved in a grand wedding. Tomorrow," he insisted again.

Jackie smiled. "We're going to be a real family, aren't we, Rory?"

She'd never called him Rory before, but it seemed appropriate. More than just appropriate, it seemed almost intimate.

"Yes," he said, and while she heard no displeasure in his voice, neither did she hear anything like the wonder and joy she felt at the prospect. "We'll be a real family."

Chapter Eleven

The house was quiet and cavernously, blackly empty. Nell and her girls had gone home for the night, and Kevin was fast asleep. The boy didn't know about the wedding yet, didn't know that his wish was going to come true. Morning would be soon enough to tell him the news.

Nell knew, though. Nell, with her smug "I-told-you-so" smile, had wished him well as if his impending nuptials resembled, in any way, a normal marriage. Reality had intruded when she'd softly suggested, her smile gone, that he confide in Jackie about Leona. About everything.

Jackie was not here. She was spending the night at the Clarks' house. He wanted her here, but as he had known she would, Mavis had insisted that it was not proper, not proper at all. Rory didn't care for what was proper and what was not, and neither did Jackie. Still, for the sake of her reputation he'd agreed it was best.

With a key taken from his bedside table, Rory unlocked the fourth bedroom's door. He hadn't set foot in this room in more than five years, and neither had anyone else. It was a tomb, a shrine, a place for ghosts.

But it was time, perhaps, to move on. To say good-bye.

He expected to feel the old familiar panic as he stepped into the room, but he discovered instead an odd and unexpected peace.

By moonlight he found his way to the dresser, where he swept back a protective sheet and opened the top drawer. Dust filled the air, tickling his nose as the sheet fell away. There, among frilly bows and satin ribbons, was a small photograph framed in silver. When he lifted it into the scant light and caught a glimpse of the face there, something akin to panic did rise within him. His heart constricted and he couldn't take a deep breath.

"Hello, Pumpkin," he whispered, touching his finger to the glass above her face.

Leona had been three years old when this picture was taken. He remembered the day as if it were yesterday. Margaret wanted a proper and formal photograph, but Leona had refused to cooperate. She'd laughed and giggled as her mother tried to make her be motionless and assume a dignified pose.

She'd finally held still, but her expression in this photo was anything but dignified. Her smile was wide and promised of so many joyous days to come, her blond curls slightly mussed.

Less than two years after this picture was taken, Leona and her mother were both gone, victims of yellow fever. Even now Rory was incensed and confounded by the injustice. Babies shouldn't die. A man should never have to bury his children.

In this very room, in the rocking chair that was now covered and still, he'd held his little girl and prayed with all his heart for her to recover. Wasted prayers, useless tears. He'd promised God anything and everything if He'd spare her, asked that his own life be taken for hers, and in a black moment he'd even asked that the life of the squalling baby in the next room be taken instead.

He'd never forgiven himself for that. Every time he looked at Kevin he was reminded of that whispered prayer, and felt the guilt that came with the remembrance.

Rory moved to the window so he could see the photograph better in the moonlight, tilting it so that it caught the silver rays. He'd loved Leona with all his heart. As his marriage had crumbled around him, he'd clung to his daughter; he'd had Leona to turn to. When he'd thought the world was a senseless place, he'd found meaning in her pale brown eyes that were so much like his own.

Margaret and Leona had died within three days of one another. He hadn't grieved for his faithless wife, but losing his little girl had almost destroyed him. He couldn't go through that again. God help him, he'd never survive.

"I'm getting married tomorrow," he whispered to the picture. "You'd like Jackie. She's pretty and smart and when she laughs the whole world is a better place."

He laid a finger that looked too big on the glass, as if he could touch Leona's cheek. "Kevin loves her, and she's good for him. Maybe I love her, too, a little."

It was good that Jackie didn't want babies, he thought as he returned the photograph to the dresser drawer. He couldn't bear to love and lose another child.

Jackie had been prepared for most every possibility in life; poverty and wealth, safety and danger, brief moments of happiness and brief moments of despair blending in with her day-to-day life.

In all her daydreams, she'd never imagined this.

Wearing her white and blue gown, she stood with Rory Donovan before a preacher in the Clarks' parlor. She held a bouquet of red and pink roses fresh from the garden. Sally had picked and arranged them herself.

As the words were spoken solemnly, she listened carefully. Only once or twice was she distracted, by a loud sniffle from Mrs. Clark, or an excited, whispered question in a familiar young voice.

There was an exclamation of dismay and the scrape of a hastily moved chair, and then Jackie felt a tugging at her skirts. She looked down in time to see Kevin creeping along, wedging himself securely between her skirts and Rory's legs.

She smiled down at the little boy. It was only fitting that he be here.

When the preacher asked for the ring, Jackie's smile faded and she glanced sharply up at her groom. There had been no time to purchase a ring. Would the marriage even be legal without one?

She supposed it would be, but she was a little disappointed. If she was going to get married, she wanted to do things properly.

Rory reached into his pocket, and his hand came up with the little finger hooked around a gold band. She did not immediately offer her hand.

"Where did you get that?" she whispered.

"Does it matter?" He seemed amused that she would even ask.

If the ring had once graced the finger of the first Mrs. Donovan, it mattered very much. If that was the case, she didn't want it. "Yes, it matters."

He took her hand, and she could either let him have it or make a scene and back away. She held very still. "I rode to Florence on my fastest horse at the crack of dawn," he whispered as the ring hovered over the tip of the ring finger of her left hand. "And pounded on locked doors and dragged merchants from their beds until I found what I was looking for." He grinned, a full-blown smile that made Jackie's heart do an unexpected flip. "I hope it fits."

It did.

It was knowing he couldn't have Jackie that made him want her so much, Rory reasoned as he watched his bride out of the corner of his eye. It was knowing he had to wait that made him grow instantly hard when she was close. Dammit, he was no randy youngster, and she was no flirting temptress, so why did she affect him this way?

Last night had been their wedding night. Even though he'd known she wasn't ready, even though he had known from the moment he'd asked her to be his wife that theirs would not be a normal honeymoon, he had spent the long night staring up at the ceiling, wide-eyed and aching and too well aware that the woman who was his wife slept so close—and so far away.

He was leaving the stables and headed for the house, and Jackie and Kevin were returning from the pond. If no one changed course they would meet somewhere beyond the ancient oak that shaded one corner of the house. How was he supposed to continue to pretend that he didn't want more from their marriage?

There was no avoiding the confrontation.

Kevin saw him and with a burst of energy ran forward.

"I almost caught the biggest fish!" he shouted when he was near. "It was *this big!*" He held his small hands as far apart as possible, and grinned from ear to ear.

"The one that got away," Jackie said with a wistful smile as she tagged along behind Kevin. "Oddly enough, every time Kevin tells me about this fish it gets a little bit bigger."

Kevin's eyes got wide. "I know! I could wish to catch it again tomorrow, and this time I wouldn't let it get away." He jumped up and down several times.

Rory's eyes were on Jackie. This waiting apparently didn't affect her at all. She was calm, so damned serene he wanted to shake her.

The three of them stood in the shade of the old oak, enjoying the breeze that ruffled the leaves and cooled their bodies. Unfortunately, the breeze wasn't nearly cool enough to ease the heat that had taken over Rory's body.

Kevin quit jumping, and his smile faded. "Maybe I'd better not wish for that fish," he said solemnly. "I only have one wish left, and I don't want to waste it on a fish, even a big one."

Jackie dropped her eyes and smiled down at a mussed red head. "Only one? I thought you had two magic beans left."

Uh-oh. "I'm dying of thirst," Rory said to change the subject. "How about we see if Nell has any lemonade?"

"Sure!" Kevin led the way to the house, and

for a brief moment, a second or two, Rory thought he'd dodged that bullet. Even though this wasn't a conventional marriage, he didn't think Jackie would take too well to the notion that he'd married her just to make Kevin's wish come true. That wasn't the case, of course, but women could be so damned sentimental. . . .

Kevin glanced over his shoulder and grinned at Jackie. "And I only have *one* wish left, since I wished for you to be my mother. I don't think I should waste my last wish on a fish."

Jackie's smile faded slightly. "You wished for me to be your mother?" she repeated. "You didn't tell me about that wish."

"No. I told Pa, instead, and it was our secret."

"Not for long, apparently," Rory muttered as Jackie glanced at him.

"Really," Jackie said lowly.

Kevin reached the open parlor door, innocently unaware of the hornets' nest he'd stirred. "Yup," he said proudly. "I wished for you to be my mother, and I told Pa, and the very next day we got married."

Jackie stopped in the parlor doorway, and amazingly there was a small smile on her face. "Kevin, you go on ahead and tell Nell we need some lemonade."

"And cookies?" he asked enthusiastically.

"And cookies," Rory said softly as the kid scurried away.

Once Kevin was gone, Jackie turned to look at Rory, the puzzling, small smile still on her face. "Kevin wished for me to be his mother the same day you proposed?"

Rory took a deep breath. "It's not like that. I didn't ask you to marry me just to please Kevin. Everything I said to you, every word, was the truth." *Everything and more,* though he couldn't admit that now. He had a feeling that if he told Jackie how much he wanted her she would flee as if the devil were on her tail. "Kevin's wish had nothing to do with it, I swear. . . . "

She reached out, almost as if she planned to place her fingers against his lips. Her hand stilled inches away from his face, and after a long moment of silence she lowered it slowly.

"I believe you," she said softly, and then she smiled. "Although," she said as she backed away and into the house, "there's something very appealing about a man who can make wishes come true."

As she disappeared into the house, Rory's gut dropped to his toes.

She was a married woman, but in the days since the small and informal wedding nothing had changed. In the mornings she gave Kevin his lessons, and in the afternoons they went fishing. In the evenings the three of them sat together in the parlor after supper, and at the end of the day she went to her own room, alone. Any last-minute apprehensions she had experienced about this marriage were proven unnecessary.

There was one rather significant change in her day-to-day life. Kevin had taken to calling her Mother or Ma or Mama, depending upon his mood at the time. It was as if he were trying each one on for size, testing to see which appellation fit best.

Kevin had been so absolutely delighted with the wedding that he'd been unable to sit still during the ceremony that had taken place in the Clarks' parlor, and before the wedding was completed he'd sneaked from his chair beside Mavis Clark to creep forward and wedge himself between the solemn bride and groom. In the days since, when he'd spoken of the ceremony, he'd referred to it as *their* wedding, including himself.

It was fitting, Jackie decided, since he was a very big reason for this marriage. The only reason, she told herself.

Still, she couldn't help but remember the kiss that had preceded Donovan's proposal. Cramped in a dark pantry she'd finally allowed a man to kiss her, and oh, what a kiss it had been! If she closed her eyes and thought very hard she could still feel it. What a wonder it had been, quite unexpectedly fine. She'd seen other people kiss, and it had always looked to her to be messy and repulsive. To be on the receiving end was very different.

As much as she longed for another kiss like that one, she steered clear of her husband. He hadn't made any secret of the fact that he'd eventually like her to share his bed, and the very idea still terrified her. She didn't think he would hurt her the way Luther had sometimes hurt his women, and she didn't believe he would force her to do anything she didn't want to do. Still, she wasn't ready to give herself so completely to a man. She'd held on to her virginity, at times like it was all she had. She might steal and lie and cheat, but her body was her own. She'd never stoop to the depths of Luther's women, or the prostitutes who lost their souls.

Even though she was married, even though she knew Rory wouldn't hurt her . . . she held on to that part of herself as if to let go would mean death. The idea of being so close to another body, of actually having a part of another person inside her, it was a little frightening, still.

"Mind a little company?"

Jackie nearly jumped out of her skin at the sound of Donovan's familiar deep voice. She didn't answer, but he lowered himself to the ground to sit beside her anyway, all six-and-a-half feet of muscle and golden skin. This close she could smell him, the now-familiar scent of his hair tonic and sweat, and horses and bourbon. Kevin glanced over his shoulder and smiled at his father, but then he returned his attention to the pond and the fish that were not biting today.

She was an idiot! All she wanted was for this man who was her husband to kiss her. She wanted his tongue in her mouth and his hands on her body, and because she wanted it so badly she felt as if she were betraying herself.

You're not a thief on the run anymore, Jackie, she reminded herself as she watched Kevin's back. *You're a married woman and this is your family.*

It occurred to her that her memory might be faulty, or that perhaps someone had slipped a splash of bourbon into her punch, and that was the reason she'd tingled when Rory had kissed her. She never had been able to drink much without it affecting her senses. There was really only one logical way to find out.

"Pretty day, isn't it?" Rory asked, his tone conversational, his eyes on the pond.

"Yes, it is. There's nothing quite like this where I grew up," she admitted softly.

"And where was that?" he asked casually.

She considered not answering, or lying, but she didn't want to lie to Rory any more than she had to. "Baltimore," she said.

"Never been there," he said, not asking any more questions. Bless him.

Jackie rolled up onto her knees, leaned over, and touched her lips to Rory's without warning. She shocked him so much he actually jumped a little, bumping their mouths together in a way that was awkward yet still pleasant. He recovered from his surprise quickly and the kiss transformed from awkward to gentle and teasing, and in an instant that roar she remembered from the pantry was in her blood, that same tingle burst throughout her body. The sensations came over her so suddenly it was as if she'd had a shock of her own.

She drew her mouth away, after a long kiss that was too quickly developing into more than she could handle. "My goodness," she whispered as she returned to a sitting position.

"What was that for?" His voice was low, and it rumbled from his chest so warm and honey-sweet it made her heart lurch.

"It was a test," she admitted.

"A test," he mumbled.

She cocked her head Rory's way and smiled at him. "Yes, a test. You see, I'm not exactly an expert when it comes to kissing, and I just wondered if it was always . . . so remarkable."

His facial features, usually so hard and un-yielding, relaxed a little. He almost smiled. "Not always."

"I didn't think so."

"Surely a pretty woman like you has lots of kissing experience to draw on," he said lightly.

Jackie shook her head. "To be honest, no one's ever kissed me but you."

She wasn't prepared for the change that came over Rory's face. He might have been sur-prised, but he certainly didn't show it. What she saw on his face was an enhanced desire that damn near terrified her. Surely he didn't find her inexperience enticing!

"I'm trying to be patient," he said lowly. "Dammit, don't torture me."

"Torture you?" She was truly perplexed.

Rory fell back on the blanket and covered his

eyes with his forearm. "You really don't get it, do you?" He didn't sound angry at all, just a little maudlin.

"Well, no," she admitted.

He sighed deeply before continuing, and he didn't move that protective arm from his face. "Every man wants a woman who is his and his alone. To know that no man has so much as kissed you . . . it makes me want to kiss you more and I can't because I know where that will lead and I know just as well that you're not ready." He peeked out from under his arm. "Are you?"

Jackie shook her head quickly.

Rory must have seen something on her face he didn't like, because he sat up quickly and all evidence of desire was gone from his face. "Did someone hurt you? Is that why you're afraid?"

She shook her head again. No one had ever hurt her; she wouldn't have allowed that.

"You know *I* would never hurt you, don't you?" His hand on her face was so gentle she was only reassured that it was true.

"I know it here," she said, laying a hand over her heart, "but I still have a hard time accepting it here." She pointed to her head. Were there other men like this one in the world? From her experience, she never would have guessed it. Rory Donovan was patient and kind, gentle and strong at the same time. Perhaps Rory wasn't perfect, but he was an honorable man. She felt safe in his house, and even in his arms. It was a miracle.

"I've never known a man like you before," she admitted.

He kissed her again, and the touch of his lips was as gentle as his hand at her face, a reassurance and a promise.

She wanted him then, forgot all her reservations and fears and put aside her memories and dark promises to simply feel and believe in everything she'd dismissed as lies. Love, pleasure, commitment. It was all here waiting for her and she was afraid to grab it. She was tired of being afraid.

"I want a kiss, too!" Kevin joined them on the blanket, his knees worming between Jackie and Rory, his puckered lips offered enthusiastically. Jackie couldn't help but laugh, and even Rory gave in to a wide smile as they shared kisses all around.

In that instant Jackie knew nothing here would ever hurt her. Rory would protect her, Kevin would love her, and she had nothing to fear. Nothing. Giving herself to Rory wouldn't make her a whore, it would make her a wife. Lying with him would not be sacrificing herself, but a sharing between the two of them.

When Kevin had garnered his fill of kisses, he scrambled off the blanket to return to his fishing. Jackie turned to Rory, and she felt inexplicably shy. She, who was never shy!

But of course she'd never been in this position before. "Tonight," she whispered, and Rory smiled.

207

* * *

Rory felt rather like a virgin himself as he waited in his bed for his bride to come to him; nervous, anxious, and downright jittery. His first wedding night had been inauspicious, and his first and only virgin, Margaret on that same night, had been less than enthusiastic. It had been an altogether forgettable night.

He didn't want tonight to be forgettable, he wanted it to be a night he and Jackie would remember all their lives.

When had they become so much a couple in his mind? When had he decided that he couldn't live without her? Long before the wedding, he was sure. Somehow she'd crept into his house and his life and even his heart.

He'd never wanted to be this close to a person again, but it was done and there was nothing to remedy it. Somehow, against all he knew, he was certain it was right. Jackie was good for him, and he was determined to be good for her, as well.

Maybe she'd changed her mind, he thought as the minutes passed. Kevin was long asleep, and he'd been waiting for—he glanced at the clock on his dresser—nigh on fifteen minutes. He grinned. He truly was nervous if fifteen minutes felt like half the night!

When she appeared, not from the hallway but from the gallery, he knew marrying and bedding her was no mistake. With the moonlight behind her and her hair falling about her shoulders and the white muslin wrapper she wore she looked like an angel; an angel come to save him perhaps. She hesitated there, for a few seconds that ticked past as slowly as the last fifteen minutes, framed by the opened French doors and illuminated by the moon. When she did finally come toward him he thought his heart would stop.

She stood beside the bed and looked down at him, and she hesitated again. He wanted to stand up, to reach out and grab her, but he knew that would be wrong. Jackie had to do this at her own pace, in her own time.

Slowly moving fingers released the knot at her waist, and she allowed the wrapper to fall to the floor. Heaven above, she was beautiful. How had he ever thought her too small? How had he ever taken her for a boy? Her skin was so flawless and creamy it was as fine as any satin, her breasts were firm and well shaped, the curve of her waist and hips perfectly proportioned.

He offered her his hand, and with trembling fingers she took it and sat beside him on the bed.

Standing, he towered over her, but here on the bed they could be equal. He kissed her first, capturing her mouth gently. Did she know how enticing it was to know that no other man had ever kissed her? The knowledge brought out a possessiveness Rory had thought long dead. She was his, completely.

The tension drained from her body. He could feel it in the response of her lips against his, and in the hand that settled over his forearm. He raised a hand to touch her breast, and felt the sharp intake of breath as she reacted to his touch. Her nipple pebbled against his hand, and she deepened the kiss, using her tongue to drive him wild.

Lifting the quilt, he silently invited her to join him beneath it, and without hesitation she came, pressing her body against his. She was warm and silky all over, and the sensation of flesh against flesh was almost more than he could bear. He was hard and ready for her now, needed her immediately, but he knew he had to wait. He welcomed her with a long and perfect kiss.

She delighted openly in the sensations of a kiss that might never end, it was so perfect, in the feel of dancing tongues and swaying lips that moved in a rhythm all their own. With every breath, with every sway of his lips over hers, he fell deeper and deeper into a pit of all-consuming fire.

With hands that trembled with desire and caution, he touched her. For his life, he wouldn't frighten or push her. Slow and easy, that was the way for this night. He caressed her breasts, ran his hands over her body from shoulder to hip, delighting in the softness of her skin. At times she released a small, involuntary moan from deep in her throat, as she discovered the joys of being touched.

He knew all would be well when she reached out and touched him, brushing the tips of her fingers over his flat nipples, raking those fingers down his side and across his belly as if she meant to learn him just as he was learning her.

His control was leaving him. *Now,* he needed her right now. But she had to be ready for him, if he was to keep his promise and not hurt her. His hand slid lower to rest between her legs. At first she tensed, but a moment later she spread her thighs for him. He caressed soft, moist folds, readying her for his entrance with probing fingers. After a single stroke of his hand she rocked against him, and he felt a deep quiver running through the body he held. She moaned once, and opened her eyes to look at him.

"Touch me," he whispered, and without hesitation she did, wrapping trembling fingers around his shaft, stroking him with those fingers until he thought he would explode in her hand.

His fingers slid into her easily. Yes, she was ready for him, and dammit he was more than ready for her.

He rolled her onto her back, and as his fingers continued to caress her she spread her legs for him. In that instant he knew, somehow, that she trusted him more than she'd ever trusted anyone, that on this night she was giving him a greater gift than she'd ever given before, than he'd ever received. He reached past her and opened the drawer of the bedside table to grab one of the French letters he'd purchased on his last trip to Florence.

"What are you doing?" she asked breathlessly as he stopped to slip the protective sheath over his shaft.

"This will keep you from getting pregnant," he whispered.

"Oh," she breathed.

Using more restraint than he thought he possessed, Rory pressed his sheathed manhood against her wetness, entering with slow and difficult deliberation. She was tight, so tight, but she admitted him into her body, relaxing and adjusting around him as she took him in. When he pressed past her maidenhead she gasped, but there were no tears and she did not retreat from him. She lifted her hips instead, and rocked against him until he filled her.

He withdrew slowly and then thrust to fill her again. She gasped and wrapped her legs around his. Somehow he could feel Jackie's wonder at the sensations that assaulted her. He felt every gasp, every shudder, and when he drove deep and she clenched around him with a startled cry, he felt her completion. As her body trembled he drove deep into her body and allowed himself the release he'd been holding back.

He realized as the pleasure faded, leaving him depleted, that he'd never been this close to a woman before. Never. He'd never felt a part of a woman, not only in body but in a deeper part of himself he was not anxious to explore. It was sure to be dangerous, but at the moment it was only comforting and somehow proper.

"Oh, my," Jackie whispered, even that coming to her with obvious difficulty. "I had no idea . . . "

With what little energy he had left, Rory laughed. "Jackie Donovan," he said as he lifted his weight from her and looked down into her flushed and beautiful face. "I could so easily—" he stopped suddenly. *I could so easily fall in love with you.* He couldn't say that, couldn't admit it to Jackie or to himself.

"You could easily what?" she prodded, wrapping her arms around his waist.

"I could very easily get used to having you around," he said lightly.

It seemed to satisfy her, for the moment.

Chapter Twelve

Sitting at the secretary in the schoolroom, Jackie penned a letter to Mina, the only person in the world she could confide in. Kevin was sleeping and Rory was at the stables, so she had a moment alone.

Mina would want to know that her friend and protégé had married. Besides, Jackie felt like she had to tell someone what she'd found, how she'd come here to steal a fabulous treasure and had come away with so much more.

She'd filled pages with details about Rory and Kevin, about the home and the unexpected peace she'd found. No one else but Mina would appreciate the change this meant for her life, no one else would feel the wonder of it the way Jackie did.

Jackie sealed the letter, including some of her earnings as governess. She didn't need the money anymore, and she owed Mina more than she could ever repay.

"Good afternoon, Miz Jackie," Nell said as she entered the classroom with a silver tray bearing tea and cookies. Jackie had to smile. Since her arrival the housekeeper had been trying to fatten her up, day after day declaring her much too thin and small.

"Good afternoon, Nell." She set the letter aside to post later and stood slowly, straightening her skirt. For some reason, Nell made her feel as if she were always being lovingly inspected. Perhaps this is what it was like to have an aunt, or even a mother. "You didn't have to do this. I was planning to go to the kitchen as soon as I finished my letter."

Nell placed the tray on the edge of the desk and threw her hands in the air. "You don't want to be in the kitchen this afternoon. I'm trying to teach those useless girls to make fudge, and they've made an awful mess. There's chocolate everywhere, I swear. On the floor, on the counter, on the girls." She lost her sour frown and laughed. "Mostly on the girls."

Jackie had recognized right away how much a part of Cloudmont Nell Logan was. If she resented having another woman in the house she certainly didn't show it. In fact, she'd been welcoming from the beginning.

Nell didn't excuse herself right away, but looked about the schoolroom as if searching for dust, running her fingers along the book-shelf and Kevin's small desk. It was, as the rest of the house always was, spotless. When Nell stood several feet away, just behind Kevin's desk, she turned to Jackie with her hands behind her back and a stern expression on her face. *Here it comes*, Jackie thought.

"It's a good thing," Nell said adamantly. "Your marriage to Mister Rory."

Jackie nodded, but Nell's expression didn't soften. She obviously wasn't finished.

"You're settling in nicely here, and Mister Rory and Kevin are both happier than I've seen them in a long time."

"Truly?" Jackie couldn't help but smile. She'd never made anyone happy before. Never.

"Truly," Nell said softly. "And I just want to tell you that if you ever need someone to talk to about . . . oh, things, you can come to me." She blushed, her cheeks turning a brilliant red.

"Thank you."

"Sometimes a woman needs a woman to talk to, and since you don't have any family nearby, well, I don't want you to think you have nowhere to turn."

It was one of the nicest offers anyone had ever made to her, an open and honest offer of friendship, a welcoming into the family and the household. Jackie honestly did not know how to respond, beyond her simple and insufficient "thank you."

Nell began her needless inspection again.

"After all, when you're in the family way Mister Rory won't be no help at all, I guarantee."

The warmth of the moment fled. Jackie didn't want to tell Nell that there would be no babies, no *family way* she'd need help through. She had a feeling the older woman wouldn't understand.

"That's a most generous offer," she said softly. "It will be nice to have someone to turn to for advice now and again."

Nell left the room quickly, headed no doubt for the kitchen and those "useless" girls. "Drink your tea before it gets cold," she ordered. "And eat a couple of those cookies. You're much too thin."

Rory undressed by the light of a low burning lamp, tossing his clothes aside much too anxiously. He'd been so certain that a night or two with Jackie would ease this restlessness, that they would settle into a quiet and sedate relationship once the long-awaited joining was done.

But it hadn't worked that way at all. He wanted his wife with a distressing intensity every time he saw her. Like it or not, he needed her. And when he touched her, well, he forgot everything but the way she made him feel.

She wasn't just doing her wifely duties, he knew. She wanted him just as badly. He saw it in her eyes, felt it in her trembling fingers when she touched him, knew it with every fiber of his being. Heaven help him, this was far more than he'd ever bargained for.

He took one of the rubber sheaths from his bedside drawer, merely glancing at the collection of keys there. For a while he'd worn the key to the case the Fabergé egg rested in around his neck, but he had returned it to the drawer a while back.

Jackie admired the egg so much, perhaps one day he'd give it to her. The very thought made him smile. He wanted to give her so many things she'd never had.

Most of all, he wanted to give her a birthday. He'd hired Pinkerton's Detective Agency to track down Jackie's family, to find out where and when she'd been born. She'd only spoken of it once, but he'd seen such pain in her eyes. She couldn't know what had driven her parents to give her up, and in her mind the only reason was that they hadn't wanted her. Rory couldn't believe that was true.

There wasn't much to go on—a false last name Jackie had taken as her own, a very big city she'd mentioned only once—and the detectives hadn't been encouraging. It might take a very long time to uncover the truth, but it was out there and he was a patient man. One day he would give Jackie the Fabergé egg as a birthday present.

He didn't hear her enter the room. Soft arms wrapped around his waist, and delicate hands settled on his midsection. Everything in him tightened, and in an instant he was ready for her.

When he turned about and wrapped his arms around Jackie, she came up on her tiptoes to kiss him lightly, warm, welcoming, inviting lips settling over his mouth. Her wrapper hung more open than closed, and her silky hair was loose and falling over her shoulders and down her back.

"God, you're beautiful, Mrs. Donovan," he whispered.

She smiled and held on tight. "So are you, Mr. Donovan. The first time I saw you I said to myself, 'Now there's a beautiful man.'"

"At the Clarks' dinner party?"

She shook her head slowly, and there was a decidedly devilish twinkle in her eyes. "Remember that golden harmonica I made off with?"

"Of course," he nuzzled her neck, laying lips on the place where shoulder became neck. He could feel her quiver in his lips.

"You were dressed much as you are now, that night," she whispered. "I closed my eyes, of course," she added, teasing, "but ultimately I had to have a peek."

He drew back slightly. "Did you now?"

"Yes," she breathed. "Are you shocked?"

He pushed the wrapper off Jackie's shoulders and laid her on the bed. "Mortified," he whispered. "Aghast. Dismayed."

"All that over a little peek?"

He kissed her throat, and trailed lips downward to take a nipple in his mouth. She arched against him, and the little moan that came from deep in her throat excited him even more.

When he took his mouth from her and rose to tower above her, to look deep into her eyes, he said, "Yes, all that over a peek. Fiddle, why didn't you wake me up?"

On afternoons when she couldn't sleep she came here. Some days, as she stood at the fence, she caught a glimpse of Rory riding or walking his horses. Most of the time he paid her little mind, but oddly enough she didn't feel ignored at all. He knew she was here, and somehow that was enough.

Ah, the man loved his horses. No job was too menial, too dirty, too distasteful, not where his thoroughbreds were concerned. She'd once looked down her nose and accused him of mucking out the stables. Now she knew that sometimes he did just that.

Today she sat on the fence and watched the horses run, but Rory was nowhere to be seen. Pity.

Jackie had known few moments of real harmony in her life, but this was one of them. A great oak shaded her chosen spot, a cool breeze washed over her, and even more importantly, she knew there were days and days and more days like this one ahead of her.

She didn't even hear Rory approaching. One

minute all was peaceful and quiet, and the next a pair of strong arms snaked around her. A single, perfect, yellow rose wavered beneath her nose.

"For me?" she asked.

"Yes." The single word was soft and gruff, and somehow reluctant.

Jackie twisted until she could see Rory's face. She liked sitting here, atop the fence. It brought her face-to-face with her husband. "No one's ever given me flowers before."

"No one?" he asked with a skeptical lift of his eyebrows.

She shook her head and then she raised the fragrant bloom to her nose.

"Do you mean to tell me that no one's ever courted you properly?" He sounded slightly indignant on her behalf.

"Well, Clint courted me, I suppose, but he never brought me flowers."

"Marsh," Rory said the name as if it were a curse, scowling and squinting his golden eyes. "There was a time, one moment, when I thought you were going to marry the bastard."

Jackie couldn't help but laugh at him as she brushed the rose gently across his cheek. "Clint's a very nice man. You shouldn't be unkind."

She thought this unusual display of what could only be jealousy was rather funny, but Rory was not amused. He stared at her hard, as he sometimes did, and she couldn't help but wonder how much, how deeply, he saw.

"I should've courted you," he said softly.

"Why?"

"Because you deserve to be courted."

She didn't, and she knew that truth too well. But how could she explain to Rory without telling too much? "Perhaps we came to marriage in an unusual way," she admitted, "but I have no complaints."

"None?"

Too many secrets, too many dark corners of her life perhaps, but none of him. "None," she said softly.

He almost smiled. "Good."

For a while Rory watched the horses with her, leaning on the fence beside her in a perfectly companionable way. His presence made her moment of harmony even more perfect.

"Remember the day you fell off this fence and I caught you?" he asked, his eyes still on his thoroughbreds.

"Of course."

He stared at her every bit as intently as he'd been watching his horses a moment earlier. "I wanted you, even then."

Impulsively, she threw open her arms and fell forward, eyes closed, head high, a smile teasing the corners of her mouth. Rory caught her.

Amazingly, she'd never doubted for a moment that he would.

Jackie glanced up from her mending for a glimpse of her husband, who frowned as he read over some report on his iron investments. How could a man be so fierce and so loving at the same time? So hard and so gentle? Every night for the past two weeks she'd gone to his bed and he'd loved her so fully and so completely she was amazed. All she had to do was look at him and her heart beat faster; it was a miracle.

"Ouch!" She drew her hand quickly away from the needle to study the drop of blood that was rising on her fingertip. That's what she got for mooning over the man she was married to rather than watching what she was doing.

"Are you all right?" Rory had placed his report aside to ask after her, and Kevin, at her feet, put aside his trains to look wide-eyed at her injury.

"Fine," she said as she popped the finger into her mouth.

Rory smiled at her, and there was such wonderful promise in his eyes.

"It's past your bedtime, isn't it Kevin?" Rory asked.

Jackie glanced at the grandfather clock. It was five minutes past, to be exact. "Your father's right," she said as she began to set her mending aside. "Come along. . . . "

"I'll do it." Rory left his chair and swept Kevin from the floor, tossing the little one over his shoulder to peals of childish laugher. "Since Mama's injured herself mending my favorite shirt, it's the least I can do."

Kevin continued to laugh as Rory ran up the stairs with his son over his shoulder, both of them bouncing as they went. When the noise abated, Jackie looked down at her mending.

She didn't deserve this. Her life was perfection, with Rory and Kevin, but in her heart she knew she didn't deserve such happiness. It wouldn't last. The punishment for her sins would be to have this perfection for a while and then have it taken away, the way she'd taken money and jewelry from unsuspecting people who had done nothing to her but try to help.

Her moments knowing true happiness were moments of weakness. She *knew* that, had always known that to let her guard down would mean ruination.

Oh, the very, very worst had happened. She loved Rory and Kevin with all her heart. If someone were to take them away from her she would die. She would absolutely curl up and die.

"Why so sad?" Rory's voice startled her, since she hadn't heard him coming down the stairs.

"I'm not sad, I'm just . . . wondering."

He sat on the floor before her, where Kevin had been a few minutes ago. "Wondering about what?"

She couldn't tell him, could she? Theirs was a business arrangement, a convenience and nothing more. If they found pleasure along with the convenience, well that was merely a lucky coincidence. The tenderness Rory displayed came from friendship and desire, not love.

"It was a lucky happenstance that brought me here," she admitted. That confession was safe, she supposed.

"Lucky for me, too," he said, taking her hand and then kissing the palm and the finger she'd injured. She tingled from the point where he kissed her to her toes. "How did we ever get along without you?"

He didn't return to his report, but sat at her feet with his back against her chair and her hand in his.

"Did Kevin go right to sleep? He was so tired."

"I helped him into his nightshirt, and he crawled beneath his quilt and was out like a light a minute later," Rory said. "I wonder if I ever fell asleep so easily? Most nights I just toss and turn and worry about horses and iron and sharecroppers."

Jackie reached out and touched his neck, raking her fingers along the warm and soft strength. This man was her weakness. Knowing that, she should be warned.

Perhaps everyone should be allowed one weakness. "You worry too much. Everything you need is right here and always will be, and you will never want for the warmth of a fire or food on your table or a roof over your head."

"Or a woman in my bed," he added, pulling her playfully to the floor to sit beside him.

"Or a woman in your bed," she whispered as she settled herself comfortably beside him.

226

He took her hand and studied the pricked finger, and after a moment's consideration he kissed it tenderly once again. There was an unexpectedly intense sensation that only increased as he proceeded to kiss each and every one of her fingers.

"Oh, you have no idea how that feels," she insisted, taking his hand and repaying him in kind, kissing the tips of his fingers, finishing with a kiss to the palm of his hand.

He picked her up and placed her on his lap, where he kissed her thoroughly. She snaked her arms around his neck and kissed him back with everything she had. How had it happened that she, who had always prided herself on her independence, had given herself so completely to this man? Heart and body and soul, she was in his hands.

She felt his manhood swell against her, and knew that he had given himself to her as well, in body if not in heart. Heaven help her, she wanted it all.

Without taking her mouth from his, she shifted until she straddled his hips. He deepened the kiss, and Jackie reached down to lay her hand over the flesh that strained against his trousers. When he moaned, she took that as encouragement and began to stroke gently.

What had begun as a simple kiss changed with every breath, with every move of their hands. Rory stroked her nipples through the cotton of her blouse, and she felt the tightening that signaled her want of him. She took her mouth from his to kiss the column of his throat, to rake her lips along the warm skin there and taste the very essence of him.

He slipped his hand beneath her skirt and in a move that was swift and sure he flicked open the buttons at her hip and slid her drawers down enough to slip his fingers between her legs and touch her even more intimately than she was touching him; probing fingers to heated flesh.

She was lost, wonderfully, marvelously, completely. Returning her mouth to his, she fumbled with the buttons of his trousers and then with the opening of his drawers, until she could wrap her fingers around his manhood and stroke in rhythm with the kiss.

In an easy maneuver she lifted one leg and slipped the drawers free, and then she positioned herself over Rory so that the tip of him was almost touching her. She wanted it, wanted him, and at the same time there was a wonderful sensation in the waiting. The anticipation of the pleasure she knew would come was a pleasure all its own. She stroked him with firm fingers and thrust her tongue deep into his mouth.

He moaned, low and deep in his throat, and Jackie opened her eyes to watch his face as she moved her hand away and lowered herself slowly to take all of him inside her.

They'd never made love by the light of day, but now the lamps were burning brightly and she could see so clearly the beauty and longing on his face. She rose and fell slowly once again, and Rory moved with her, rocking up and more deeply into her than he'd ever been before.

She was compelled to move faster, to find that primal rhythm she and Rory played so well together. Her body drove her, and all thought left her mind as her body searched and demanded, rose and fell until it found completion in pleasure so intense she cried out against Rory's mouth. Her body tightened and throbbed around his, and then she felt his own release, the hot and welcoming explosion of his manhood deep within.

She settled her head against his shoulder. This was more wonderful than any time before. She had seen his face in the light and known he wanted her, she had wanted him with such intensity she had done things she'd never thought herself capable of, and, oh, to feel his hot flesh against hers, to feel the release of his seed inside her . . .

She raised her head slowly. What had she done? She looked at Rory's satisfied face and knew he hadn't yet realized what had happened. Still lost in the power of their bodies, he hadn't yet realized that they'd broken their agreement. He didn't want more children, and she didn't want the pain and danger of childbirth. They had agreed.

She knew when he understood what had happened. There was a start of a frown on his face, a puzzled question in his eyes as he locked them to hers.

"We shouldn't have . . . " he began.

"I know," she whispered. She should say she was sorry, even though she alone was not at fault. And besides, she found perversely that she was not sorry at all. If this joining led to a baby, well they would just have to accept and handle it, wouldn't they? Perhaps having a baby wouldn't be so bad after all.

Rory didn't look as if he were particularly sorry, either. In fact, he appeared to be wonderfully satisfied and completely relaxed. "Just this once," he said softly, "it should be safe enough."

"Yes," she whispered as she placed her head against his shoulder. "Just this once." One time was enough for some women to conceive, she knew, but many more took their chances and didn't get pregnant. Why, it took some women years to conceive a child . . . and it took others only once.

"Once you touched me I didn't even think—"

She kissed Rory quickly, covering his mouth with hers and kissing him long and deep. She didn't want to hear him say he was sorry, she didn't want to listen to his reasoning when she could find none in her own mind. He stole her reason with his touch, made her forget all her fears.

At this moment in her life she would gladly throw caution and reason and sanity to the wind. She would sacrifice it all for a never-ending kiss like this one.

Chapter Thirteen

"You must tell me what it's like to be married," Sally insisted as she removed her summer gloves and tossed them onto the piecrust table in the parlor.

What to say? Jackie wondered as her smiling friend spun about to face her expectantly. *It's wonderful, exciting, confusing* . . . "I rather like it," she confessed.

Sally's smile only got wider as she came close to clasp Jackie's hands in her own. "I'm getting married, too," she said, her voice high with excitement.

Jackie led Sally to the parlor sofa for what promised to be a long afternoon visit. "So, Telford finally asked you to be his wife," she said with a burst of spontaneous laughter. "It certainly took him long enough!"

"Oh, not Telford," Sally said with a wrinkle of her nose. "I decided he's not my type at all. It's Clint Marsh I'm going to marry!"

"Clint?"

Sally perched on the edge of her seat, obviously too excited to sit back and relax. "He started coming around more and more, and at first he just moaned about how you'd married Rory, but before you know it he was coming around and he didn't even ask about you at all!" The accompanying smile was brilliant. "The more we visited, the more we discovered we had in common. Oh, we could talk and talk for hours, and we did. I don't think I realized how handsome he was until a moment a few weeks back when the light hit his face just so, and my heart nearly stopped." She sighed deeply, remembering.

"He asked me last night, after supper," Sally continued, "and I wanted you to be the first to know. After Mama and Papa, of course," she added.

"That's wonderful." Jackie was sure Sally and Clint would make a perfect couple, and they both certainly deserved someone special. They deserved one another.

"It is!" Sally agreed. "Can you believe it? Everything we wished for will come true. Perhaps our original plans were a tad askew, when we chose Clint for you and Telford for me. Telford turned out to be an awful bore, and

Clint realized that he loved me, and Rory turned out to be not so unsuitable after all. Now you have Rory and I have Clint and we can be special friends forever and give parties and, oh Jackie, our children will grow up together!"

Jackie's heart sank even as Sally threw her arms around her neck. *Children*. Oh, they were an awful lot of trouble, and there was the pain and danger of childbirth and the responsibility that came with being a parent and the commitment. It was a lifelong undertaking. Rory didn't want babies, and neither did she.

Did she?

Suddenly she was a little jealous of the children Sally and Clint would have, little ones like Kevin, babies to hold and love. Children made a family complete, they made a family real and whole. At this moment the rewards of childbirth seemed well worth the risk.

Not that it mattered. Rory was adamant. Perhaps he simply didn't like children. When she'd come here he certainly hadn't had much time for his son. Maybe one day he would change his mind. Thinking of that impulsive evening in this very parlor she wondered if perhaps he wouldn't have a choice but to accept what came to them.

Rory would make a wonderful father, of that she was certain. He was strong and protective and even though he tried hard not to show it there was love in his heart. A father's job was to provide and care for his children, and Rory was more than capable. Yes, he would make a wonderful father.

But would she make a wonderful mother? Her own mother had abandoned her child to a man like Luther, selling Jackie or giving her away. What if deep inside she was like the woman who had given her life? What if she looked at her own child and felt nothing? She'd often wondered what kind of woman could walk away from her own child. . . . What if deep in her soul she was capable of that atrocity?

It wasn't true, and she knew it! Kevin had shown her she could love and care for a child. She could, if the unthinkable happened, love and care for her own baby, protecting it from harm, from hurt, from the ugliness in this world. Nothing could ever tear her apart from her child.

Jackie sat back, rather amazed at the rush of maternal instinct that coursed through her veins and left her winded and dazed.

While she was contemplating the impossible, Sally leaned close and whispered, "Tell me what it's like."

Startled, Jackie straightened her spine. "What?"

"Lovemaking," Sally said, her voice so low Jackie almost had to read her lips to understand. "Tell me what it's like."

There was no immediate word that came to mind that was adequate to describe lying with Rory, and if she had managed to come up with one it would be much too embarrassing to share. Jackie Beresford, embarrassed? Nonsense.

Sally waited expectantly, eyes wide and ears

open. Goodness, Jackie thought as she searched for the proper response, she had to say something.

"Well, I rather enjoy it," she confessed, her voice as low as Sally's had been. Once she'd begun, it wasn't so difficult to continue. "To look at a man, at the way he's made, you wouldn't think it would work properly, but believe me it does."

She'd never before had a girlfriend to whisper delicious secrets and forbidden knowledge to, and suddenly she decided she liked it. She liked it a lot.

"Oh, Sally," she whispered. "It's marvelous. I never felt so fine in all my life."

Sally's smile faded. "Jackie, what happened to your accent?"

She'd been so excited she'd let it slip completely away. What was she to do now? Goodness, she didn't want to spend the rest of her life faking an English accent! "Rory and Kevin have been influencing me, I suppose," she said. "Why, Rory says I sound more like a true Southerner every day."

It was explanation enough for Sally, who was more interested in hearing the details of the newlyweds' physical relationship. Her curiosity about the one apparently far outweighed the other. "Is it really marvelous? Are you sure? I heard Ruth Daniels whispering once about the trials of the marriage bed, and what a woman has to endure in order to please a man."

Jackie grinned. "Believe me, sharing Rory's

bed is not a trial, and I don't feel as if I've been made to *endure* anything."

Her husband chose that moment to enter the parlor, sweaty and dirty from his work with the horses and yet as handsome as always.

Sally, at the sight of him, squealed as if she'd been caught, and the squeal was followed by a burst of laughter. Her face turned an alarming shade of red and she slapped her hand over her mouth as another burst of laughter threatened.

"I've obviously missed something," Rory said with a touch of dry humor, striding to the sofa to kiss Jackie on the cheek.

Sally almost choked as she tried to contain her giggles.

"Just a little silly girl talk," Jackie said as Rory pulled slowly away from her. If they were alone she'd get more than a kiss on the cheek. He looked as if he wanted to give her a proper kiss as badly as she wanted one. "Nothing you'd be interested in."

At this, Sally turned red all over again.

Rory excused himself and made his escape, and Jackie watched him as he left the room, her eyes on his broad back and the dark blond hair that curled slightly at the nape, at the fascinating cut of his jeans and the masculine grace of his every step.

"Oh, Jackie," Sally whispered when he'd disappeared from view, heading for the stairway to clean up from a hard day's work. "You truly do love Rory, don't you?"

Jackie looked closely at her friend. The redness was almost gone from Sally's face, and the smile had faded to a near normal grin that was warm and welcoming. Here was someone to share secrets with, the deepest, darkest secrets of her soul.

"I do," she whispered.

Rory frowned at the letter in his hands, but no matter how fiercely he stared, the words made no more sense than they had the first time he'd read them.

If the Pinkerton's agent had information about Jackie, why wasn't it included with the letter? Why on earth was the man insisting on a face-to-face meeting?

"What's wrong?"

His head snapped up at the sound of Jackie's voice. She sat in her favorite chair, doing her best to stitch a sampler. She'd been working on it for days, dragging the linen and thread out at the end of the day when the three of them gathered in the parlor. It was obvious by her frustration and the number of knots on the back of the piece that this was new to her. He wished she would put it away and read a book or play a game with Kevin, but she was damned and determined to finish this newest project.

He folded the letter carefully. "Looks like I'm going to have to go to Birmingham for a few days."

"When?" She placed the sampler in her lap and looked at him hard. He couldn't hide from her. Those blue eyes looked right through him, cutting and clear and constant. Would she miss him while he was gone? Yes, he knew it was true. Damn if she didn't look like she was dreading his leaving as much as he was.

"Next week."

She sighed and picked up her sampler. Yes, she would miss him, and dammit he would miss her. Too much.

"Trouble with your iron investments?" she asked, bending over a particularly stubborn letter and stabbing at it with her needle.

"Yes," he said, lying quickly and easily. If the news was bad, she would never have to know. He hadn't gone to all this trouble just to distress her. He would hear what the Pinkerton's detective had to say, and then he'd make his decision on whether or not the information should be shared with Jackie.

Since the detective had insisted on meeting in person, and the tone of the letter had been less than cordial, Rory had a sinking feeling the news would not be what he wanted. If Pinkerton's had only succeeded in proving that all Jackie's fears about her family were true, she would never have to know.

"Look, Pa," Kevin said, coming off the floor with a stack of drawings grasped in his hands. He leaned over the arm of Rory's chair with the top drawing displayed proudly. It was a frog, and a damn fine one, even if the legs were a little misshapen.

More easily than he'd ever thought possible, Rory lifted Kevin off his feet and settled the boy in his lap. "I had no idea you could draw so well," he said.

Kevin made himself comfortable, squirming until he was well seated and leaning against Rory's chest. "Look at this one," he said proudly, displaying the next picture, which was a simple drawing of the house surrounded on all sides by huge trees, snakes, a frog, and a lizard or two. The house slanted slightly to one side, and a swirl of scribbled smoke came from the chimney.

"Very good," Rory said in a serious tone of voice, as Kevin moved that picture to the back of the stack and revealed the next.

The river flowed in the background, and there on the bank stood two fishermen, a very tall one and a very small one. Their catches of the day were as tall as they were, and they displayed the prizes with huge smiles on their faces. A woman stood beside the little fisherman. She was almost as tall as the bigger fisherman, and had a decidedly feminine shape.

"This is you," Kevin placed a finger on the tallest figure, "and this is me," he said as he moved to the small fisherman, "and this is Mama." His finger brushed the woman he had drawn.

"Very good," Rory said gruffly.

Before Jackie had come, there had been no drawings, no peaceful evenings, no family at all. She had somehow forced him to put aside feelings of anger and guilt to move forward at last, to open himself to the possibilities of life once again. She'd brought joy into his house. The change was good for Kevin, he admitted, and good for himself as well.

"You know," he said, taking the picture from Kevin. "I think we should make a frame for this, so I can hang it in my study."

The kid's eyes got big. "Really?"

"Really," Rory said. "Now, go show those drawings to your mama before she stabs herself with a needle again."

Kevin scrambled off Rory's lap, ran a few steps, and jumped into Jackie's lap as she laid the sampler aside. "Pa and me are going to make a frame for this one," he said as he held the drawing of the three of them up to her face.

"Wonderful idea," she said, and then she exclaimed again and again over the perfection of the drawing.

The evening was cool, compared to the heat they'd been experiencing during the daytime hours. A breeze wafted over Jackie as she walked from her room to Rory's, and she stopped to look out over a moon-washed landscape.

This was home. She found herself at the railing, leaning over and looking down to the ground where she'd fallen on the eventful night that now seemed so very long ago. A lifetime ago. She wrapped one arm around the column she'd climbed in order to gain entrance to this house, and swung forward.

Ah, she didn't miss her old life at all, didn't long for lonely nights and frantic prayers to

Nicholas of Myra, didn't yearn for stealth and deception. The Fabergé egg that still sat in Rory's bedroom remained fantastically beautiful and priceless, but she no longer craved it. She no longer *needed* it.

She knew Rory was behind her even before he wrapped his arms around her waist and laid his lips on her neck.

"It is a beautiful sight, isn't it?" he whispered in her ear.

"Yes," she breathed, keeping her voice low.

Rory held her tight. "I can't tell you how many sleepless nights I've looked out over this land, thinking of the future and remembering the past. See that rise over there?" he pointed, his arm snaking past her shoulder. "When I was seven I was pretending to be an Indian charging over the hill on a stick horse, when I took a nasty tumble and broke my arm."

"An Indian!" she said with mock alarm. "Rory Donovan, I would have taken you for a cavalry man."

"On other days, I was," he revealed. "And a pirate and a cowboy and Robert E. Lee. I could never tell my father about that last one."

"Your father the scalawag?" she asked lightly, turning in his arms to find herself against a warm, bare chest.

"My father the scalawag," he confirmed in a soft voice. She lifted her face to look at him, and he rested a single finger beneath her chin. "Tell me, Jackie, what did you pretend to be when you were a little girl?"

"Nothing," she confessed, the fun instantly gone out of the game. Rory found comfort in memories of his childhood. She did her best, always, to forget hers. "I never . . . pretended as a child." She'd more than made up for that oversight as an adult, hadn't she? She couldn't tell him that!

Her wrapper hung more open than closed, and her shameless husband was as naked as the day he was born. Their skin touched here and there, in hot, sensitive places that came more alive with every slowly passing heartbeat.

Rory had fond memories of his past to cling to—she didn't. She wanted to forget the past and plan for the future, and more than that she needed to celebrate right now. It was so easy to do.

She traced lazy fingers down his sides to his hips, over skin so warm and hard to her touch she was certain there was nothing quite like it on earth. After years of avoiding human contact of any kind, she found she now craved it; not just any touch, though, but the touch of this man.

Rory untied the sash and pushed the wrapper she wore off her shoulders, allowing his fingers to follow the trail of descending muslin over her shoulders and arms and hips. How very quickly she had become so accustomed to his touch that she needed it. Familiar and loving he caressed her, and when he placed his mouth on hers she was in her own Heaven. She had given herself completely to her husband, heart and body and soul. She was his, and he was so much a part of her that she was no longer the same person who had climbed into his bedroom to take his most prized possession. She was better now, happy, content. Whole.

His arousal pressed against her belly, hot and hard, and the kiss became more insistent. She was ready for him, and as the kiss went on she was more than ready; she was anxious. When he placed his mouth on her breast and sucked on a sensitive nipple she forgot everything but the way he made her feel.

Lost in a whirl of sensation, she gave herself over to Rory, body and soul. Every time he touched her she was born again, into a better world. Every time he kissed her she was changed, transformed by a shocking bliss that started deep within her and grew until there was nothing else.

She ended up on the floor of the gallery, her wrapper beneath her and Rory cradled between her legs, the tip of his arousal brushing against her. Mindlessly she opened her thighs wider and rocked against him so that the desired fullness teased her as he began to enter.

His breathing was coming hard, his hooded eyes were locked on her. He hesitated, and even in the moonlight she could see the question in his eyes.

Was he ready to take the chance? Was she?

"Yes," she breathed.

He drove deep, burying himself inside her, and she wrapped her legs around his hips and moved with him, savoring the feel of his skin against hers, lifting her hips to accept his hardest thrusts. He took her to the brink of this world, to a place where there was no one but the two of them, joined, together always, never alone.

She arched her back and stifled a cry when the completion seized her, and she went over an edge into a warm oblivion where there was nothing but sensation and forever love, and Rory came with her.

Everything about this night was sharp and clear. The scent and crispness of the air, the feel of the man above and inside her, the moment of silence, the jumble of emotions she embraced and fought at the same time.

"I love you," she whispered as he relaxed and placed his head against her shoulder. "God help me, I'm sorry, Rory," she said as he lifted his head to look at her. "I know it's not what you wanted." She waited for him to protest, to tell her that theirs was not a love match. She didn't give him the chance. "This is supposed to be a business arrangement, not a . . . not a . . . " He silenced her with a soft finger over her lips. Obviously he didn't want her to say it again.

But he didn't look angry. What she could see of his face was calm and satisfied, and as handsome as always. He took the finger from her lips and traced her face with it, touching her chin and her jawbone and her neck.

He came to her gently, with soft lips that feathered small kisses on her mouth. "Heaven help us both, I love you, too," he whispered as his mouth left hers. "And I'm not sorry at all."

When he smiled, she knew everything would be all right. Forever. He loved her! In that instant the last little bit of Jackie's shield, the remaining armor that had protected her from the rest of the world all her life, shattered.

Chapter Fourteen

His bag was packed, and he'd said good-bye to Jackie four times and Kevin three. This was a fine turn of events, Rory thought as he stood in the foyer and stared at the closed double doors. He traveled all the time, for a few days or even a few weeks, and he'd never had such a hard time taking his leave.

Just a couple of minutes earlier Kevin had ordered him to wait here, and then the child and Jackie had scrambled up the stairs, whispering to one another all the while. They were a couple of plotters, they were. Hadn't they plotted and successfully staged a war on him? On his heart, to be specific, a heart he'd been so sure was forevermore numb.

"I hate to say I told you so," Nell said as she

sneaked up behind him. He turned to see her smug smile. "But I told you so."

"What are you talking about?"

"I told you to marry that girl, and I was right."

Rory gave his housekeeper, the woman who had practically raised him, a wide smile. "It must be nice to always be right, Nell, and difficult to maintain your humility. However do you manage?"

The expression on her face was one of dignity and annoyance. "I manage quite nicely," she said as she took a step closer. "It's a great responsibility, you know."

"I can imagine."

She stood before him and lowered her voice. "I hate to spoil your fun, but there's one thing that's been bothering me mightily."

Another useless helper in the kitchen, he imagined. "You know you can always come to me."

Whatever her problem was, it was serious. Her dark eyes were narrowed and her mouth was firmly set. This was Nell Logan prepared for battle. "You know how I hate to stick my nose into other people's business, Mister Rory."

He managed not to laugh, but couldn't stop the wide smile that spread across his face. "Of course."

"This isn't funny," she insisted. "I just wanted to know if you've told your wife about Leona."

Rory's smile died. "I told you I don't ever want to talk about that. It was a long time ago."

"I take that as a no," Nell said sharply. "And

it is just what I was afraid of. It's a part of who you are, and your wife has a right to know. Now's the time to tell her, not later when you have other children and the past comes back to haunt you."

Nell could get away with a lot in this house. She was more family than employee, and he deferred to her on many occasions. But not this time. She'd brought this subject up once before, the night before the wedding, and he'd humored her. Perhaps he should have made it clear to her then that he had no intention of *ever* telling Jackie the secrets he'd buried so deep.

"No," he said softly. "I haven't told her, I won't tell her, and neither will you. Do you understand me?"

She raised her eyebrows at his commanding tone, and lifted her chin. "Why not?"

He didn't have to explain himself to this woman or to anyone else. The truth was, he was afraid he'd break down and cry like a baby if he had to relive his daughter's death again. He was afraid all the pain would come back, that horrid, deep down pain that had made him want to die. What if it didn't go away this time? A man surely couldn't live with pain like that. Best to keep it buried, deep and dark and silent.

Kevin saved him from coming up with an answer for Nell. He came flying down the stairs with a piece of paper fluttering in his hands. "This is for your hotel room, so you won't forget us while you're gone."

Kevin came to a skidding halt in front of Rory and offered up a new drawing, this one of the three of them standing in front of the house, hand in hand. As usual, the boy was in the middle.

"As if I could ever forget you two." Rory said as he studied the drawing. He lifted Kevin and planted yet another kiss on his cheek, and was rewarded with a vigorous hug. A hug Rory knew he didn't deserve.

Nell left without saying another word that anyone could understand, though she mumbled grumpily. No one else seemed to notice.

Rory's happiness was marred by the memories Nell's question had raised, even as he placed Kevin on his feet and offered his arms to Jackie again, as she came to him for another good-bye kiss.

As she drew her lips away she brought a hand from behind her back and presented him with a gift of her own. "I made this for you," she said shyly.

He took the linen handkerchief from her fingers and unfolded it. His initials had been embroidered in one corner, in blue thread the color of a robin's egg. Knowing how she struggled with her needlework, he ran a rough finger over the perfectly crafted letters. "Thank you," he said softly as he placed the handkerchief in his breast pocket.

"I'm going to miss you terribly," she whispered.

"I'll miss you, too." They both displayed a

touch of wonder at these confessions. Perhaps Jackie, who'd had no family before coming here, had never had to say good-bye to someone she loved, not even for a few days. As for himself, he'd tried so damn hard *not* to love anyone again . . . and he'd failed miserably.

This was far, far more than he'd wanted from this marriage, but how could he deny what he felt and what he saw in Jackie's eyes? It had happened so quickly, his defenses had been too easily breached. Jackie was too much a part of who he was now.

For all their precautions, there was always a chance one of their nights together would result in a child. He knew that, and still he found himself coming to her again and again, forgetting about the protection a condom offered, so caught up in the rush of desire that overwhelmed him when she touched him that he could think of nothing else.

Rory didn't want another child, didn't want to take the chance of loving and losing that way again, but he couldn't make himself be sorry he'd found Jackie. If there was a child he would have no choice but to accept it, for Jackie's sake. But he doubted very much that he could ever completely love a child again. He would keep a part of himself back, he would protect his heart this time.

He hugged his wife tightly one last time and said good-bye again, and with his bag in hand he stepped into the sunshine where one of the stable boys waited with the buggy.

Maybe one day he would have to tell Jackie all the ugly details of his past, but not today. Not today.

This was a fine turn of events! She missed her husband, she who had never wanted a husband at all, much less one she depended on so completely she couldn't seem to make it through two whole days without mooning like a lost calf. Rory had been gone for a little over forty-eight hours, and she craved the sight of him and the sound of his voice so much it was frightening. How had she ever gotten so involved?

Jackie sat in the shade and watched Kevin fish. He wore his father's hat on his head to protect his face and neck from the hot sun, the same wide-brimmed hat Rory had placed on his head that day by the river. The child had not relinquished the hat since, and it did come in handy for the fair-skinned child on these sunny days.

In the silence of the afternoon, she heard approaching footsteps and the swish of a skirt, and she turned her head to see one of Nell's helpers, a young girl by the name of Eleanor, running toward her with her skirts in her hand and a frown on her face.

"Oh, Mrs. Donovan," Eleanor said as she drew near. "There's been a terrible accident. Nell's hurt."

Jackie shot to her feet and called to Kevin. He was sometimes reluctant to leave the pond, but he took one look at her face and obeyed without question.

"What happened?" she asked as the three of them hurried toward the house.

"She fell down the stairs," Eleanor said with a sob in her voice. "I don't know what happened, but there was a terrible crashing sound, and Corinne and I ran to see what had happened and there Nell was at the bottom of the stairway."

"Corinne is with her now?" Jackie asked breathlessly as they neared the house.

"Yes, ma'am," Eleanor confirmed.

That was little comfort. Corinne had a tendency to become distraught over the smallest detail. Jackie had a feeling a true disaster would send the girl into a dither.

Sure enough, it was Corinne who was sobbing, and Nell who was comforting, even though the older woman was lying on the floor, still dazed by what appeared to be a nasty fall.

Jackie shooed Corinne out of the way and knelt beside Nell. She'd had a few nasty falls herself, including the one from the Cloudmont gallery. "Where does it hurt?" she asked, taking Nell's hand.

Nell shot her an irritable and impatient glance. "Everywhere."

That was actually a very positive answer. Jackie checked for broken bones and found none, though the left wrist was badly sprained. There was a small knot on the side of Nell's head, and several scrapes. As Jackie checked her patient over, Nell tried to sit up. Her eyes closed as she approached a sitting position, and she eased herself back onto the floor.

"Your back?" Jackie asked, and Nell nodded.

Corinne and Eleanor were in an absolute frenzy. They sniffled as they stared down at Nell, and held onto one another for comfort, their two fair heads together, their normally plain faces contorted with distress. Jackie felt a rush of anger at the two girls who were proving to be so worthless in this crisis.

But then again, they were unused to any crisis more horrible than a stubborn stain or a burnt pan of biscuits. She had to remind herself of this as she instructed them, her voice calm and easy, to help her move Nell.

"We can't move her!" Eleanor insisted, horrified at the very suggestion.

"Well, we can't very well leave her here, can we," Jackie countered. "She needs rest."

"I'll be fine in a minute," Nell said weakly. "If I can just catch my breath I'll be fine."

Jackie looked down at the crotchety woman who was so much a part of Cloudmont. Nell had been the first to make Jackie welcome here, had offered an ear and a shoulder. She wouldn't allow the injured woman to go about her duties as if nothing had happened.

"You're going upstairs and you're going to rest."

Nell protested, "There's supper to prepare and I haven't finished with the cleaning—"

"Corinne will prepare supper and Eleanor will see to the cleaning, just as soon as you're settled in my room."

"Your room! Nonsense. I have my own little house—"

"It's too far away for me to watch over you and Kevin, so you'll have to make do with my room for a few days."

"A few days!" Nell snapped, showing a spark of life. "Nonsense! And besides," she said, lowering her voice. "Corinne can't cook. Eleanor, neither."

"Anyone can make a pot of stew, even me," Jackie answered as she directed the girls to either side of the injured housekeeper. She wasn't going to take no for an answer. Together, the three of them helped Nell to her feet, and more carried than assisted her up the stairs to Jackie's room. Although Nell protested the entire time, when she was settled in the big, soft bed, she closed her eyes and took a long, deep breath.

"All right," she said softly. "Perhaps I can rest here for a few minutes."

Jackie shooed Eleanor and Corinne from the room, and then she removed Nell's shoes and covered her with the quilt. "You'll rest here for a few days, and I don't want any arguments on the matter."

"But the girls—"

"The girls and I will be fine," Jackie insisted softly. "Give them a chance to do well."

Nell grumbled.

"Give us all a chance to take care of you for a change," Jackie said softly.

Nell grumbled some more, but she didn't try to leave the bed.

This was one of the nicest hotels in Birmingham, and one of the finest rooms in it, but compared to home it was sorely lacking. There was no life here, no comfort. It was simply a cold and impersonal place to sleep.

The Pinkerton's detective James Fullerton, who sat across the small table, was distant and sedate. When he'd arrived at Rory's suite just a few minutes earlier he'd refused a drink curtly and suggested that they get directly to business, but now he seemed reluctant to proceed. This couldn't be good.

Fullerton fingered the leather case in his lap. "This Jacqueline Beresford is your"—he cleared his throat and glanced toward the window—"ummm . . . wife?"

"Yes."

The man worked up the courage to look Rory in the eye. "How long have you been married, Mr. Donovan?"

This definitely wasn't good. "A few weeks."

The man nodded solemnly.

"Were you able to find her family?" Rory asked.

Fullerton shook his head. "I'm afraid not. But we were able to gather quite a bit of information about her past. Are you interested in what we found?"

Was he? He'd instigated this investigation to find Jackie's family for her, to at least find out where and when she'd been born and who her parents were. That wasn't what the detective had found. Obviously Fullerton had found something of interest, but Rory knew if he was smart he would say no. Jackie had lied about many things, including her age and her nationality. What else was she hiding?

It was in the past, he reminded himself. Did he want to know? "Yes," he said softly.

Fullerton reached into his leather bag and withdrew a sheaf of papers. "First of all let me assure you that the information we gathered is confidential. We have not gone to the authorities and will not." The size of the stack the detective placed on the table, face down, distressed Rory more than he'd expected.

"Jacqueline Beresford," the detective began coldly, "aka Jacqueline Barkley, aka Jackie Bernard, aka Juliet Billings, aka Jasmine the Magnificent."

Rory's heart sank and his stomach clenched, but he didn't show his distress. "Jasmine the Magnificent?"

"Fortune teller," Fullerton said, rifling through the papers until he found the sheet that detailed the short career of Jasmine the Magnificent, fortune teller and psychic medium. She'd set up shop in Charleston for a short time, bilking unsuspecting people who wanted to speak to their departed loved ones.

The detective began at the beginning, and

more distressing information followed the revelation that his wife had pretended to be a fortune teller to swindle money from grieving customers. Jackie was a known thief in Baltimore, where she'd apparently been raised by a fellow thief and con artist named Luther Maynard. She'd left Maynard at an early age and struck out on her own, eventually teaming forces with Mina Trayton, a known prostitute.

Details followed, scanty details that left months and even years unaccounted for. His wife had apparently conned and robbed her way up and down the East coast, playing on the sympathies of the wealthy and walking away with a small fortune each and every time.

Pretending to be lost.

Pretending to be destitute.

Pretending to be helpless.

Fullerton continued to speak, placing one page after another on the table that separated them, but after a while Rory ceased to hear the words.

He only had one question, and he couldn't bring himself to ask it. *What kind of scam was she pulling now?*

"Mr. Donovan?"

His head snapped up from the last page Fullerton had placed on the table. How many times had the man called his name? "Yes?"

"Should we continue the investigation? With what we have so far, it's only a matter of weeks, I'm sure, before we find out where and when she was born."

Did it matter anymore? "Yes. Continue."

Rory didn't move from his seat as Fullerton took his leave. He was stunned, all but immobilized by the news.

Did Jackie want the Fabergé egg so badly that she'd marry him to get close to it? Or did she have a bigger reward in mind?

He knew she'd been a virgin when she'd come to him; there were some things that even Jackie couldn't fake. He should've been able to find some comfort in that fact, but there was none. The giving of herself was just something new to add to her repertoire, evidently. A new scam, a more complicated game.

She called Sally her friend, when she'd been using the Clarks all along the way she'd used countless other wealthy families. She pretended to love Kevin.

She pretended to love him.

He'd known all along that loving Jackie would hurt in the end, he just hadn't expected it to hurt so damn much. He closed his eyes and placed his forehead on the table, trying to find comfort in the dark, trying to forget. All he saw was her face, and the way she'd looked at him when she'd said she loved him.

Just as clearly he could see the way something in her had changed when he'd told her he loved her. God, what an idiot he was! It was just what she wanted, wasn't it, what she'd wanted all along; a besotted husband.

Some kernel of hope that was buried deep inside made him want to believe that what the detective had discovered was in the past, that Jackie was a different person now. She wasn't playing a game this time, she really did love him and all she wanted from him was what he'd offered. His home, his protection, his name . . . his love.

No matter how hard he tried he didn't quite buy it.

Chapter Fifteen

"But I'm tired of stew!" Kevin insisted as Jackie stirred what was in the pot. "We had it last night, and the night before that, and the night before that, and—"

"Enough!" Jackie said, glancing over her shoulder to smile at Kevin. "Stew is the only thing your mama knows how to make."

She slipped off her apron and spoke to Eleanor. "Keep an eye on the stew. Stir it every now and again and don't let it boil too hard."

"Yes, ma'am," Eleanor said meekly from her position at the worktable.

"And Eleanor," Jackie said from the kitchen doorway. "Last night's biscuits really were superb. Let's see if we can't do that again tonight."

Eleanor smiled shyly, keeping her eyes on the dough before her. "Yes, ma'am."

Kevin followed Jackie as she hurried up the stairs. "Mama, when can we go fishing again? We haven't been fishing in days."

"I know," she said as she reached the second floor. "You've been so good to help me with Nell. She loves her frog pictures, I know because she told me so, and when you read that story to her this morning, she was entertained and so very proud of you."

Jackie bent down so she was face-to-face with Kevin. "I'm proud of you, too," she said softly. "When Nell is better and your father is home, we'll pack a picnic and spend all day at the river, just the three of us."

Kevin pouted. "I don't want to wait," he said. "I want to go to the river today."

"Well, you can't go today. We have to take care of Nell, and make sure that Eleanor doesn't burn the biscuits, and see that Corinne gets your father's study clean for his return. He should be back any day now."

Kevin sighed and rolled his eyes. "We used to have fun every day."

"We'll have fun again," she promised.

When would Rory be home? She'd expected a telegram, perhaps, advising her of the date of his homecoming, but so far she'd had no word from him at all. It had been nearly a week!

What would he say when he came home and

found her in his bed? Nell was recuperating in Jackie's room, and in spite of her protests she needed to stay there a few more days. Jackie had been spending her nights in Rory's bed, glad of the comfort his space offered.

But he'd never asked her to move into his bed. He seemed perfectly content to maintain separate bedrooms, to love her for a while and then allow her to slip back to her own room. There had been a few nights that she'd fallen asleep in his bed and remained there until morning, but it wasn't the same.

One day, she told herself, he would ask her. But for now, she didn't want him coming home to find her simply *there*. She wanted to be invited in.

Jackie glanced at the closed door of the fourth bedroom. What could be behind that door? A room that was simply long unneeded and unused, perhaps. It probably wouldn't take more than an afternoon's work to make that room suitable. She could allow Nell to remain in her room, and be settled into this one before Rory returned.

His business in Birmingham was finished, and tomorrow morning he would board the train and head home.

Rory won another hand and raked in his winnings. He could have returned home days ago, but he'd found excuse after excuse to stay in the city. A card game in this exclusive club, a meeting with a fellow investor, a tour of a newly built plant.

In truth, he wasn't ready to go home. More specifically, he wasn't ready to face Jackie.

"Hello darlin'." A slender hand fell easily on his shoulder. "Looks like luck is with you tonight."

Rory looked up and into the face of the double-jointed widow he'd mentioned to Nell so long ago. Vera was a handsome woman, with chestnut hair and green eyes and an hourglass figure. She'd been married once, she'd told him during one long night, but her husband had died years ago. After that, she'd supported herself as a courtesan.

"Looks that way," he said, mustering a weak smile.

"Buy me a steak dinner?" she asked, and there was the offer of something more in her eyes and in her crooked smile.

"I told you last night, I'm a married man now."

She sighed. "A faithful husband, how dreadfully boring."

Suddenly he looked into her eyes and saw something he'd missed before. Sadness, a hint of desperation. He'd seen that look in Jackie's eyes, when he'd first met her. He couldn't recall seeing it in a long time, though.

"Doesn't mean I can't buy you dinner."

He escorted Vera to the small and exclusive club restaurant and ordered steak for both of them. She was bubbly and flirtatious, perhaps thinking he'd changed his mind. He hadn't.

Heads always turned for Vera. She had a stately, almost regal air, and the clothes she chose to wear, like the emerald green silk she wore tonight, were made to show off her hourglass figure to its best. She was both a lady and a whore; it was a fascinating contrast.

When their steaks were done and they sipped strong coffee, Rory leaned across the small table, and in a lowered voice he asked her. "Why are you here?"

"Sugar, I heard you were still in town and I rushed right over. . . . "

"No," Rory interrupted impatiently. "I mean, why are you *here*?"

Vera's bright smile faltered and finally died. "What do you mean?"

"You're smart, you're pretty, you should be married and raising kids, not—"

"Hold it right there," she snapped. "Buying me dinner doesn't give you the right to insult me."

"It's not an insult," he assured her. "I want to know."

She was tough, Vera was, in the same way Jackie was sometimes tough. "Hey," she said with a falsely bright smile. "A girl's gotta do what a girl's gotta do."

He had to know more. He wanted to know everything. "Would you . . . steal?"

She narrowed her eyes, suspicious at this line of questioning. "Are you accusing me of something?"

Rory shook his head.

"Just wanna know how far I'd go?" she asked.

"I guess so."

She waited, studying him carefully as if trying to decide how much it was safe to reveal. "You wouldn't know what it's like not to have a home, not to know where your next meal is coming from."

"No, I wouldn't."

"There was a time when I would have done anything," Vera said softly, "for a bowl of grits and a bed to sleep in. When my husband died he left me nothing but debt and a few bruises to remember him by. I was all of nineteen years old, and I didn't have anywhere to turn."

"You said you had a sister."

Vera laughed loudly, and several heads in the restaurant turned their way. "I don't have any sister. The girl I told you about is a friend. We . . . share customers now and again."

"So you had nobody," he said softly.

Vera shook her head. "Nobody and nothing. And then a man came along and offered me money for sex. Seemed easy enough at the time. Just that once, I told myself, sure that something else would come along soon. It didn't, and that man had a friend who wanted to meet me, and then that first man came back again, and the next thing you know . . . " her voice trailed off, and he didn't want or need to hear the rest.

She looked him square in the eye. "You're a good man, Rory. Big as you are I don't think you'd ever hurt anyone smaller than you, which is damn near everybody." She flashed him a humorless smile that didn't stay. "You don't strike me as the kinda man who would take advantage of someone who was down on their luck, or take your anger out on the closest woman, or try to make yourself feel big by making someone else feel small." She paused. "There are a lot of men in this world who are not so good as you." She leaned across the table and lowered her voice to a whisper. "Would I steal? I wish to God I had."

She'd found the key in Rory's bedside drawer, along with several others. The first thing she'd done was open the doors on both walls and allow fresh air to circulate. This room had been closed up for a while, but aside from a little dusting and airing out, not much would be required to make it livable. She'd have to strip off all the sheets that protected the furniture, and move a few of her things in here, and by this evening she'd be set.

While she didn't like this room as much as her own, it was pleasant enough. The walls were a pale yellow, and with a few vases of flowers here and there and her things on the dresser and her clothes in the wardrobe, it would suit very well.

Kevin and Nell, her two uncooperative charges, were both napping, and so far Corinne and Eleanor had managed to avoid disaster. It was the quietest afternoon she'd enjoyed since

Nell's accident. She wouldn't have minded a nap herself, but there was still so much to be done.

Surely Rory would be home soon, she thought as she stripped off a sheet and uncovered a lovely rocking chair with an embossed back. The rosewood rocker had a broad seat and wide arms, and it was so inviting she had to try it out, just for a moment.

It was very comfortable, and rocked easily. She closed her eyes, just for a moment . . .

Rory approached Cloudmont with much less dread than he'd felt just a day before. He tried to understand—he *wanted* to understand. Had Jackie seen her crooked past as her only option? Perhaps she had. *A girl's gotta do what a girl's gotta do.*

There had surely been other options for her, but he found he was grateful that she hadn't taken the route Vera had chosen. She'd come to him a virgin, in spite of her circumstances, in spite of the fact that she'd evidently spent several years in the company of a known prostitute. She'd chosen thievery over the unpleasant option of selling her body, and for that he could only be thankful.

The sight of Cloudmont from his seat in the hired carriage comforted Rory in spite of everything he'd learned in the past week. This place was more a home to him now than it had been in a very long time, perhaps more of a real home than it had ever been, thanks to Jackie.

The grass was greener, the trees more majestic, the blooming flowers more fragrant.

But as he drew close, his heart constricted and his mouth went dry. Would Jackie still be here? By leaving he'd given her the perfect opportunity to make off with the Fabergé egg and anything else that struck her fancy. She could have taken her time and packed as many bags as the train would carry, stealing his treasures, his money, his heart.

He cared little for his treasures, and there was always more money to be made . . . but he wasn't sure his heart could stand another beating.

The carriage stopped in the circular drive, directly before the wide double doors. He waited a moment, half-expecting Jackie and Kevin to come barreling out the door to welcome him home. Surely they'd seen the carriage approaching.

All was quiet, so quiet the house might be completely empty. Rory stepped from the carriage and flipped a coin to the driver as he muttered an absentminded "thanks."

He stood in the drive as the rig and horses headed for town, waiting for a sign, listening for the sounds of laughter. Just a few days ago he'd been so sure his wife was false in her affections, that her avowed love was part of an elaborate scam. Right now he prayed he was wrong, that she was anxiously awaiting his return.

Inside all was still. He closed his eyes and strained to listen, and after a moment's wait he heard the muted clatter of pans and a burst of girlish laughter that drifted through open doors and windows from the kitchen. Nothing more.

It was afternoon, the time of day Kevin always took a nap. Jackie sometimes did. He'd looked in on her a time or two, finding an unexpected comfort in her complete tranquillity. If she was there now, he thought as he began to climb the stairs, sleeping in nothing but her chemise and stockings, he would climb into that bed with her and let her welcome him home properly. The thought brought an unexpected smile to his face, and granted him the assurance that she *would* be here.

He was almost to the top of the staircase before he noticed that the sunlight hit the hallway floor at an odd angle. That particular section of the upstairs hallway was always in shadow—his heart thudded—because the door to Leona's room was always closed and locked.

But it wasn't closed and locked today. The door stood open, and from his position near the top of the stairs he could see the end of a sheet-covered dresser, smell the fresh air that wafted through an outer door that was always kept shut. Another step and he could see the thin curtains at the French doors dancing in the breeze.

He dropped his bag there in the hallway and stepped to the door. The room was flooded with bright light, and it was as it had been the last time he'd seen it—but for the fact that

Jackie was sitting in the uncovered rocking chair.

She was motionless. Her eyes were closed, her head listed slightly to one side. She'd fallen asleep in the chair where he'd rocked his dying baby; she slept peacefully in the very spot where he'd cried and begged and prayed in vain.

Taking a few silent steps he placed himself before Jackie. He could barely breathe, but he knew he had to do *something*.

"Get up," he demanded, his voice a hoarse whisper. She didn't move, so he spoke again, his voice louder, his heart thudding so hard in his chest he could *feel* it against his ribs. "Get up!"

Her eyes fluttered and opened, and she smiled at him. What game was she playing? Where did this cruel maneuver fall in her scam?

"You're home," she said sleepily, but she made no immediate move to vacate the chair.

Rory reached down and took her wrist and yanked her into a standing position. She practically fell against him, tender and yielding and warm.

There was such a look of peace on the face she lifted to him, as if for a kiss. She was all rosy cheeks and bright eyes and softness. But what was she hiding beneath the softness?

"Get out," he ordered gruffly as he released his grip on her wrist.

Jackie's smile faded and she stepped to the side, away from him and away from the rock-

271

ing chair. "What did you say?"

"I said get out," he said softly. "You don't belong here."

The stricken expression on her face should have made him feel guilty . . . but it didn't. When she spun around and left the room she'd had no business entering, he felt a surge of relief instead. She really didn't belong here. No one did.

When she was gone he touched the arm of the rocking chair. It was warm, still, where Jackie's hand had rested. He should've burned this chair years ago, cleared out this room and buried the memories along with Leona's body. But he hadn't, had he? He'd clung to the horrid memories as if without them he would have nothing left inside. Even bad memories were better than emptiness, weren't they?

He closed the doors that led to the gallery, putting an end to the fresh air and bringing the gentle swing of the thin curtains to a standstill. He stood over the rocking chair with the sheet in his hand, ready to recover it and the past, but he hesitated. After a long moment he turned and sat slowly.

Leona had loved this chair. She'd looked so very small sitting in it, her little feet barely clearing the end of the seat, her head far below the elaborately carved headrest. How many nights had he sat here, telling her stories, listening to her prayers, assuring her that he loved her, waiting for her to go to sleep after a bad dream.

He rocked once. Leona had never liked being alone. She'd needed people around her; she'd needed laughter, *life*. The rocking chair began to move rhythmically. Dammit, he tried so hard not to think of her. When he did he was tormented with visions of a child who would never grow up, a young woman who would never be. He'd never get the chance to bandage her scraped knees or buy her first grown-up dress or take her to her first dance. He'd never get to intimidate her beaus or interrogate a man who asked for her hand in marriage. There were so many *nevers* he was afraid the regrets for a life lost would never cease.

"Pa?" The soft voice startled him, and he turned his head to see a sleepy Kevin standing in the doorway. The boy rubbed his eyes and frowned as if he'd had a bad dream of his own.

"Go back to bed," Rory said softly. Of all people, Kevin should definitely not be in this room. What if he heard the ghosts of the past? No, it wouldn't do.

"But—" his eyes studied the room quickly.

"Don't argue with me," Rory said gruffly. "You obviously haven't finished your nap. Go back to bed."

Kevin stood silently in the doorway for a long moment. His eyes got big, and he scratched his cheek as if it itched. "I just wanted to know where Mama's going."

"Mama's not going anywhere."

"But—"

"Mama's not going anywhere," Rory said again, his patience gone.

"She left," Kevin said, and his lower lip trembled slightly.

Rory placed two fingers to the bridge of his nose. The headache had come all of a sudden, sharp and pounding. He would have to explain it all to her now, wouldn't he? "She's probably gone for a walk, that's all," he said.

Still, Kevin didn't leave. He fidgeted and scratched his cheek again. "Why did she take a bag of her clothes on a walk?"

Rory burst from the chair and almost knocked Kevin down as he made his way to the stairs.

Chapter Sixteen

Get out.

It would have been best, less painful, if Rory had simply shot her. Jackie walked down the road, headed for Florence. In her tapestry bag there were a couple changes of clothes, her jewelry, and . . . no money at all. She'd have to withdraw funds from her account at the bank in Charleston, something she never did, but this was an emergency situation.

Two lonely tears rolled down her face, and she hated Rory for causing them. She never cried! Not for real. She was great at producing false tears, could call them up at a moment's notice when necessary, but these . . . these were real, painful and uncontrollable. More tears followed, blinding, ugly, tormenting tears. No matter how hard she tried, how sternly she ordered herself to stop, they continued to fall.

A few months ago she could have walked away from Rory and Kevin—from anyone—without a second thought or a single backward glance. Jacqueline Beresford didn't need anyone. She was strong, hard, unfailingly independent, and no man made her cry! Ever! More tears ran down her cheeks, and an unwanted sob escaped.

Get out!

Rory must've discovered her past while he was in Birmingham. How? She didn't know, and in truth it didn't matter. He knew she was a thief and a liar, and he didn't love her anymore . . . if he ever had.

You don't belong here.

She knew that and always had, right? Something within her had been waiting for this all along. If only she'd listened to the little voice that had kept telling her this wouldn't last.

The speed and length of her stride increased. She didn't belong at Cloudmont; she didn't belong anywhere.

"Jackie!"

At the sound of that familiar voice she tensed and increased her pace. She didn't want Rory to see her crying, didn't want him to know how much he'd hurt her. His big feet made a racket on the road behind her as he drew closer, pebbles skittering across the dirt, his boots pounding against the hard ground. What did he want?

No doubt to check her bag to make sure she hadn't made off with any of his belongings.

"Jackie, please stop." He was closer now, much too close. "You don't understand . . . "

She increased her pace, knowing it would do little good against his longer stride. "I understand 'get out' quite well," she said, trying to keep her voice calm. I also comprehend the meaning of 'you don't belong here.' "

"I'm sorry. I didn't mean—"

How could he be so thoughtless? "There are some things you can't take back," she interrupted. *I need you, I love you, get out.* "You can't just change your mind and make it go away."

"Jackie, stop."

"No." She wouldn't stop, she wouldn't so much as glance over her shoulder for one last look.

She waited for Rory to ask again, or else to slow down or stop or disappear. But he was silent for a few long minutes, and his step didn't so much as falter. He was right behind her, too damn close.

"It's the room," he said, and he was so near he could no doubt reach out and grab her if he wished. He didn't. "Seeing you there sitting in that chair, with the sun shining in and the breeze bringing life into the room, it was more than I could bear."

"I had no idea you were so sentimental about the first Mrs. Donovan," she snapped. New tears sprang to her eyes. She didn't dare turn to face him!

"It wasn't Margaret's room," he said softly. "It was Leona's."

"Leona," she repeated. "A mistress, no doubt. Did she come before or after the first Mrs. Donovan? Was she the love of your life, Rory? The woman who broke your heart?"

"She was my daughter."

Jackie stopped in the middle of the road. *Daughter?* "You don't have a daughter," she whispered.

"I did." Rory stood close behind her, so close she could feel his presence. He didn't touch her or come around to face her, but spoke to her back. "She died a few days after her mother. Yellow fever. I sat in that rocking chair and held her as she died. I prayed to God to save her, to take my life instead of hers." His hand rested on her shoulder, so very lightly. "She was so young."

She dropped her bag onto the dirt road and turned to face her husband. His face was blank, as if he were hiding behind a welcomed numbness.

"Why did you never tell me?"

Rory reached out and brushed her tears away with his thumb. He didn't want to answer, she could see that plainly enough. He was wrestling with himself, with his conscience and maybe even his soul.

"I didn't want to talk about it, ever," he finally

said softly. "I've kept everything locked in that room, all these years. It seemed best just to leave it all there."

"Oh, Rory." She laid her palm against his chest, felt the beating of his heart and the heat that poured off of him on this hot summer day. She'd spent all her life avoiding closeness, so why was it that his simple touch comforted her? "You can't lock away the past and pretend it didn't happen." Strange words coming from her. Wasn't that exactly what she was doing? Ignoring the past, pretending she could start over and her former life would stay buried.

"It would be an easier world if we could," he muttered.

She looked up and into honey-brown eyes that were sharp with sadness and alive with wonder. "Maybe that's true," she whispered.

They stood there for a long moment, wrapped in the heat of the afternoon, his hand on her face and hers against his chest. Jackie was afraid if the contact was broken too soon something precious would be destroyed. She curled her fingers against his shirt.

"They buried Margaret without me," he whispered. "I wouldn't leave Leona, not even for a few minutes. I was afraid that if I left her side she'd die. My strength was hers, my will, and without it . . . "

Jackie rested her head against Rory's chest, and he wrapped his arms around her and held on tight.

"Without it she was helpless," he finished. "Foolish nonsense, I know . . . "

"No," Jackie whispered. "Not foolish at all."

He held her tight, and she did her best to give him her strength, her will.

"I prayed for her, offered my life in exchange for hers, and in those last desperate hours I . . . I asked God to take the life of the baby crying in the next room, and to spare my little girl."

"Kevin?"

Rory nodded. "I've never forgiven myself for that."

Jackie wrapped her arms around his waist and held on tight. "You were desperate and exhausted, and not yourself to offer up your son in exchange for your daughter."

He whispered something so low, so mumbled, that she couldn't decipher it.

"What?"

He forced her away from him, held her shoulders firmly and stared down into her eyes. If anything, his look was more distraught than before. "Kevin's not my son," he said distinctly.

He'd never spoken the words aloud, not to anyone. Nell had to suspect, but she'd never mentioned it, either. He'd only spoken of it with Margaret the one time.

"I hadn't been in Margaret's bed for more than a year before Kevin was born," he whispered. A few days ago he'd been hurt and angry at Jackie's deception, mere minutes ago he'd been afraid she wouldn't be waiting for him at home, and now . . . now he was sharing with her the most painful confessions of his life.

If she could put her past aside and start anew, why couldn't he?

"I hated him for a long time," he whispered, admitting to his transgression for the first time. "A helpless baby, a blameless child . . . I looked at a baby and wanted him to pay for his mother's sin. I stared into deep brown eyes so like his mother's and wondered who the real father was. The traveling photographer who'd taken our family pictures, the lad I'd hired to help with the stables that summer, or perhaps the penniless beau who was, by all accounts, the love of Margaret's life. I don't think she knew herself who the father was."

She held on tight, and he needed that—her arms and her warmth, her heartbeat. "Where are they now? Do they know?"

Rory shook his head. "The photographer and the stableboy moved on long before Margaret discovered her pregnancy, and her old beau . . . he died less than a week before she did, and if he suspected the child was his he took it to his grave."

He'd often wondered if it was a blessing or a curse that Kevin looked so much like his mother. There was no clue in the child's appearance as to who the real father might be.

The news he'd shared with his wife was shocking, scandalous, horrifying, but Jackie looked at him with nothing but love in her eyes. "In every way that counts you are Kevin's father, just as I am now his mother. Forgive yourself for mistakes you made long ago, and look to the future."

It sounded so simple and inviting. "Can we do that?"

She gave the question a moment of consideration, thinking, no doubt, of her own past. Would she share with him all the sordid details of her life before coming to Cloudmont, as he had shared his deepest secrets with her? He wanted her to, more than he'd ever wanted anything. If she could come to him and tell all it would prove that she trusted him completely, and right now he needed that trust.

"I believe we can," she said softly. "Perhaps our household isn't conventional, but that doesn't mean we're not a family. We *are* a family. I love you, and I love Kevin, and together we can face anything."

Anything. Her past and his sins. Her secrets and his fears.

Jackie wasn't going to confess all to him now. She was waiting for him to agree, to forge a bond here in the middle of the road, to swear to a covenant as sacred as their marriage vows. He wanted to ask her, *but what of* your *past, wife? Do you trust me enough to tell all?* He didn't dare. "So you forgive me?"

She smiled and came up on her toes to kiss him. "Of course. Love conquers all, you know," she whispered as she pulled her mouth from his.

"Does it, now?" He stole another quick kiss.

"That's what I hear." Her faint smile died and she looked into his eyes as if she were searching his soul for answers. "I never believed it until I met you."

He could forget everything when he held her; her past, his vows, the silly businesslike arrangement that had started this marriage. She was his, and he wanted to brand her here and now, to mark her body with his.

He scooped Jackie's bag from the road and led her into the tall grass, down a steep slope and away from the house.

"Where are we going?" she asked as he hurried her along.

"Over there." He gestured, with the hand that held her bag, to an ancient magnolia tree in the near distance. The weighted limbs hung nearly to the ground, and the thick leaves and creamy flowers hid the trunk completely from view.

"Why?"

"Why?" he repeated, dropping the bag and scooping Jackie into his arms. "Because I want you, now. If we go back to the house it will be hours before I get you alone again, and I can't possibly wait hours."

She wrapped her arms around his neck and smiled seductively, and with that smile she managed to instantly put so much behind them. "Are you going to seduce me?"

With the sheen of tears still in her eyes, she

could smile and ask such an outrageous question. "Most definitely," he mumbled.

"Marvelous," she sighed. "But out here in the open, in the middle of the day? Really, Rory, I had no idea you were so daring."

"We won't be in the open, exactly," he said as he set her on her feet near a break in the magnolia leaves. He held a branch aside and motioned for her to enter.

She stepped through the opening and into the leafy enclosure, looking up and around and marveling at the private space. "It's like a small room," she said as he stepped in behind her, "and it smells heavenly."

Sunlight broke through the space between the ground and the lowest limbs, through narrow breaks where the thick leaves didn't quite touch, illuminating the enclosure with a faint glow that was as magical and seductive as any moonlit night.

"I used to hide here when I was a kid," he said, reaching out to calmly unfasten the pearly buttons of Jackie's bodice. "When I had chores to do and didn't want to do them, or when I knew I was in trouble, I would come here and pretend this was a secret cave where no one would ever find me."

"Did they ever find you here?" She reached out and flicked a few of his shirt buttons through her fingers.

"No." He drew her closer and slipped his hand into her dress, cupping a full breast and teasing the nipple that hardened against his palm. "I always got hungry and went home by suppertime."

Their mouths came together for a kiss; a deep, slow, intoxicating kiss that heightened his already raging desire for his wife. Her tongue danced with his, tasting and probing gently, promising him everything she had to offer.

No matter what had happened in the past, he needed her. She was his *life*, the only beauty, the only passion, the only soul.

He pushed her dress off her shoulders and freed her arms, so that the fabric fell to her waist. The chemise was cut low, and with a simple hook of his fingers it slipped below her breasts.

He'd once thought her breasts small, he remembered as he circled a nipple with his thumb, but they were perfectly shaped, slightly rounded and firm, and so very responsive to his touch. He felt Jackie's deep quiver as he flicked a thumb across one nipple, and when he bent to take that peak into his mouth a faint cry of pleasure escaped her throat.

He lowered her gently to the ground, pushing her voluminous skirt up. Hooking her drawers with his fingers he slid them down and off.

Her trembling fingers found his trouser buttons, and as he joined his mouth to hers she flicked them open until his arousal sprang free. Gentle fingers explored and stroked, cupped and caressed until he was ready to explode.

Intimately, lovingly, he touched her as she touched him, his fingers stroking the folds of flesh that were wet for him, that awaited his entrance. Jackie's hips rocked against his hand, and her tongue drove deep into his mouth, and when he slid a finger into her tight sheath she moaned deep in her throat.

He covered Jackie with his body, and she cradled him possessively with her legs, arching to accept him as he thrust deeply within. With that thrust he marked her, as he'd longed to do. He made her his own once again, branded her with this act that was primal pleasure and sacred pledge and avowal of love.

He withdrew slowly and then thrust again, driving deep. And then again, deeper than before, and then again. Her completion came with a cry and an arch of her back, and he felt her ripples of pleasure caressing him, wringing everything from him. Her response spurred his own, and he branded her again with his seed, pumping everything he had and everything he was into her welcoming body.

For a long moment they lay very still, their bodies entwined and entangled. The first movement that followed was the soft stroke of Jackie's hand against his back. "Oh my," she whispered, every trace of her British accent gone. There was even, perhaps, a hint of a Southern accent there. "That was quite . . . remarkable."

With a lazy finger he brushed a wayward strand of hair from her face. She was so very beautiful, so full of life and love and expectations. "It was, wasn't it?" he agreed softly. "I missed you so much while I was gone, there were moments I hurt with it." It was the truth. Even when he'd wondered if her love was part of a scam, even when he'd been certain it was, he had still yearned for her.

"Was your bed too big and cold and lonely?" she asked.

"Yes," he breathed.

"Mine, too." She wrapped her arms around his neck. "It was irritating and puzzling and amazing, because it was much more than missing you. I came to believe that you took a part of me with you, because I was not *complete* while you were away. A part of me was gone."

Rory placed his lips against Jackie's and kissed her again. This was no scam, no con, no dastardly game. She wanted to leave her past behind . . . the same way he now did. Everything was brighter at this extraordinary moment.

He drew his mouth from hers, and as he watched her smile faded away. "I think I understand now why you don't want other children," she whispered. "Losing a child must hurt more than anything I can imagine." Her eyes filled with tears. "I wish I had been here for you, then."

"So do I," he whispered.

"I would have done everything in my power to take some of the pain away," she said, and he knew that she would have tried with everything she had.

"I know."

"But Rory," she said, a hint of panic in her voice, "If we continue to lie together without anything between us, there will be babies. Lots of them, I would imagine."

It had been his greatest fear for years, loving and losing, opening his heart only to have it destroyed . . . but Jackie made him feel as if life was worth living, as if taking a chance was the only way to truly live.

"You said you didn't want children, either," he said. "Have you, by any chance, changed your mind?"

She bit her lip, opened her mouth to speak and then apparently thought better of it. Her eyes bored through him, searching his soul again. "Yes," she finally whispered. "More than anything I want to have your child. I don't know why I want this so much, after years of being certain I'd never have a family, but I do. Don't be angry."

He kissed Jackie deeply, and the shaft that was still buried within her body began to harden and grow. Rocking slightly, he stroked her inner core. He wanted her again, but this time he would love her slowly, without the frenzy that had driven him the first time. He took his mouth from hers to kiss the column of her neck, to suckle gently where neck curved to shoulder. She responded with a pleased sigh and exploring hands that delved beneath his shirt to touch his flesh.

"I guess this means you're not angry," she whispered breathlessly.

"Of course I'm not angry. I want you to have everything you want. Everything."

Her hands slid down his back, and slipped beneath his loosened trousers to caress and clasp his buttocks, to urge him on. He rocked his hips rhythmically, slowly, and Jackie began to rock with him.

Together, they made the world and the past disappear, for a while.

Chapter Seventeen

With the house in view, Jackie checked her skirt again and raised a hand to her hair. Most of the wayward strands had been straightened, but without a mirror to check her reflection in she knew she must look a mess.

"You look fine," Rory said, and she glanced sideways at her husband only to catch him grinning widely.

"I look a fright," she whispered.

Rory stopped her as they reached the front door. With both hands on her shoulders, he studied her with a critical eye. "You look beautiful," he said softly. "Well-loved and sinfully content." He kissed her quickly, and when he came away he brought a strand of grass from her hair.

She checked her skirt again and found more

contrary bits of grass and a nasty grass stain. "I suppose I could tell Nell I stumbled and fell," she muttered.

Before she could open the door Rory snaked his arm around her waist and pulled her against his chest. His lips landed on her neck. "What do you care what Nell thinks?" he whispered as he dragged his mouth across her flesh.

"She'll be shocked—"

"To know that I find my wife irresistible?" he finished. "Perhaps. A little shock now and again will do the old bat good."

"Rory Donovan!" She circled in his arms and looked up with what she hoped was a censuring gaze. Her smile probably counteracted the severity. "How dare you speak that way about poor Nell. She's been laid up in bed all week after taking a nasty fall down the stairs."

Should she tell him now that Nell's presence in her bedroom was the reason she'd intruded into Leona's domain? No. She didn't want to mention anything that would ruin this wonderful moment.

"Was she badly hurt?" Rory's eyes narrowed and his smile died. He could bluster all he liked, but he cared deeply for Nell Logan. There was more love in his heart than he knew.

"No, just bruised and battered a bit," she assured him. "But the shock of realizing that the very proper gentleman Rory Donovan would sneak off with his wife in the middle of the day and seduce her beneath a magnolia tree, well, it might be more than she could bear."

"She's tougher than that," Rory said as he reached past her to throw open the door.

Jackie stepped into the house with a renewed sense that this was her home, for now and always, her place in the world. Until she'd come to Cloudmont she'd never wanted or expected a place of her own, more than just a shelter for the body and the heart, and now . . . now she understood what home really meant.

She understood so much about Rory, now that she knew about his daughter's death and his first wife's infidelity. He was a giant of a man, tall and broad and strong, but underneath he was still just a man, with a heart that could be broken as easily as hers. He needed her every bit as much as she needed him.

There was a commotion at the top of the stairs. Nell stood there, with Corinne and Eleanor on either side, supporting her as she tried to descend the stairs. The girls were apparently uncertain about the endeavor, but Nell was insistent.

"I'm fine!" she snapped. "There's just a little twinge in my back, that's all. I've been in bed long enough!" Their progress was slow but certain as they descended one step and then another.

"Obstinate as ever, I see," Rory said as he climbed the stairs quickly.

"I want my own bed in my own house, and if you call that obstinate then yes, I'm an obstinate old woman!"

Rory very gently swept Nell off her feet, to

muttered protests. "Put me down. You can't carry me! I said . . . oh, you . . . " By the time she finished they had reached the bottom of the stairway.

Rory did not place his charge on her feet. "Mrs. Donovan," he said formally. "Do you release your patient to her own bed and her own house as she so vehemently desires?"

"I suppose," Jackie sighed. "Corinne and Eleanor and I can take turns checking in on her. . . . "

"That won't be necessary," Nell snapped. "I'll be back in my kitchen by tomorrow morning."

Rory headed for the back of the house, Nell still in his arms.

"Where are you taking me?" she snapped.

"Home."

"I can walk, you ninny!"

Jackie smiled as the voices faded away. Rory would see Nell settled in her little house, and even though she'd protest during the entire trek Jackie was sure that she would be grateful to be home.

Corinne and Eleanor retired to the kitchen to get supper underway, and Jackie climbed the stairs with every intention of indulging in a quick cleanup and perhaps a change of clothes. But before that, she'd check in on Kevin while he napped.

It was a shock to learn that Rory was not Kevin's real father, but it didn't change her feelings for the little boy, not one iota. If anything, it deepened her love. Like her, Kevin had been set adrift without his real parents to watch over him. Like her, he had Rory to watch over him, always. Rory might doubt his love for the boy, but Jackie didn't. They were father and child, in every way that mattered. And she was mother and wife, and if she was very lucky she would be a mother again, one day. Rory didn't seem to mind that they risked that possibility on a regular basis.

She'd meant every word she'd said in the shelter of the magnolia. A child of Rory's would make her world complete, and she wanted that child with all her heart. Who would have thought that Jacqueline Beresford harbored a deeply buried maternal instinct!

She was grinning when she stuck her head into Kevin's room, but her smile faded when she saw that the bed was empty. All was quiet, but she searched the other three bedrooms, just in case, and circled the gallery. He was not upstairs.

Her cleanup forgotten, she hurried downstairs. Though she knew Kevin never willingly entered the schoolroom, she checked there first. All was quiet. A quick inspection of the parlor and Rory's study revealed no sign of the child, either. She looked everywhere, even under the dining room table as she passed on her way to the kitchen. While on the brick walkway she glanced into the garden and beyond, but all was still and quiet.

In the kitchen, Corinne and Eleanor were arguing about whose turn it was to make biscuits.

"Where's Kevin?" Jackie interrupted, and they turned wide eyes her way as their argument ceased.

"I thought he was with you and Mr. Donovan," Eleanor said softly. "He wasn't upstairs when Nell called us to help her down the steps."

"No," she said, trying not to fret. Kevin had probably sneaked down to the pond for a little fishing. Still, until she saw him she wouldn't completely quit worrying!

Rory came in through the kitchen door, having left Nell in her little house.

"Did you see Kevin while you were outside?" Jackie asked curtly.

"No." He was accustomed to Kevin's escapades, and seemed not at all concerned. "He's not here?"

She joined him at the opened door. "He's probably gone to the pond," she said sensibly. "Come with me?" For some reason her heart thudded unnaturally in her chest. Something was wrong; she knew it. "Please?"

He'd been so sure that Jackie's worries were unfounded, and that Kevin would be fishing contentedly at the pond. But when they came upon the silent and still body of water, it was evident to Rory that he was mistaken. Kevin was nowhere in sight.

"Just because he's not here, that doesn't mean something's wrong." He tried to calm

Jackie, but his own heart wasn't taking this too well. Where was the kid?

"Something is wrong," Jackie insisted. "I can feel it."

"Mother's intuition?" he glanced down at her frowning face, keeping his tone of voice light and trying not to let her see that he was beginning to be as worried as she so obviously was.

"I suppose." She began to pace. "He's afraid of the horses, so I don't imagine he's at the stables."

"Kevin's afraid of the horses?" He hadn't known . . . he should've known. . . .

"Yes," Jackie said curtly. "The only place he likes to go is here, and—" she stopped pacing and her face went pale. "The river," she whispered. "Oh, he's asked every day this week if we could go to the river again."

They ran, Rory in the lead and Jackie keeping pace and staying close behind. Why hadn't he known the kid would run? Kevin had been so upset that Jackie had left. *Where's Mama going?* Rory cursed himself as he ran. He should've known better than to assume that Kevin would sit patiently at home and wait.

He'd worked up quite a sweat by the time they reached the riverbank. There was no sign of Kevin at their usual fishing spot, and that gave him a moment of relief. Maybe they'd been wrong, maybe Kevin was hiding somewhere in the house, maybe he'd fallen asleep under the stairs or under the desk in Rory's study. There were a hundred possibilities to explore. He had almost convinced himself of this when Jackie, who'd been walking along the bank silently, whispered his name.

The river was low, and the shallow water lapped several feet below the grassy brink. There was a straight drop of four or five feet from the point where Jackie's shoes peeked over the ledge to the muddy river's edge. He stood beside her and looked down at a fishing pole that bobbed in the water, its line snarled in a tangled growth that was peeking out of the water.

"This just means he was here," he said. His voice was calm, but his heart was beating so fast he could feel it thudding in his chest. His stomach knotted. "It doesn't mean anything's happened."

"Then where is he?"

Isn't this just what he'd been trying to avoid by keeping his distance from the boy? God help him, he couldn't lose another child. Not now, not when he'd rediscovered so much he'd thought long lost. He couldn't let himself dwell on the horrible possibilities. There was not only his own agony to deal with, but his wife's as well. How would Jackie survive if Kevin had not?

"I'm letting my imagination run away with me," he muttered. "Kevin is fine. Kevin is just fine."

He left Jackie's side and stalked along the river's edge. "Kevin!" he shouted, looking to the stand of trees to the west. The kid could be in there, hunting critters, hiding, playing a game without knowing that he was torturing his parents. He called again, and again, and Jackie started walking in the other direction, calling for Kevin in a voice that was surprisingly strong.

Nothing in the grove moved, but Rory headed in that direction, anyway. Before he entered the shade of the trees he glanced out at the river. It flowed unerringly, strong and deep, treacherous and beautiful. The trunk of a fallen tree was caught on a high spot, and it bobbed in the water like a small floating island.

Rory turned from the trees and stalked toward the riverbank. His eyes were playing tricks on him, surely. He took off his shoes and dropped his jacket on the ground, his eyes on the log. Surely he was mistaken. Still, he needed a closer look to be certain.

"Rory!" Jackie was running toward him, but she wouldn't be here in time to stop him from entering the water. He had to confirm what he saw before he told her.

He jumped from the bank and into the shallow water, and after taking two long strides he pushed himself into deeper water. The current wanted to take him, but he was a strong swimmer, and he compensated for the current by training his sights upstream of the log.

How many years had passed since he'd really prayed? He remembered too well the last time, even though he'd tried for years to forget. He prayed now, with everything he had, to be wrong. The tepid water flowed over his body as he pushed and fought the current. It was strong. If Kevin had fallen into the water and gotten caught up in this current he wouldn't have had a chance.

He reached the log and shot out a hand to grab a roughened end, stilling his progress. The river swirled and pushed at his body, so he held on tight as he reached out to grab the item that had caught his eye from the riverbank.

It was Rory's own hat, battered and soaked. He remembered well the day he'd placed it on Kevin's head, a beautiful, memorable day of fishing and picnics and capitulation. Since then, this wide-brimmed hat had become the boy's lucky fishing hat.

He closed his fingers around the ruined brown felt and ripped it from the log. It wasn't fair . . . it wasn't right! Kevin was just a kid, and he'd paid a hundred times over for his mother's sin. Rory had made him pay, hadn't he? With every rebuff, with every cold refusal. The distance Rory had chosen to protect himself had robbed a child of his only chance at a real family, at real love . . . until Jackie had come and taught him what it meant to be a family.

And now . . .

Jackie called his name now, frantic, worried, not knowing yet what he'd found. How could he show her this evidence that Kevin had gone into the water?

He didn't have the strength to let go of the log and swim back to shore. Not yet. His body was numb, his eyes clouded with tears. "One more chance, God," he whispered. "If you're listening, if you've ever listened, give me one more chance to make things right."

Jackie's voice became more frantic, and Rory took a deep breath and pushed away from the log and toward the shore. His progress was slow, but then he wasn't driven as he had been when he'd seen the hat and headed for the damning sign.

In fact, he dreaded his arrival at the bank. He didn't want to show Jackie what he'd found, didn't want her to lose heart and hope as he had when he'd seen Kevin's hat.

But eventually he reached the shallows, and he stood to face Jackie. The hat was crushed in his hand, a wad of wet, ruined felt. A few steps and he was standing in the mud. He heaved himself up onto the grassy bank with the last bit of his strength, and Jackie was there to help him to his feet.

"What on earth were you thinking?" she said as she laid her hand on his soaked shirt.

He didn't want to tell her . . . but it wouldn't be fair not to, would it? "I saw this," he said weakly, holding the lucky fishing hat out to her.

There was immediate recognition in her eyes, and then fear, and then tears. "No."

"It just means Kevin dropped his hat in the water," he said, trying to reassure her. "It doesn't mean . . . " His words trailed off to nothing.

He wrapped his arms around her and held on tight. "We'll get together a search party," he whispered. "Maybe he landed on the bank upstream, and he's lost. Just lost, not . . . not hurt." It was possible, but he'd felt the power of the current and knew a boy like Kevin wouldn't have much of a chance against it. Still, there was a chance. . . .

Jackie gripped his shirt with delicate, shaking hands, and buried her face against his chest. She was no fool. She knew as well as he did that the odds were slim. "Yes," she whispered shakily, "a search party."

Rory buried his face against Jackie's shoulder, holding on tight for a moment longer as he gathered his strength. Without her he would fall to the ground, break into a million pieces, disappear. . . . There would be nothing left of him.

The soaked hat was taken from his hand. He felt the gentle tug as the battered evidence slipped from his fingers. There was a warm and gentle pressure at his back, against the wet fabric of his shirt, as if a small hand had settled there. It was a familiar touch that made his heart lurch.

"Pa?"

Chapter Eighteen

At the sound of that familiar and tentative voice, Jackie released her grip on Rory and looked down. Kevin had one hand at her back and the other at Rory's, completing the circle of their family. His face and his clothes were covered with mud, and tufts of red hair stuck straight up from his head.

"I fell," he said softly as they stared down at him.

Rory took a deep, stilling breath, and knelt before the muddy child. His hands were trembling, and as Jackie watched he balled them into fists to stop the uncontrollable tremors. "I should whale the tar out of you," he said in a low and menacing voice.

Kevin's eyes got wide as he stared at his father, dark brown eyes wide in a mud-covered face.

"Do you have any idea how worried we were?" Rory lifted one trembling hand and brushed a drying clump of mud from Kevin's cheek. "Didn't you hear us calling you?"

Big tears welled up in Kevin's eyes, and he sniffled once. "You were mad, so I stayed in the woods."

"Of course we were mad!" Rory said with little patience as he settled big hands on Kevin's shoulders. "We thought you were . . . " He wrapped his arms around Kevin and pulled him close. "We thought you were lost."

"I was lost, a little bit," Kevin said as he wrapped his arms around Rory's neck. "I dropped my hat in the water, and I tried to get it before it went out too far, and then I fell in the mud and I couldn't climb up because the bank was too high, so I walked down the river's edge until I came to a place where it wasn't so high, but it was a long ways. I came up in the woods."

He glanced up at Jackie. "Are you mad, too?" he asked solemnly.

"I'm furious," she said, dropping down to wrap her arms around them both. Rory was soaking wet and Kevin was covered with mud, and she laughed as she held them both close.

Kevin turned his face to hers, and they were nose to nose. "I thought you were gone," he said, his tone of voice accusing.

"No," she said softly. "I just went for a walk."

"I thought you weren't coming back," he said softly.

Jackie kissed a muddy cheek. "I'm your mama, and mamas don't walk away and not come back."

"Promise?"

"Promise," she answered quickly.

Kevin grinned, his white teeth, gap and all, ridiculously bright against a muddy face.

When Rory stood he lifted Kevin with him, apparently afraid to let the child go even for a moment. Kevin settled in nicely, his arms around his father's neck and his thin legs hooked around his father's waist. Jackie gathered Rory's jacket and shoes from the ground, and together they headed for home.

"How many times have I told you not to come to the river by yourself?" Rory asked sternly.

"Lots," Kevin conceded.

"Well, we'll discuss this later." Rory's voice was gruff. "Man to man. I don't want your mother to be subjected to what I have to say to you."

"That bad?" Kevin asked.

"That bad."

Jackie was happy to walk alongside them, her relief at Kevin's safety finally settling in.

He was a big child and had to be heavy, but Rory showed no indication that he planned to put Kevin down anytime soon. Perhaps he found comfort in holding his son, after believing that he was gone forever.

There were no doubts in her mind that Rory loved this child as if he were truly his own. If he could only forgive himself for his moment of mad weakness, he would realize the truth himself. The way he held the boy right now, perhaps he already had.

Sally had said that blood can't be denied, but she was wrong. The free giving of a heart was stronger, much stronger, than blood ties, and the realization gave Jackie hope for her own future.

They were well on their way home before Rory changed the subject. "I think maybe I should teach you to ride. That'll give you something to do besides fishing and making your mother and me worry."

"You mean, ride a horse?"

"Naturally."

Jackie sighed. She'd told Rory that Kevin was afraid of horses! What on earth was he doing?

"I don't like horses," Kevin said, pouting.

"Why not?"

"They're big and mean."

Rory grinned widely. "Then we'll have to get you a pony that's small and sweet."

"A pony?" Kevin's eyes lit up.

"I can't have any son of mine afraid of horses," Rory admitted. "We'll start you off with a gentle pony, and as you get bigger, the ponies will get bigger."

Jackie grinned widely. *Any son of mine.* What a meaningful phrase that was!

"Okay," Kevin agreed readily. "Will you teach Mama to ride a pony, too?"

"Nope." Rory glanced over his shoulder and smiled at her. "Mama gets a fully grown horse. A sweet mare, I think."

"I've never ridden a horse in my life, and I see no reason to start now!"

"And when you can both handle your mounts well, we'll take Sunday rides all over the county. We'll travel to fairs and picnics and barbecues, and when people see us coming they'll say 'Here come those Donovans.'"

"And we can go to different parts of the river, can't we?" Kevin asked, excitement in his voice.

"Perhaps," Rory answered, lowering his voice. "But you are never again to go to the river alone, do you hear me?"

"Yes, sir."

Jackie slipped her hand into the crook of Rory's elbow. It had been a momentous day all around, but one recently spoken phrase still reverberated in her mind. *Here come those Donovans.*

This day had been the longest of his life, a day filled with anxiety and love, insecurity and peace of mind.

He could no longer deny that he loved Jackie and Kevin, that he was vulnerable once again. All these years of fighting that encumbrance, and now . . . now that burden made him whole again.

The three of them had bathed and then eaten like they were starved. Kevin in particular had ingested an uncommon amount of stew and a plateful of biscuits, as well as two slices of chocolate cake. He was a growing boy, after all.

They'd had their "man-to-man" talk, a gentle dressing down where Rory attempted to explain to Kevin how worried his parents had been. He'd done his best, but Kevin had not completely understood. He'd nodded and muttered yes sir and no sir when appropriate, but to the child it was a scolding, and nothing more. One day, Rory thought, when Kevin had children of his own, then maybe he would understand the panic and the pain.

Jackie came to him by way of the gallery, as she always did. She entered the room, walking past fluttering lace curtains, and came straight into his arms.

He no longer cared about her past. No matter what she'd done to survive, she was here now. She was his wife, Kevin's mother, a Donovan through and through. Perhaps one day she would tell him about her life before she came to Cloudmont, but if she didn't, if she never mentioned her past . . . he didn't care.

"When are you going to pack up your clothes and hairbrushes and frilly things and move into this room where you belong?" he whispered.

She lifted her head and smiled at him, chin on his chest. "When you ask me properly."

"I have to ask?"

"Yes," she breathed.

He stroked her silky fall of hair, stared into eyes that were wide and hopeful. He was glad he'd left a lamp burning, so he could see those trusting eyes. "Jacqueline Donovan, love of my life, keeper of my soul, thief of hearts . . ." She closed her eyes and smiled, and he planted a quick kiss on her lips. "Stay with me always. I want you close, day and night. I want to know where you are, be able to reach out and touch you in my last waking moment at night, and I want your face to be my first vision each and every morning. This is your home, your room, your bed." This moment was as important as their wedding day, this whispered invitation as binding as their wedding vows. He kissed her again. "Is that proper enough?"

"It's more than I ever expected," she whispered.

He put out the light, and together they crawled into their bed, in their room, in their home, and for the first time in years Rory Donovan was completely at peace.

Jackie had enough pretty dresses to satisfy any woman, but both Sally and Rory insisted that she indulge herself with a new dress for the upcoming wedding. She had finally agreed to spend the afternoon at a Florence dress shop with the bride-to-be, as the dressmaker measured and made final plans for the elaborate wedding gown Sally desired.

"It's going to be simply marvelous," Sally insisted as she draped herself in white satin. "Seed pearls and satin and silk flowers, and the veil! Oh, Jackie, you will simply love the veil!" Sally lifted her chin and danced about carefully.

Mavis Clark stuck her head out of the back room. "Sally, would you put that satin down before you wrinkle it! Sit next to Jackie and be patient!"

Sally obeyed her mother's instructions. At least, she sat down. Asking patience of Sally was asking for an awful lot.

"I think your dress should be a deep rose, perhaps a crushed strawberry satin," Sally suggested. When the dressmaker was finished with Mrs. Clark, Jackie would be next.

"I don't know. Rory has a fondness for blue." She would be perfectly satisfied to wear her blue gown to Sally and Clint's wedding. Why did she need a new gown? Everyone would be looking at Sally, anyway.

"But you already have a blue gown," Sally whined.

Her frugal ways stayed with her, in spite of Rory's fortune. She'd had nothing growing up, and after a successful scam she'd always put as much of the money away as she could, saving for her retirement and her little cottage. A few nice dresses were often necessary for her occupation, but enough was enough!

"I don't see why that blue gown won't suit for

310

your wedding," she said sensibly. "I've only worn it twice."

"Twice!" Sally was clearly horrified. "Everyone's already seen it! For my wedding day, you must wear something new, something no one's seen."

It was easiest just to relent. Sally was determined, as was Mrs. Clark, as was Rory.

The new pony had arrived, and Rory and Kevin were spending the afternoon at their first riding lesson. She'd much rather be there, watching, than endure a fitting for a gown she didn't need!

When Mrs. Clark was finished, Jackie was ushered into the back room. She would be allowed no privacy, and shouldn't have expected any. Sally insisted on coming along, and Mrs. Clark had to make her preferences known.

Jackie stood upon a stool in her chemise and stockings and high-top boots, as the dressmaker circled her once, twice, and again. She'd never been so nervous, not even when she'd climbed into Rory's bedroom.

Measurements were taken first, and then the dressmaker began to show her samples of fabric. The green was immediately dismissed by Mrs. Clark as being too dark, and just as Jackie was about to choose the blue, Sally whisked it from the dressmaker's hand. The Clarks took turns removing fabrics from the offered selections, while Jackie stood on the stool, silent. Finally, they had narrowed the choices to three.

A sunny yellow, Sally's rose, and a luscious lavender.

Jackie touched the lavender satin. "I've never had a gown this color before."

The dressmaker, Mrs. Rawson, held the swath near her face and Jackie glanced into the mirror. "It's a good color for your skin tones," she said, "and it makes your eyes sparkle."

"It is quite a lovely color," she conceded. "I suppose if I must have a new gown—"

"You must!" Sally insisted.

"Then I choose this fabric."

More discussions on beading and lace followed, another discussion Jackie was excluded from. She was able to insist, once, that the design be kept as simple as possible. She considered herself to be too short and too delicately built to support yards of lace and pounds of beading. She'd surely look like a kid playing dress-up.

With all the important decisions made, they walked down the street toward a little café for a cup of tea and a slice of cake before returning home. Sally and Mrs. Clark chattered on about the wedding plans, and Jackie was content to listen.

What was wrong with her? She was so happy, but every now and then it was as if a cloud moved across her rosy vision. She didn't deserve this wonderful life; her past would catch up with her, Rory and Sally and all the rest would find out who she really was and they would hate her.

"Look at this hat!" Sally squealed, coming to a sudden stop at the window of a milliner's.

Lost in thought, Jackie took two steps before turning around to see the hat in question. She caught a glimpse of the beribboned straw hat, but what caught her attention was the man behind them who bowed his head and stepped hurriedly into the pharmacy.

Goodness, her mind was playing cruel tricks on her. The man who'd stepped quickly into the shop and out of her line of vision had looked an awful lot like Luther.

If he'd known Ruth Daniels would be in attendance, he would have refused the dinner invitation. The widow had always seemed harmless enough in the past, but he did not like the way she looked at Jackie.

Still, Jackie didn't seem to mind at all. She ignored the cutting glances and sweet, mild barbs Ruth sent her way, and concentrated on her conversation with Sally and Clint.

This had been meant as a small gathering of friends, the Donovans, the Clarks, and Clint Marsh. Rory no longer felt threatened by Clint, since he was doting so absolutely on his bride-to-be.

And then Ruth had stopped by unexpectedly, and Mavis had no choice but to invite her to join them.

One thought ruined this lovely afternoon. If Ruth Daniels knew what Jackie had been before coming to Cloudmont, she would gladly make their lives miserable.

When the meal was done, Rory escorted his wife to the veranda, her hand in his. More than anything he wanted to protect his wife, but he didn't know how. If she would tell him the truth, confess to everything, perhaps he could protect her from the Ruths of the world. As it stood he had to pretend he didn't know, and that became harder every day.

If Ruth had any manners at all she would have excused herself from the gathering, but of course she didn't. Rory sat in a chair beside Jackie, and to his dismay Ruth seated herself at his other side.

"Well," Ruth said in a voice that commanded the attention of the entire party. "I haven't seen you since your marriage, Rory dear," she said sweetly. "How very interesting that you decided, after all these years of being a widower, to marry the governess. It's rather like a romantic novel, isn't it?"

Sally obviously missed the sarcasm, for she jumped right in. "Oh, it is. Their story is a grand romance, a fairy tale, a . . . a . . . " She searched for something suitable.

"A stroke of incredible luck," Rory finished for her, bringing Jackie's hand to his lips for a brief kiss. He even smiled at his wife, ignoring Ruth and the mild, unladylike spluttering that was going on at his side.

314

The conversation turned to wedding plans, and Ruth was silent for a while. Mavis and Sally were consumed with their discussion of clothes and flowers and music, and their bright conversation dominated the afternoon.

Ruth fumed the entire time. Finally, she leaned close to Rory and whispered harshly. "And what of Georgia and Florida? Will you continue to see them?"

It was an odd question, but then Ruth had been very odd lately. "I suppose I will, now and again," he said softly, so as not to interrupt the Clark women. There would be horse auctions and races and buyers to visit across the South, and he would have to continue to travel, on occasion.

"And what does your bride think of that?" Her voice and her eyes were sharp.

Rory grinned. "I imagine I'll ask her to join me, if the idea appeals to her."

Ruth's face paled. "That's despicable," she hissed.

Jackie leaned slightly forward and looked past him to the distraught widow. "Whatever are you talking about?"

"Georgia and Florida," Ruth whispered. "Your depraved husband intends to ask you to join him the next time . . . the next time he . . . "

"How thoughtful of you," Jackie said cheerfully.

"You wouldn't mind?" he asked, wondering what she would think about leaving Kevin behind for a few days. Then again, perhaps the boy could come along, too.

"It sounds very exciting," she whispered in a conspiratorial voice.

Ruth decided that was the moment to take her leave, and she did so with her nose in the air and her face beet red. Rory wasn't sorry to see her go.

He and Jackie left soon afterward. As they rode toward Cloudmont in the phaeton, Jackie had the most wicked smile on her face, and every now and again she would laugh out loud, for no reason. They were halfway home before she decided to speak.

"I suppose I must tell you," she said as she wiped away a tear caused by laughter. "Oh, I never should have done it, I know that, but I couldn't resist. You'll be shocked," she warned.

"I don't shock easily," he assured her.

She took a deep breath. "Well, when Ruth visited last, she tried to warn me off."

"What do you mean, warn you off?" He didn't like the sound of this, not at all.

"She said men like you might sleep with women like me, but you don't marry them."

If he'd known that earlier he wouldn't have made an effort to be kind to the witch! Knowing what he did about Jackie's past, that must have hurt, badly. "She's a desperate, lonely, bitter woman. I hope you didn't listen to her."

"I did," Jackie confessed softly. When he glanced to the side he saw that wicked smile blooming again. "But I got even. I told her I wouldn't even think of marrying a rascal like yourself, and then I told her about one of your many escapades."

"Escapades?"

"Yes, I told her about those naughty twins Georgia and Florida, and how I caught the three of you in the ladies' parlor."

The house was in view, now, and none too soon. "In other words, you made up a tale to shock her."

Jackie was still smiling widely. "Yes. I described, in great detail, how I peeked into the parlor and saw you sitting in that wing chair by the window. You were naked, of course."

"Of course," he mumbled.

"And Georgia and Florida, those wanton girls, were naked as well, and they were doing the most outrageous things to you."

"Like what?" he whispered huskily.

"Oh, I didn't need to go into a lot of detail. I just mentioned a lot of bare legs and moaning and hands and mouths going this way and that."

"This way and that."

Alvin was waiting for them at the carriage house, and Rory gladly handed over the reins.

"Mr. Donovan," the shy young man said as Rory turned away, "Miss Corinne asked me to tell you that she's taken Mister Kevin to her house for the afternoon. She has two brothers about his age, she said, and she thought they might like playing together."

"That's fine," Rory said, as he took Jackie's arm and led her into the house. "Georgia and Florida," he muttered as they went in through the front door. The house was silent, still, empty. Good. "No wonder Ruth damn near had a conniption fit when I said I'd ask you to join me."

Jackie giggled again, and he led her into the ladies' parlor and stood before the wing chair by the window. "This chair?"

She sighed deeply. "Yes."

He left Jackie standing there while he closed and latched the double doors, and he even closed the French doors before he returned to her. Crossing his arms over his chest, he stared at her. As always, she stared right back.

"Show me," he whispered.

Chapter Nineteen

For the fourth day in a row, Jackie woke feeling horrendous. Her stomach pitched this way and that, and her head pounded. She rolled carefully from the bed, so as not to wake Rory, and made it to the lavatory just in time to heave violently.

She was never sick! She didn't get colds, nothing upset her stomach—she had an iron constitution! Until now, she thought as a wave of nausea swept over her again. Just a few days after her trip to Florence with the Clarks, the morning after she and Rory had joined the Clarks for Sunday dinner, she'd awakened to her first unpleasant episode, and every day since she'd been stricken.

Something was seriously wrong with her.

The nausea eventually subsided, but Jackie sat on the floor of the small room and contemplated the worst.

She was dying. Some dread disease was destroying her body. The nausea would get progressively worse, until she spent her last days bending over a bowl and emptying her guts. She'd never in her life been weak, but after each episode she felt as if every bit of her energy and life had been sapped from her body.

She didn't want to die, she thought as yet another wave assaulted her. Rory needed her, Kevin needed her, she'd just found happiness and it wasn't fair.

Maybe this illness was her punishment for lying. She knew in her heart that she should tell Rory everything about her past, but she couldn't do it. She couldn't bear to have him look at her with pity and hate and revulsion in his eyes. Love was growing there, more every day, and she didn't want to do anything to stop that growth, to destroy that love.

But this punishment seemed severe. Pain, weakness, maybe even death. She rolled her eyes to the ceiling. "Nicholas of Myra," she whispered. "You're a poor excuse for a saint."

It was barely dawn, and Rory and Kevin slept soundly. Jackie dressed quietly, stepping into a simple yellow house dress that buttoned up the front. Perhaps a cup of coffee would restore her— The thought caused an unexpected roil of her stomach, but with a stilling hand over her abdomen and a slow, deep breath, the nausea faded away.

She and Sally were to pick up their new dresses this afternoon. Perhaps she should plead illness and excuse herself, and have the lavender gown delivered.

But if she did beg off Sally would be disappointed, and in truth the horrid nausea never seemed to hit in the afternoon. Even her afternoons had been changed. She'd been uncommonly tired, the past couple of days, and had been taking naps to rival Kevin's.

Jackie made her way downstairs slowly, hanging on to the handrail and taking small, delicate steps so as not to disturb the relative calm her innards were experiencing. Nell would be waiting in the kitchen, Jackie knew. She could hear the muted banging of pots as she stepped onto the brick porch.

"Good morning," Nell said brightly as Jackie pushed into the kitchen. The smell of bacon cooking caused another unexpected bout of nausea. She closed her eyes and clutched at her stomach and prayed for the unpleasant sensation to go away.

Corinne and Eleanor had not yet arrived for the day, so Nell had the kitchen to herself.

"Not feeling well again this morning?" Nell asked with a lilt of cheer in her voice, and when Jackie opened her eyes she saw that the housekeeper was smiling widely. How could she be so cruel?

"Not well at all," Jackie confessed.

Nell gave off a contented hum that was much like the opening note of a joyous song.

"I'm so glad my illness pleases you," she said, fighting back another small but nasty roil.

Nell removed her sizzling skillet from the stove and came to Jackie, placing a gentle arm around her shoulder. "Poor girl, you have no idea what's happening to your body, do you?"

Jackie allowed Nell to lead her to the kitchen table as if she were an invalid, leaning against the older woman until Nell placed her carefully in a straight-backed chair. "What if I have some awful disease?" she asked, voicing her fears aloud for the first time. "At first I thought I'd eaten something bad, but it's been four days. Four days! And it's not just the nausea," she revealed in a lowered voice. "Sometimes in the afternoon I'm so tired I can barely keep my eyes open. It isn't natural!"

"It's perfectly natural when you've got a baby growing inside you," Nell said in a soothing voice.

Jackie's lips parted in surprise, but no sound came forth.

"Do you mean to tell me you didn't even suspect?"

Jackie stared wide-eyed at the housekeeper. "A baby? Carrying a baby makes you sick to your stomach? And tired?"

With a comforting pat to Jackie's shoulder, Nell returned to the stove to heat a pot of water. "All that and more. I always hated the swelling.

Your fingers and ankles and bosom will likely be the worst. They always were for me. Oh, and nature's call will come much more frequently, as if the little tyke is sitting on your bladder and jumping up and down to amuse himself."

None of this was sinking in. A baby? Jackie glanced at her flat stomach, still unable to believe what Nell was suggesting. "You mean I'm not dying?"

"Of course not. A cup of sweet tea and a slice of plain toasted bread will make you feel all better," Nell promised. She turned from the stove and stared at Jackie, hard. "You really had no idea?"

Jackie shook her head. "I've never been around a . . . a . . . woman in the family way before." She looked at her flat stomach again. It didn't seem possible that there was a child growing in there. A baby made from her joining with Rory, a tiny life that would grow inside her day by day. "How can I know for sure?"

Nell harumphed as she collected the tea. "Well, if you won't take my word for it I suppose you could consult a doctor."

"A doctor," Jackie repeated. It made perfect sense. "Next week, after Sally's wedding, I'll see a physician in Florence."

What would Rory say about this baby? He surely understood the possible consequences of their unprotected encounters, but was he really ready for this? "Don't mention this to my husband," she said softly. "I don't want to tell him about the baby until I'm sure." Rory had lost enough. It would be best if she didn't mention the possibility until she knew, without a doubt, that there was a baby. "There's no need for him to worry needlessly."

By the time Nell set Jackie's tea and toast before her she was already feeling better. As she finished the bread slowly, she was more and more certain that death was not waiting around the corner for her. A baby!

Jackie glanced skyward, and a smile she would have thought impossible moments earlier spread across her face.

Nicholas of Myra, I take back every unkind thought I've ever had about you. You're a fine saint.

By the time Jackie and the Clarks arrived at the dress shop in Florence, her nausea was gone and almost forgotten. Ah, it was a beautiful day. Spring was fading and summer was here. The days were longer, the nights milder, the trees greener.

"Why are you smiling like that?" Sally asked as they entered the shop.

She didn't dare to tell anyone before Rory, and since she hadn't seen a physician and had her suspicions confirmed yet, there was no way she could share this news with Sally.

"I just can't wait to see my new gown," she said brightly. "Mrs. Rawson is a genius to have all these gowns finished so quickly! Goodness, she didn't even start on mine until last week."

Sally only raised her eyebrows at Jackie's uncustomary enthusiasm. "She is quite good."

Sally's wedding gown was fabulous and extravagant, and Mavis Clark's beaded gold and beige mother-of-the-bride gown was exquisite. Jackie tried on her gown last.

As Jackie had requested, the dressmaker had kept the design simple. There was a touch of lace at the sleeves and waist, but the cut was elegant and there was no elaborate beading as there was on the other two gowns. Jackie stood before the mirror and looked hard at her reflection. Rory would like it, she decided.

She tugged once at the neckline, which was a fraction lower than she'd expected. Was it her imagination, or were her breasts larger than they'd been last week? Nell had spoken of swelling, and if Jackie wasn't mistaken, it had already begun.

The Clarks complimented her and the dressmaker on the perfection of the gown. Apparently none of them noticed that she was different today.

With their purchases stored in the Clarks' carriage, they walked down the sidewalk to their favorite café for a cup of tea. Jackie was ravenous! What would Sally and her mother say if she ordered two slices of cake with her tea, and then gobbled them up as if she hadn't eaten for days?

Sally stopped to admire yet another hat in the milliner's window, and Mavis Clark joined her daughter in her admiration. Jackie stepped on slowly, dreamily, enjoying the perfection of the day, wondering with every step if the child growing inside her was a boy or a girl.

When had she become so certain, doctor or no doctor, that she was carrying a child? She wasn't sure when the transformation had taken place, but she was now convinced that it was true. Maybe she didn't have to wait until she saw the doctor to tell Rory.

"Miss, I believe you dropped this?"

The voice behind her was familiar, familiar in the kind of way that made her insides tighten and her throat close. It couldn't be— She spun around slowly and came face-to-face with a man who offered her a lace handkerchief. His eyes were smiling, even if his lips were not.

The years had not been kind to Luther. He was smaller than she remembered, and he'd lost a lot of his hair, and there were deep wrinkles around his eyes and his mouth. He held the handkerchief out to her with a gnarled hand.

She couldn't speak to save her soul. What was he doing in Florence, Alabama? Where had he come from?

"Cat got your tongue, girlie?" he asked in a lowered voice. A quick glance to her side showed her that Sally and Mrs. Clark were still discussing the merits of yet another bonnet. "Not even a hug and a hello for your poor old Uncle Luther?"

"You're not my uncle," she squeaked out, appalled as always at the idea of being bound by blood to this man.

He allowed himself a small smile. "Well, that's the truth, isn't it? But I did raise you, you ungrateful girl, and how do you thank me? You run off just when you get of an age where you might be of use to me."

"Go away," she whispered.

"Not so easy, my sweet. You've done well for yourself." He looked her up and down slowly, taking in the expensive clothes, the jewels at her ears and fingers. "Very well." His dark eyes locked to hers. "I want my cut."

"What?"

Sally and Mrs. Clark were headed her way. Dear God, she didn't want them to know this man! She didn't want them to know she'd lived years of her life in his care!

"Just after dark," he whispered. "In front of the stables at that fancy house of yours."

She shook her head, unable to speak.

"And if you're not there," he promised, "I'll come knocking at your door. I'm sure your fine husband would like to meet me."

He swung toward Mrs. Clark. "Does this handkerchief belong to one of you ladies? I was quite sure it was hers, but she says not."

Mrs. Clark dismissed the crude Luther haughtily, collected her girls like a clucking mother hen, and headed for the café.

"Look, Mother," Sally said, real concern in

327

her voice. "I believe that horrid man frightened Jackie. She's gone quite pale."

Of course she was pale. She felt as if she were about to pass out, right here on the sidewalk.

Luther was here. Somehow he had found her, and he was going to ruin everything! Rory would find out about her past, and he would hate her then, wouldn't he?

She saw spots before her eyes. Goodness, she was going to faint! She couldn't faint! Her stomach revolted, and she dashed into an alleyway to throw up her lunch. With one hand pressed against a brick wall for support, and the other flattened against her chest, she stood there long after the nausea subsided.

Luther could so easily ruin everything, and Jackie knew it too well. She would lose Rory, Kevin, her home . . . her life.

Sally and Mrs. Clark comforted her, and when she was ready they led her away. As if from a distance, Jackie heard Sally voice her concern, saw Mrs. Clark watching silently and with an understanding smile.

Mavis Clark had guessed about the baby, but she couldn't possibly have guessed that Jackie's life was about to fall apart.

Rory knew, with every fiber of his being, that something was wrong. Jackie smiled as she listened to Kevin's account of his afternoon riding lesson, but it wasn't her usual, real, true smile. It was forced, fake, and it didn't reach her eyes.

Those eyes kept flitting to the window, and

as the day faded and the night turned gray, the smile became more and more forced, and Rory could see something he remembered from the old Jackie. Desperation. He hadn't seen that look in her eyes for a very long time.

"When are you going to start your riding lessons, Mama?" Kevin asked from his comfortable position on the floor, and Jackie practically jumped out of her skin.

"Riding lessons? I can't take riding lessons."

"You agreed that once Kevin was proficient you'd allow us the opportunity to teach you the finer points of horsemanship," Rory reminded her. "He's a quick learner."

Kevin beamed at the praise.

"But . . . but . . . " she fixed those desperate eyes on his face. Yes, something was definitely wrong. "What if I fall?"

"I'll catch you," he promised softly. "I'll always be there to catch you when you fall."

She didn't seem at all reassured. "Can I start on a pony like Kevin's?"

"Well, I had intended to start you on a new mare I have. She's gentle, just right for you."

"Is she small?"

Was Jackie really so afraid of riding a horse? Fearless Jackie, who'd climbed a column to gain access to this house, who'd lived her life existing from day to day, who'd done things he could barely imagine. Everyone should be allowed one fear, he supposed. "Very small," he assured her.

"Next week," she said as she glanced at the

window once again. "We'll start the lessons next week."

When it was Kevin's bedtime she asked Rory to put the child to bed. Usually it was a job she gladly did herself, but tonight she was distracted. She offered her arms for a hug, first, and Kevin flew into them, as always. It seemed to Rory that Jackie held the child a bit tighter than usual tonight.

As he led Kevin from the parlor with the promise of a bedtime story, Jackie rose from the serpentine-back settee and faced the window.

"I think I'll take a walk," she said softly. "The fresh air will do me good."

Rory paused in the doorway, as Kevin headed for the stairs. "Wait a few minutes and I'll come with you."

"No." Her head snapped around, and she fixed intense blue eyes on his face. "I could use a few minutes to myself, tonight. I'll be upstairs shortly."

Something was definitely wrong. Rory tucked Kevin in and told him a brief bedtime story, but as he performed the nighttime rituals he was thinking of his wife. She was happy here, wasn't she? He did his best to love her, to take care of her. From what he knew no one had ever taken care of her before, and to his thinking it was past time someone did. Long past time.

He had put her past aside because all that mattered was today. He'd never dreamed that he would think this way, that he would be able to let go of the past and embrace the present and the future. Jackie had given him that gift, and he wanted to give her the same.

When the story was done and Kevin closed his eyes, Rory stepped to the French doors that were open to allow the cool night breeze to fill the house. He continued on, across the gallery and to the railing that encircled the house.

He grasped the banister with both hands and looked out over his land, searching tonight for a figure of a woman walking across the grass and through the trees. Perhaps he could join her now, take her in his arms and kiss her lips and take away whatever pain she still carried within.

Circling the gallery, he searched for Jackie. She enjoyed Nell's garden, but she wasn't there tonight. She loved the aromas of the magnolias and the honeysuckle on the south lawn, but she wasn't lingering there, either.

He hadn't even considered that she might go to the stables, but as his eyes scanned the lands of Cloudmont, that was where he saw movement. The swirl of a full skirt, pink in the twilight, caught his eye. As his eyes focused on the scene before him he saw his wife standing at the corner of the stables. She didn't walk on by, but paced anxiously there, her steps short and quick.

Dammit, he would go down there right now and make her tell him what was wrong!

Before he could move from his post at the

rail someone else appeared, a shadowy figure of a man. Jackie stopped her pacing and faced this man.

Rory's heart sank. This wasn't someone she'd happened across; she'd been waiting for him. They put their heads together, Jackie and this mysterious man, and with every passing second Rory's heart grew heavier and heavier.

His wife was meeting secretly with another man.

Frantic to believe in her, he searched for a simple explanation, anything to explain away her behavior this evening and the undeniable fact that she had arranged a rendezvous with another man. No matter how hard he tried he couldn't think of a single one.

Perhaps Margaret had met her lovers at the stables. The very idea hardened his heart.

The man lifted both arms and placed his hands on Jackie's shoulders. She backed away and shrugged those hands off, and with a quick glance toward the house she took her companion's arm and together they rounded the corner of the stables and disappeared from view.

Rory entered the house through Jackie's old bedroom and dashed through the dark room and down the stairs, moving so quickly he barely felt the steps beneath his feet. He was such a fool! With all the evidence he had against her, all the proof that she was not who she pretended to be, he trusted her, still. Once again, he'd been proven wrong, but by God, the woman wasn't going to cuckold him right under his nose!

He left the house through the study doors, and stalked toward the stables, not knowing what he'd do when he caught up with Jackie and the man she'd slipped away from him to meet, not capable at the moment of any rational thought at all. The moon lit his way, as he headed unerringly toward the spot where he'd seen his wife with another man.

She came around the corner, alone, long before he reached the stables, and when she saw him she increased her step, gaining speed until she was running at him. Maybe he was wrong, Rory thought as she approached quickly. Maybe she would fall into his arms and tell him everything. His assumptions were wrong; he prayed to be wrong.

Jackie did fall into his embrace, throwing her arms around his neck and burying her face against his chest. Rory wrapped his arms around her and lifted her gently, so that her feet dangled inches from the ground.

Whatever had happened, whatever was wrong, she could tell him anything. As long as she was honest with him, as long as she didn't lie. . . . God, he'd had enough of lying in his life, and so had she. The truth, that's all he asked for. The truth.

"What's wrong?" he whispered.

Jackie took a deep breath and exhaled slowly. "Nothing. Nothing's wrong." She held on tight.

"Can't a woman be glad to see her husband and want a hug?"

"Of course." His heart sank. *Tell me!* "But I thought I heard voices, and I wondered if maybe something was wrong."

"Voices?" she repeated weakly.

"I might have been mistaken . . ."

"Yes," she whispered. "You were mistaken. It was the wind in the trees you heard, perhaps, or a squirrel or a raccoon."

He set Jackie on her feet and looked down into eyes that lied so well. He could see the lie, though, in the depths. "The wind."

She clasped the front of his shirt with both hands. "Kiss me."

He obliged, taking her mouth with his, losing his fears and his hurt in a savage joining of their mouths. Jackie's response was as wild as his own, as she held him tight and plunged her tongue deep into his mouth, as she nibbled at his bottom lip and moaned as the fire grew hotter, out of control.

"Love me," she whispered, and Rory picked her up and carried her toward the house.

He entered the big house as he'd left it, quickly, through the wide open study doors and up the stairs. Jackie was already unfastening the buttons of his shirt as he set her on her feet beside their bed.

He reached out to quietly shut the door, and Jackie was wrestling with her own buttons when he returned to her. She was truly desperate, now. Her hands trembled, and in the moonlight that broke through the opened French doors he could swear he saw the sheen of tears in her eyes.

As he reached out to her he wondered if this was Jackie's way of saying good-bye.

Chapter Twenty

She wanted to wipe away the memory of Luther's face and words with Rory's touch. She wanted to forget everything for a while, and simply let Rory love her.

His skin was hot in her hands, the flesh of his chest and arms she pressed her palms against as he finished unbuttoning her dress and peeled the fabric aside. He tugged the bodice away quickly, and she heard the whisper of a small rip as the fabric gave way.

He laid his mouth over the linen of her chemise and over her breast, sucking the nipple and the wet fabric deep into his mouth even as he continued to undress her. Her knees wanted to buckle, so she held onto him for strength.

I'll catch you if you fall.

337

More than anything, she wanted to believe that Rory would be there to catch her, tonight and always.

He ripped the last of the clothing from her body and together they fell onto the bed. This time his mouth closed over bare flesh, without the barrier of thin linen between her nipple and his tongue. He suckled and laved until her wish came true and all she could think of was this. His hands on her, his mouth, the promise of his fullness deep inside where she ached for him.

Blindly, she unfastened his trousers and slipped her hand inside to grasp his arousal. Her fingers grasped and stroked his hot, silken steel, and with every caress his kiss became more intense, his hands more daring. When he suckled at a nipple and slipped a finger inside her, she arched off the bed and moaned aloud.

Rory shucked off the rest of his clothes and covered her body with his. She cradled him with her thighs, and he teased her wet opening with the tip of his shaft.

"I need you," she whispered hoarsely. *Now and forever. Catch me . . . catch me when I fall.*

"Do you?" He teased her, rocking just slightly forward and beginning to enter before rocking back.

"Yes. I love you." *More than you'll ever know. Catch me. Love me.*

"Do you?"

"Yes."

He plunged deep, filling her waiting body with one strong thrust. Tonight he was relentless, thrusting deep and withdrawing almost completely before filling her again. He seemed to know when she was on the edge of completion, because he withdrew and stilled, tormenting her with gentle, shallow strokes and then stroking deep again.

Their fulfillment came at the same time. Jackie felt Rory's shudders and took his moans into her mouth as her inner muscles flexed and squeezed around him, as the release he provided crackled through her body with the force of a bolt of lightning.

She wanted to hang onto this moment and what she'd found here, wanted to cherish the love and peace of mind and sense of belonging she'd never known before coming to this place.

"Yes, I do love you," she murmured as he relaxed and fell atop her.

He was still and quiet over and within her. She heard his deep breathing, and felt his heartbeat pounding against hers.

If she were not such a coward she would tell him everything. Here, now. Did he love her enough to forgive everything she'd done? Did he love her enough to forgive everything she had yet to do?

Writing that letter to Mina had been a stupid, sentimental thing to do! She'd told a friend that she'd heard from Jackie, and word had gotten around. The news had spread to Luther, of course. Knowing Mina would never tell him anything, he'd searched her room while she was out and found the damned letter. He'd read about the marriage and the Fabergé egg, and he wouldn't be satisfied until he had the treasure for himself.

He could have it, for all she cared, as long as he left her and her family alone. She could explain away the disappearance of the egg, if she had to. She could make up a story about an intruder, break the glass, give the sheriff a mystery he would never solve.

And then Luther would leave her alone.

On any other night, Jackie's easy departure from the bed probably would not have disturbed Rory. But tonight, what little sleep he'd experienced had been brief and restless.

Had she thought a rousing bout of sex would exhaust him so completely that he wouldn't hear her leave? No doubt that was the case.

She slipped into the clothes that had been discarded on the floor, very slowly and quietly stepping into the chemise and pulling the dress over her head. Wouldn't she be surprised when she reached the door and he sat up to ask her where she was going?

With his eyes half-closed, Rory watched his wife by the illumination of the moon. His heart ached for what he'd thought they had. Faith, a new beginning; love. Finding out it didn't exist at all was as painful as losing something real.

Once Jackie was dressed, she stopped at his bedside. He prayed to be wrong. *Let her bend to kiss me and open her heart. Let her confide in me the way a wife should confide in her husband.*

She bent down slowly, and for an instant he thought his prayer would be answered. Then she very carefully slid open the drawer of his bedside table and reached in to recover a key.

His heart stopped. He'd been right all along. She wanted that damn Fabergé egg, and she'd been willing to do anything for it. Anything.

Out of the corner of a half-opened eye he watched her insert the key into the lock at the base of the glass cover. It clicked softly, once, as she turned the key, and she glanced over her shoulder to look at the bed. Rory didn't move.

She soon returned her attention to the be-jeweled egg. The glass case was lifted slowly and set aside, and at last she laid her hand on the object of her desire. Not him, not love, but a priceless jewel-encrusted egg. A thing, a possession; a curse.

Cradling the egg in her hands, she headed for the door. She didn't look at him or at the bed, not once, but kept her eyes on the object she'd finally managed to steal.

Dammit, she could have made off with the prize weeks, months ago! Why wait until he was in so deep that he would be devastated by her betrayal? Why wait until he loved her?

The truth came to him with blinding clarity. What man would send the authorities after his wife? It would be damned embarrassing, wouldn't it, to be forced to admit that your own wife was a thief who'd only married you for a priceless treasure? Better simply to let her go.

Better simply to let her go.

She'd been gone from the room only a minute before Rory left the bed. Damned if he'd make it that easy for her!

Naked as he'd been when she loved him last, he followed her, halting at the top of the stairs. She stood in the foyer below, the egg in one hand, the other hand on the doorknob of the massive front door.

"Going somewhere, my dear?" he whispered.

Her head snapped around. It was dark here, without the light of the moon, but he could see her dark figure well enough. Too well, perhaps.

"Rory," she said softly. "This isn't what it looks like."

He took a step down. He was almost interested in hearing the lies she would weave to cover this one. Almost. "Isn't it, Jackie Donovan? Or do you prefer Jacqueline Beresford, or Juliet Billings, or maybe you'd prefer Jasmine the Magnificent?"

He knew! He knew everything. Jackie watched as Rory descended a few more steps, until he stopped in the middle of the staircase. A shaft of moonlight from the window beside the door illuminated most of his face for her, and when she looked into his eyes she wished with all her heart that he'd remained at the top of the stairs, lost in darkness.

He hated her. She could see the disgust in his face, in eyes that had once shown her only love. This was what she'd been dreading when she'd kept her secrets from him, this loathing.

"You know," she whispered. Luther, damn him, must have spoken to Rory in spite of his promises, in spite of their infernal deal.

"Of course I know." He smiled, but it wasn't a real, true smile. It was a smug, self-righteous grimace. "You outdid yourself this time, Jackie the Magnificent." He leaned against the rail casually, propping his elbow on the polished banister and leaning ever so slightly to the side. "And you were magnificent," he said lasciviously. "Passionate and adventurous, as a lover should be, as hot-blooded as any woman I've ever bedded. It was a fun game, while it lasted, in fact I found it very exciting. Why else do you think I put up with your charade for so long?"

"Rory—"

"There are a few tricks of the trade I haven't taught you, yet," he said as if she had not spoken. "Tricks that might come in handy on your next encounter."

"Don't," she whispered.

"When you get tired of the next man," he said cruelly, "come on back for a day or two. Climb into my bedroom and I'll show you a few moves that will drive your men wild. Learn enough and you can sleep your way into any man's life and walk away with every treasure your heart desires. Do it right, and they won't even care." He descended one step. "But then you already knew that, didn't you?" he whispered.

She glanced down at the heavy, ugly egg in her hands. Well, there was no need to give this treasure to Luther. Rory already knew everything, and just as she'd suspected he hated her for it.

After taking a few tentative steps she stood at the foot of the stairs. Without saying a word she very carefully placed the Fabergé egg on the bottom step.

"What's wrong with you?" Rory asked gruffly. "Does it spoil the game if you get caught? Is this some kind of thief's code of honor?"

She backed away slowly.

"Take it," he ordered.

She shook her head once.

"Take it!" he took a single step down, plunging his hate-filled face into darkness once again. "Come on, Jackie, you earned it."

With those final words he broke her heart. She'd earned it! On her back. Under the magnolia tree, in his bed, on the gallery. With those words he made her what she'd sworn never to be; a whore, a woman who sold her body. All these years she'd protected her heart and her body, and the man she'd finally given them both to despised her.

She backed slowly toward the door, and Rory matched her step for step, descending the stairs.

"Take it," he whispered as she reached the door and he reached the step just above the stair where the egg rested.

She turned and ran, throwing open the door and escaping into the night. She'd run before, hard and fast, fearing for her life and her freedom. But she'd never before run this hard, she'd never before felt as if her heart and her soul were shattering with every step.

After the door slammed Rory gave in to the weakness in his knees and sank down, sitting on a step and leaning his shoulder against the railing.

He scooped up the Fabergé egg from the bottom step, where she'd placed it so carefully. Why hadn't she taken it with her? He'd caught her red-handed, sneaking out of the house with her prize, so why, after he'd told her to take the damned egg, had she left it behind?

He ran his fingers over cold, hard gems he could barely see in the dark. This is what she'd wanted all along, so why the hell had she looked at him like *he'd* been the one to betray *her*, and then placed the treasure at his feet as if she offered her battered heart and soul on a silver platter.

The closed door loomed large and ominous, and he stared at it, half-expecting Jackie to burst back in at any moment, hoping, dreading, that in the next heartbeat she would open that door and come back.

But would it be for the egg, or for him?

The tears rolled down her face and still she ran. Rory wasn't following her, she knew that, and still she ran. God help her, she couldn't stop.

Her heart pounded, the tears flowed, and the ground beneath her feet was hard and unyielding. Her body ached, and still she ran. She ran until she felt as if she couldn't run anymore, until she could barely move. And still she ran.

The night was quiet, undisturbed by her pounding heart and her labored breath. She couldn't escape from Cloudmont fast enough; she couldn't get far enough away.

Not that she thought Rory was following her. Why should he? He was finished with her, he'd had his fun and he still had his precious treasure. He'd probably gone back to bed, already, taking his bejeweled egg with him.

Luther was waiting behind the stables, and he could wait there all night. If he wanted the egg he would damn well have to steal it himself!

Somehow she ended up at the magnolia tree where Rory had made love to her that afternoon not so long ago. She slipped beneath the leaves and into an enclosure that was pitch black, hiding from the world as best she could.

With the tree trunk at her back she closed her eyes and took a deep breath. What would she do now? Where would she go? She couldn't go back to the life she'd led before meeting Rory, she just couldn't.

Her knees buckled, and she sank slowly to the ground. *What do I do now? Where do I go?* These questions had never bothered her before. She'd always been satisfied to drift aimlessly, to get on a train and see where it took her. Free as the wind, she'd reminded herself many times.

Unencumbered by responsibility of any kind, she'd drifted from one place to another.

Somehow she knew she'd never be that carefree again. Maybe she'd never been carefree; maybe she'd simply been searching for something more all along.

Before dawn her tears stopped. Jacqueline Beresford would not be beaten by any man, not even Rory Donovan. She might love him, might always love him, but she didn't *need* him and she refused to allow him the opportunity to hurt her again.

By the gray light of morning, she left the shelter of the magnolia tree and found the road, and with her head high she started walking toward Florence.

Chapter Twenty-one

After a sleepless night, Rory dressed as if he were getting ready to do battle, slowly, deliberately. He stepped into dark trousers and pulled on a plain white shirt, and standing before the mirror above his dresser he tied his tie into a perfect knot. It would be best to approach this day as if it were any other normal, ordinary day.

Nell would not understand why Jackie was gone, and dammit, he couldn't explain it to her. He barely understood himself. But Nell would insist on explanations, wouldn't she? She'd want details, reasons, the truth.

Facing the rest of the world with the news would be hard enough, but what would he tell Kevin? Damn her, how could Jackie leave that boy without a word when she knew how much the kid loved her? He knew Jacqueline Beresford, thief and professional liar, was capable of many things, but he didn't think she was deliberately cruel.

Think again.

He descended the stairs to the aromas and noises of breakfast being prepared and served; familiar sounds, familiar odors. Every breath was an effort, but he made sure the effort didn't show. He made sure he was in control, long before he faced Nell.

She must have been looking and waiting for him, because before he was comfortably seated she was there bearing his coffee and wearing the most ridiculous grin on her wrinkled face.

"Is Miz Jackie sleeping in this morning?" Nell asked brightly as she poured his coffee. The old woman leaned close and whispered. "She certainly needs the rest."

He reached out and took his cup of coffee, and sipped before he answered. "No," he said as he placed the cup on the table. "Mrs. Donovan is not sleeping in."

"She's not ill again, is she?" Nell left the dining room on that odd question, only to return a few minutes later with a plateful of his favorite breakfast foods: eggs, sausage, biscuits.

"Ill?" *Again?*

"Well, I guess it's only to be expected—" she stopped suddenly. "Never mind," she snapped. "It's nothing at all. Should I send up a tray?

Eleanor can make her some tea and toast and have it to her in a flash."

Tea and toast? Rory shook his head. "Mrs. Donovan is not upstairs," he said calmly. No one had to know how painful this was, not even Nell. "Mrs. Donovan is gone."

"Gone where?"

Nell expected a simple answer. *She's gone for a walk. She's gone to visit her friend Sally. She's gone to town.* Unfortunately, Rory didn't have a simple answer. "Just gone," he said softly.

Nell sighed deeply and pulled out a dining room chair for herself. She plopped into it heavily. "Gone?" she repeated.

"Yes."

She gave him a look that was censuring and harsh and just short of demonic. "What did you do to that poor girl?"

Rory set his fork aside and took a deep, stilling breath. Dammit, he was going to have to explain again and again, so he might as well get used to this . . . but deep inside he wasn't ready. Unfortunately, it didn't matter if he was ready or not.

"That *poor girl* is a thief. She came here for the express purpose of stealing the Fabergé egg I keep in my bedroom. Don't look so shocked. We were all taken in, and I suppose we should learn from this experience—"

"Hogwash," Nell interrupted. "That poor girl is your wife, and if I'm not mistaken she's carrying your child." Her voice was mercilessly sharp. "What did you do to drive her away?"

"She's . . . what?" he pushed his plate away. God, he might never be able to down a bite of food again. His stomach was one big knot, his throat closed on him. "What makes you think she's carrying a child?"

"She's been sick at her stomach," Nell revealed in a low voice, "these past few mornings. And haven't you noticed what long naps she's been taking in the afternoons, and that she's been eating nearly twice as much at supper as she used to?"

"No."

"Well, I've noticed. She suspected, too, but didn't want to tell you until after she'd seen a doctor." Nell stared at him with parsimonious, puckered lips. "She didn't want you to worry needlessly."

There was only one way for him to survive hearing this news, and that was to deny it. "It was a part of her scam, a way of gaining your sympathy," he said softly. "She's not pregnant. She can't be."

"She *can't* be?" Nell said in a disbelieving voice as she rose from her chair. "Why on earth not?"

He wasn't sure he had an answer for her.

It was a simple matter to arrange for a transfer of funds from her Charleston account. The bank manager was very helpful, but then she *was* Mrs. Rory Donovan, and the Donovans had been good customers for many years.

Jackie buried her hurt deep, under a facade she'd utilized many times in the past. She was confident, she was independent . . . she was invulnerable. She plastered a smile on her face and went about her business. The business at hand was getting out of Florence as quickly as possible.

With a ticket on the eastbound afternoon train purchased, she went to the dress shop where her beautiful lavender gown had been made. It was unfortunate that she would be unable to wear that gown. What a waste.

Mrs. Rawson had a few ready-made dresses that suited Jackie just fine. A dark blue traveling outfit, a plain cotton dress in yellow, another in green, and the appropriate underthings. She packed all but the traveling outfit in the leather bag she'd purchased at the general store just a few doors down.

She changed clothes in the back of the dress shop, gladly shedding the pale rose-colored dress Rory had taken off of her the night before.

"Get rid of this," she said softly, handing the dress to Mrs. Rawson's helper, Annie. "It's torn."

Annie looked carefully over the gown. "Just a few small tears here and there," she said with a hopeful lilt to her young voice. "I could fix it for you in a jiffy."

She didn't want it! Dammit, she wanted to shed everything of this place before she left. "No, thank you. I'm rather in a hurry."

"Seems a waste," Annie said wistfully. "It's such a pretty dress."

Jackie gave the dressmaker's assistant a wide smile. "Would you like to keep it for yourself? We're about the same size, and that shade of pink would be lovely on you."

Annie lifted wide eyes to Jackie. She was obviously a girl who'd had little beauty in her life, and in that one glance Jackie saw who the girl really was. Annie worked hard, behaved like a proper young lady, went to church regularly, and if she was lucky one day she'd marry well and settle down to have baby after baby. Her life was set, planned, the kind of existence Jackie had always abhorred. Yet, right now she thought Annie a very lucky girl.

"Are you sure, ma'am?"

"Very sure."

And what of her own baby, if there really was one?

Funny how the very prospect of a child changed one's outlook on the world, Jackie thought as she headed for the train station, her back ramrod straight and her small bag grasped securely in her hand. There would be no more thievery, no more scams to make it from one town to the next. Children needed security, stability, love and honesty. Her child's mother would not be a thief.

She had managed to get through the entire morning without shedding a single tear, but one fell as she thought of Kevin. He would hate her for leaving him, when she'd promised she would not. *Mamas don't walk away.* What would Rory tell the child? The truth, most likely, the whole, ugly truth.

Yes, Kevin would hate her, too, she imagined. More than anything she wanted to deny that fact, but she couldn't. The two Donovan men would despise her. Just as well. Perhaps the hate would ease their pain, a little.

There were several hours to spend in Florence before the train pulled out. Jackie spent an hour window shopping as if nothing was wrong, admiring frivolous hats and pretty dresses and lace fans. She had lunch alone at the café where she and the Clarks had enjoyed tea and cake on two occasions.

Perhaps she'd write Sally a letter, once she was settled, and explain everything. *Everything.* The staged meeting at the resort, the diamond earrings, the way friendship and love had changed her life forever. Of all the people she'd ever known, Sally was most likely to forgive. She was young, and sweet, and kind. Oh, she would miss that girl's silly laugh.

She thought of everyone she was leaving behind, but Rory. Her constitution couldn't take that sort of trauma right now. There would be time enough, later, for recriminations and tears. All the time she'd ever need. All her life.

He was a coward. Rory bent over blurred numbers he could not read, his aching head in his hands. When Kevin had asked where Mama was, Rory had lied. On a trip, he'd said with an insane calmness. She'd been called away suddenly, he said.

He guessed that it would be easier to tell Kevin that his mama wasn't coming home after she'd been gone for a while. The pain would be muted, the hurt not so acute. In that time he'd do his best to be both mother and father to the boy. They'd go fishing more, and he'd read to Kevin at bedtime, the way Jackie sometimes did.

No matter what she'd done, she had given him his son. For that reason he could forgive her . . . a little.

He was such a fool. Knowing what Jackie was and what she'd done, knowing that she'd lied all this time . . . he still missed her. He missed the sound of her laugh, the sight of her smile, the possibility that she might come around any corner at any minute.

There was an insistent knocking at the door, but Rory did not rise to answer it. Nell could get it, or she could send one of the girls she employed to answer the door. There was no one he wanted to see, not today.

Eleanor came to the door, all twittery and shy. "There's a . . . ummmm . . . gentleman here to see you, sir."

"I'm not seeing anyone this afternoon," he said, returning his eyes to the meaningless numbers on his desk.

She twittered a little more and left him alone to his misery again, as apparently relieved to be out of his presence and he was to have her gone. Not relieved enough, apparently, since she was back a few minutes later.

"He says it's important, sir."

"I don't care—"

"He says it's about Mrs. Donovan," she said quickly.

Rory leaned back in his chair. The Pinkerton's agent, perhaps, with more news? Useless information, facts he did not want to know. "Send him in."

The man Eleanor led into his study was not the same detective Rory had met in Birmingham. As a matter of fact, if this man was a Pinkerton's agent they had lowered their standards. He was oily and every bit as fidgety as poor Eleanor, but his eyes snapped about the room, taking in everything as if he were evaluating each and every object.

A small, middle-aged man with sparse, graying dark hair, he carried himself with an air of cocky self-importance. He might once have been a tolerable-looking fellow, but today his health did not appear to be good. There were circles under his eyes, and his skin had an unhealthy, yellow tinge.

"Mr. Donovan," the oily man said, extending his hand across the desk. Rory declined to take it, and eventually the offered hand dropped.

"What do you want?" Rory asked in a low voice.

An insincere smile faded. "Right to business,

I see. Well, that's the way I like things myself."

Rory said nothing, but stared the man down.

"My visit concerns your Mrs. Donovan," he said in a lowered voice. "Is she about?"

"No."

The man nodded. "Just as well. This is a problem that might best be handled man to man, just the two of us. Women are so sentimental and foolish at times. They just don't have a good head for business, like you and I."

Rory was quite sure he had nothing in common with this man, but he remained silent, hoping the visitor would get to the point and then get out of his house.

"You see," the man continued, "I hate to see a fine man like yourself taken in by the likes of Jackie. She's not quality, you see. She's a common street girl, a thief, an ungrateful liar. I'm sorry to be the one to inform you, but she's pulled the wool over your eyes, Mr. Donovan."

One word caught Rory's attention. "Ungrateful?"

"I raised her like she was my own, I did, tragic little orphan that she was. I did my best, and now that she's got all this"—he raised his hand and it wafted, palm upward, for a moment—"she doesn't want to repay her poor old uncle who's in ill health. A man who sacrificed everything for her, a man who—"

"You must be Luther," Rory said lowly, everything the Pinkerton agent had told him coming together in a sickening way. This was the man Jackie had met last night at the stables, the man she'd been going to meet after the household was asleep.

"I see she told you about me."

"No."

The little man smiled. "Well, you'll have to ask her sometime about her Uncle Luther and all I did for her. It was such a surprise when those detectives came knocking on my door asking about her, and an even greater surprise when I found out about Jackie's good fortune. It seems only right that the girl should share."

"You were blackmailing her, weren't you?" Rory asked without moving.

"Blackmail is such a nasty word," Luther said with an ugly smile. "Jackie, she isn't cooperating, see. She thinks she can forget her Uncle Luther, pretend she's a fine lady and play at being quality and forget the man who made her what she is today. She thinks she can ignore me, but she's wrong."

Luther was much too confident. He had this all planned out, down to the last detail. Rory felt sick, and he couldn't see straight for a moment. Jackie had been cooperating, hadn't she? She'd been trying to buy her life back with the Fabergé egg, she'd been willing to risk everything to get rid of this man.

"See," Luther continued smugly, "I figure a man as important as you won't want your friends and neighbors to know that his wife was a pickpocket and a thief, and that she lived for several years with a prostitute in Baltimore. They might begin to worry about their valuables . . . or their husbands."

Rory was across the desk so fast that Luther didn't know what hit him. The little man crashed to the floor as Rory delivered a blow to the gut and then another to the chin. "You son of a bitch," he said as he held Luther to the floor. "How dare you come here and threaten my wife."

"She owes me," the little man squeaked out. "I raised her like she was my own daughter, and how does she thank me? She runs away just when—" There was a spark of fear, at last, in Luther's dark eyes.

"Just when what?" Rory prodded in a low voice.

"It doesn't matter," Luther said softly. "Just forget I was ever here."

Forget? Not likely. Too much was coming together, like the pieces of a nasty puzzle he didn't really want to solve. "What did you do to Jackie to make her afraid of a man's touch?" She had been afraid when she'd come here, hadn't she? Shy, terrified, withdrawn in a way, in spite of her strength and audacity. He had sensed that coming to his bed took courage on her part. . . .

"I didn't touch her!" Luther protested. "Damn high and mighty bitch wouldn't let me near her."

Rory answered by slamming Luther's head against the floor.

"I swear it's true!" the slimy man shouted.

"She bit me! See? I even have a scar to prove it." He offered up his hand, and pointed to a faint, white scar on the pad of his thumb.

He'd never known what bloodlust was until this moment. He could kill this man with his bare hands, and without a twinge of guilt. If ever a man deserved to die—

Rory lifted his head to find that the doorway to his office was crowded with people. Nell and her girls and a wide-eyed Kevin stood there, all of them visibly frightened. Kevin had his eyes fastened not on the man on the floor, but on his father. There was fear there, in those wide eyes, and that was the sight that stopped Rory from literally killing the man beneath him.

"Nell, bring me some rope and send Alvin after the sheriff. This man needs to be charged with extortion."

Luther smiled up from his position of weakness. "What stories I'll tell," he said, enjoying his revenge. "Boy," he yelled, tilting his head back and looking at Kevin. "Did I ever tell you about the time Jackie—"

Rory grabbed Luther's chin in his hand and yanked his head down. "You say one word about my wife," he whispered lowly, "one word, and I will kill you." No one could hear him but the man on the floor, and that was the way he wanted it. "Not here, in front of these good people, but later, as you sit in the jail cell you deserve. I will pay the sheriff to look the other way while I beat you to death an inch at a time, even if it takes every cent I have. One word."

Wisely, Luther believed him.

When the blackmailer was hog-tied and gagged, Rory headed for the front door.

"Mr. Rory," Nell called out as he grabbed the doorknob. "You're not going to leave me here with this varmint!"

"He's not going anywhere," he assured her. "I tied him good and tight, and the sheriff will be here soon enough."

"But . . . but where are you going?"

In the open doorway he turned to look at Nell, and at the small figure of a boy close behind. "I'm going to get my wife and bring her home," he said, and then he slammed the door behind him.

Chapter Twenty-two

Her stomach was in knots again. *A perfectly natural side effect of your condition,* she told herself as she boarded the train. *Perfectly natural.*

But it was afternoon, not morning, and the knots in her stomach were very different from the nausea she'd experienced so much of late. For the first time in her life Jackie was truly afraid. Just yesterday her life had been so secure, her future so certain, and now . . . now she was lost, truly lost and alone.

"I have you," she whispered softly as she took her seat. Her hand rested over her flat stomach. "I'm not really alone." But she didn't have Rory, or Kevin, or a home. *I can make a home,* she thought. *Anywhere I want to be. A cottage by the sea or a cabin in the woods. I'll make my own home for me and my baby.*

The railroad car was crowded, with families and single travelers like herself. They carried small bags and baskets of food, toys for the little ones, and they were dressed in their very best. Most of them were smiling, excited about the journey to come. Jackie felt as if she were separated from the other travelers. She was in a daze, still.

Perhaps they sensed the wrongness around her, for as the car filled no one took the seat next to Jackie.

Something within her, some stubborn spark of hope, tried to force her to look out the window and study the platform for a familiar fair head. Rory would surely stand out above all the rest.

But she didn't so much as turn her head. Rory wasn't coming after her, what a foolish notion! He hated her, as she'd known he would. If she went to his door and begged for forgiveness he would send her away, or call the sheriff and have her arrested. She stared straight ahead, and when she couldn't stand it anymore she dropped her head and stared at her clasped hands.

He'd wasted precious hours, going to Sally's house and looking for Jackie there. At first he hadn't believed Sally's protestations that Jackie was not hiding in the Clark house. Where else would she have gone but to her friend? But as Sally's concern grew, Rory had had to accept the fact that his wife was not there.

So where was she?

The truth had hit him with sickening clarity. She really was gone. He'd told her to leave and she'd taken him at his word.

The streets of Florence were bustling. The shops along the main thoroughfare did a brisk business, and he stepped impatiently around shoppers who moved too slowly for him. He'd check the hotel first. She had to have a place to stay, after all. And if she wasn't at Sally's . . .

No one at the hotel had seen her, and the clerk stared at him as if he were crazy as he gave name after name. Jackie Donovan, Jacqueline Beresford, anyone named Jackie or Juliet or Jasmine. The clerk finally told Rory, quite forcefully, that no lone woman had checked in on this particular day.

He walked toward the train station. Would she run so far so fast? Would she escape on the train just hours after he'd so stupidly confronted her and sent her on her way? Perhaps. He was almost there when he saw her on the opposite side of the street, walking away from the train station at a brisk pace. She moved stiffly, and her hair was covered by a ridiculous straw bonnet, but he recognized that pink dress. Just last night he'd practically ripped it off of her.

Shooting across the street and barely missing crashing into an old woman who balanced three hatboxes in her hands, he chased his wife. "Jackie!" he yelled, but she didn't so much as falter in her step. He caught up with her quickly, and called her name again, but she didn't respond.

She was angry. Of course she was angry, he'd made an ass of himself and had hurt her. Would she even believe him when he said he loved her and begged her to come home?

"Come on, Jackie." He reached out and laid a hand on her shoulder, placed his fingers over the pink cotton of her dress.

With a squeal she spun around, and he realized that this was not his wife. A young girl stared up at him, terror in her eyes. He stepped back.

"You're not Jackie," he whispered.

"No, I'm Annie," she continued to eye him suspiciously.

He apologized and stepped back, his heart sinking with the renewed certainty that he'd never find his wife. "Where did you get that dress?"

She smiled shyly, then. "Oh, a woman gave it to me this morning. Isn't it lovely?"

"Yes." Maybe this girl knew where Jackie was. Maybe this search wasn't hopeless after all. "My name's Rory Dononvan, and when I saw the dress I thought you were my wife." He wondered how much of the truth Jackie had told this girl. "I'm looking for her, and it's very, very important. Do you have any idea where she might be?" He held his breath.

Annie's smile widened. "Oh, I imagine she's already left for her trip, though she didn't exactly say what time her train was leaving."

He turned and ran toward the train station, knowing that chasing after that damned dress might have cost him precious time. When the sidewalk became congested once again with shoppers who were walking too slowly to suit him, he cut into the street and ran even faster.

It was time for the train to pull out, and as he ran through the depot and jumped onto the platform he had to push past last-minute arrivals and tearful relatives saying good-bye to get to the tracks.

Was she on this train? If only he could be sure. She might have taken an earlier one, or she might have planned to leave later. He searched the windows as the train began to move, cursing the glare of the sun and the people who got in his way. He ran, trying to outpace the train so he could get a glimpse into the front cars. The train moved faster and faster, and so did he.

He saw a dark head that might have been Jackie's. It was bowed, and she didn't look out the window like most of the other passengers.

"Jackie!" he yelled as the train picked up speed and left him behind. He couldn't hear his own voice over the train's engine, so he was sure that even if that dark-haired woman was Jackie, she wouldn't hear him. He shouted her name again, anyway, and then he was left standing on the platform as the train sped down the tracks and eventually disappeared from view.

Rory searched the crowded platform and the station house, looking for a familiar head of hair, listening for a familiar voice. With every passing, disappointing second, he was more assured that he'd lost her. He was too late.

Until long after dark he searched for her, but his heart was heavy by the time he mounted his horse to head home, and there was no hope left. He'd missed her. She was gone, and Jackie could disappear in the blink of an eye. She would change her name, take on a new accent, and disappear.

It was late by the time he arrived at Cloudmont, and he silently tossed the reins of his stallion to Alvin, who was standing outside the stables. The boy took one look at Rory's face and wisely decided to maintain his silence as well.

Nell and Kevin were waiting in the parlor, as he had expected they would be, and they both stood quickly when he entered the room, anxious eyes searching the empty space behind him. They both looked very disappointed when they realized he was alone. Nell's face fell, and Kevin's half-grin melted away.

"I missed her," he said gruffly. "She'd already left on her trip."

Tough, no-nonsense Nell teared up immediately, but Kevin had no idea what this news meant. He was disappointed, but he didn't yet know that his mama wasn't coming back. Ever. He returned to his drawings.

Rory tried to reassure Nell as she walked past, escaping from the parlor, perhaps to shed more tears in private. "She'll be back," he said softly, reassuring her and trying like hell to re-assure himself. "When she calms down and re-alizes that I didn't mean what I said, she'll come home."

Nell gave him a censuring glance with tear-filled eyes. "If you believe that nonsense you don't know your wife very well. Love her, and she'll love you back with all her heart. Hurt her, and she'll run forever."

Forever.

"Don't look so shocked." Nell continued an-grily. "What else could you expect? Heaven above, did you see and hear that· odious man who raised her?"

"How much did you hear?"

"Enough," she hissed. "Enough to know that if you managed to convince Miz Jackie that you don't want her she won't be coming back." With that Nell stormed off, and Rory entered the parlor where the three of them had spent so many quiet evenings. He sank into his chair, the energy leaving him all at once so that he was surprised he'd made it this far without collapsing.

Kevin glanced up now and again, but said nothing. He gave up his drawing for a wooden train that snaked its way across the rug to a soft *choo-choo* Kevin provided himself.

Tiring of the train as well, he sat up and stared at Rory with wide eyes. "Are you sick?" he finally asked with real concern.

"No." Rory shook his head. He would have to be both father and mother to Kevin, now. He had so much wasted time to make up with his son, so many wasted days to recover. "I'm just . . . sad."

"You miss Mama, too, don't you?" Kevin asked, wide-eyed and innocent, not realizing that the trip was a permanent one, that his mama wasn't coming home.

"Yes," Rory said softly.

He looked at Kevin, really, truly looked. For years he'd avoided just this, a careful inspection that revealed his mother's face, a wistful hope, and deep, trusting eyes.

"Your father is a stupid, stupid man," Rory whispered.

Kevin left his place on the floor and came to Rory's chair, and once there he laid a small hand on a tense forearm. The little fingers waved softly, as Kevin patted Rory's arm in a gesture meant to comfort.

"You're not stupid."

"I'm afraid I am." Much more stupid than he cared to admit, more than he dared to confess, even to himself.

Kevin gave Rory's arm one last pat, a more energetic tap this time, and then he darted from the room. His footsteps were fast and loud on the stairs, and a minute later he descended those stairs just as quickly and loudly, his shoes banging against the steps as he ran. When he came back into the parlor, he planted himself in front of Rory's chair.

"Maybe this will make you feel better," he said, offering a single dried bean on his little palm. "It's my last one, and I was saving it for something special, but I think you should have it."

Rory shook his head. "You keep it, son. One day you might need it."

But Kevin had made up his mind. "No, I want you to have it." With a small, insistent hand, he took one of the large fists that rested on Rory's thigh and lifted it a few inches, peeled open the reluctant fingers, and placed the bean in the center of his father's large palm. "Do you remember the rules?"

Rory stared at the dark little bean in his hand. "No," he said. "I don't remember."

Kevin placed his hands on Rory's knees and leaned slightly forward. His voice was lowered as he shared his magical secrets. "First you hold the bean tight and wish for the one thing you want most in the world. Wish with your heart, Mama said. Then tell your wish to someone you love and give them a hug, and then . . . and this is the hardest part . . . sometimes you have to be patient."

Rory folded his fingers around the bean and closed his eyes. Magic! There was no such thing as magic, but he would humor the boy,

371

for now, and pretend that there was magic to be found, even here, even though he knew there was no such thing. . . .

But then again, a few months ago he would have said there was no such thing as love, a few weeks ago he would have sworn there was no way he would ever want another child. If magic was watching the impossible happen, then maybe . . .

He squeezed his eyes tight and made his wish, putting aside reason and reality for a few precious, hopeful seconds, and then he opened his eyes slowly. Kevin was still standing there, leaning forward with his little hands on his father's knees.

Rory reached out and scooped the kid off the floor and onto his lap. He held on tight, cupping a red head snugly against his shoulder. His son smelled of soap and cinnamon, of sunshine and ink. It was such an unexpectedly comforting aroma, familiar and heartwarming.

"I want Jackie to come home," he whispered hoarsely. "I want her back."

Chapter Twenty-three

Jackie had always loved Charleston, but today she was only anxious to leave it. Just yesterday she'd closed her account at the bank, much to the bank president Mr. Odell's dismay, and now she was headed west.

In the end, she'd been unable to keep all that money. One shouldn't start a new life on stolen funds, she'd decided. Her child would not live in a house built on such a shaky foundation. She'd kept enough for a meager start elsewhere, and Mr. Odell had been most helpful in helping her to distribute the rest in a charitable manner.

Her bag was packed, and she had already purchased a ticket on the afternoon train. She wasn't going far. The western part of Tennessee would be suitable, she'd decided. She'd never been there before, so she should be safe.

Besides, she wanted her child to grow up where there were magnolia trees and wild violets, ponds full of fish and vast pastures where horses ran.

Pulling back the green velvet curtains, she looked down at the bustling street below. Her baby wouldn't be born or raised in a city. There was too much danger there, too much uncertainty.

She sat down at the desk in her hotel room to write another letter to Kevin. Every day for the past week she'd written him, trying to explain why she'd left, assuring the child that she loved him, swearing that when she'd promised not to leave she'd meant it. . . . But it was hard to explain to a child about broken promises.

When it was finished, the letter joined the others in a pocket of her leather pouch. There was also a letter to Sally, and one to Nell.

Maybe one day she'd have the nerve to post them.

A bellboy led Rory to his hotel room, explaining as they walked up the stairs that he was lucky to have found a bed available. The room had just been vacated, within the hour, the kid said.

Rory didn't care. Once again he was too damn late. Jackie had closed her account at the bank, and she was gone. The bank president had been unable to tell him where she was going. She hadn't shared that information.

If only he'd thought to question the president of his own bank, just a few days sooner, he would have been here yesterday when she'd closed her account. If only . . .

The bellboy left him alone, and even though Rory was exhausted he went not to the bed but to the window. He pulled back the green velvet curtains and looked down on the street below, watching for a petite woman with a head of dark hair, searching for the familiar turn of a head. Nothing.

This was his punishment, he decided, for not trusting Jackie, for not teaching her to trust him.

Reluctantly he fell into the bed. He was drained by false hope and disappointment, and tomorrow he had to begin again. Baltimore, he decided as his eyes drifted closed. He would head north.

Just before he fell into a restless sleep he caught a whiff of lavender so strong, so tantalizing, he could almost convince himself it was real.

"Mrs. Donovan, would you read me this letter?"

Jackie looked up from the assortment of ribbons she'd been straightening to find Cletis Hovater staring at her over the next shelf. "Of course." It was as much a part of her job as selling notions and canned goods, the reading and writing of letters for the customers of this country general store who could do neither for themselves.

Before she'd arrived, nearly two months ago, that job had fallen to Mrs. Nagle, the owner's wife, but as she had a gruff voice and a tendency to cough frequently, and her handwriting was not as fine as Jackie's, the chore had been passed on.

They sat in ladder-back chairs near the stove, Cletis leaning forward expectantly and Jackie with her posture stern as she began to read the love letter from a girl in the next county. The choice of words and the spelling were crude and simple, but the meaning was clear. There were no lies, no hidden meanings.

Everyone here, Mr. and Mrs. Nagle and all their customers, assumed that Jackie was a widow. The fact that she still wore her wedding ring and that she always wore black contributed to the supposition, as well as the fact that she always either burst into tears or threw up whenever anyone asked her about her husband. Oddly enough, it wasn't an act.

No one asked about her husband anymore.

They didn't know yet that there was a baby on the way. While her stomach was rounded slightly, she kept the evidence well hidden under voluminous skirts, and she'd discovered a fondness for high-waisted fashions.

Eventually they would see the truth, though, and when they asked her about her baby's father she would probably burst into tears or throw up.

There were so many nice people here in this

rural Tennessee crossroads. They'd welcomed her with open arms, taken her in, given her a job and a place to live. It had been coincidence that she had found herself in this small rural community, in this particular store, on a day when she was feeling particularly lost and Mrs. Nagle had been in bad need of a little help. More serendipity, she supposed.

"Please write me back," she finished reading in the accent that was her own. Part Baltimore, part proper English with a little bit of a Southern drawl, this voice was her own. "Your letters brighten my day. Your friend, Rosena."

Cletis, a tall, lanky man with too much dark hair, grinned from ear to ear. "Will you write back for me, Mrs. Donovan?"

"Gladly."

His obvious joy faded when he was faced with the prospect of choosing the words. "I don't know rightly what to say. Rosena is . . . oh, Mrs. Donovan, she's the light of my life. There's not another woman in the world like her, and without her I just couldn't go on." He spoke with the passion of youth, and the innocence of a man who'd never had his heart broken.

Jackie collected the paper and ink from behind the counter, and with a book on her lap as a writing surface, she retook her seat. "Why don't you tell her exactly that in your letter?"

He looked terrified at the prospect. "Just blurt it out like that? Why, what if she laughs at me? What if she thinks I'm some lovesick fool?"

377

Taking a deep breath, Jackie picked up the letter from Rosena and reread a particularly glowing passage. When she set it down Cletis was smiling again. "Forgive me for intruding, but this young lady loves you. You owe her your honesty. If you love her, make it plain."

"I do love her," he said softly, apparently not wanting anyone else to hear. "So much it kinda scares me."

"Then tell her," Jackie said, her limited patience coming to an end. "For goodness sakes, Cletis, ask her to marry you and be done with it."

"Do you think I should?"

Jackie took a deep, calming breath. "If you love her and want her as your wife, then ask." *If you don't, let her go before you break her heart and her spirit.*

Cletis looked hard at the wedding band Jackie continued to wear. "Did you love your husband very much?"

The knot in her throat kept her from answering. Her eyes filled with tears so that Cletis's face was blurred, and without warning her stomach twisted and turned. She'd forgotten people completely in less than three months, so why was Rory still so damned real to her? Why did it still hurt so much?

"I'm sorry," Cletis said, standing and backing away. "I forgot." He looked at Mr. Nagle, who was manning the front counter. "I forgot," he said again.

Jackie burst from her chair and ran out the

front door, hoping the cool autumn air would calm her stomach, hoping the chill would clear her head. She ran well beyond the front porch, where two old men, regulars at the store, sat playing their daily game of checkers. She rounded the corner and leaned against the side of the building, forcing her stomach to behave.

"Cletis!" one of the old men snapped as the front door swung open noisily again. "Did you ask her about her husband again, you nitwit?"

Her innards revolted, and Jackie lost the fickle control she'd found, bending over and emptying the contents of her stomach onto the ground.

Rory deposited his two sacks there by the door to the country store. Two elderly bearded men stared at him, hard, taking in his dark suit and shiny boots.

Maybe this was the wrong store. Jackie would be as out of place here in this rustic place as he was, but he had seen the letters, the letters she'd written to Sally and to Nell and to Kevin, and they'd been posted from here. She hadn't written him, but then why should she?

He heard her voice as he stepped into the store, and even though he was terrified of what her reaction would be when she saw him, he smiled. God, he'd missed that sound!

He walked toward the back of the store, where the voice came from.

"You have made me the happiest woman in

379

the world," she said with an unnatural stiffness. "Of course I will marry you, of course I will be your wife."

His heart thudded to a halt. Dammit, she was still married to him!

"I love you madly," she finished. He rounded a corner and saw her, sitting in a chair with a piece of paper before her face and a rapt listener before her. "Your future bride, Rosena."

When she finished reading the man before her jumped from his seat and whooped loudly, then spun around three times, shouting to the ceiling.

"What's going on back here?" A woman and three men came to the rear of the store, and that was when Jackie looked past the joyous man and saw Rory.

Her smile faded, her face went deathly pale, and she dropped the letter so that it fluttered to the floor.

The newly engaged man scooped the paper from the floor and kissed it, then held the precious letter to his chest. "I'm getting married, Mrs. Donovan, what do you think of that?"

"That's wonderful, Cletis," she said woodenly.

Suddenly, everyone realized that Jackie was staring at the stranger in their midst. An older gentleman stepped forward. "Can I help you, mister?"

Rory didn't take his eyes from Jackie's face. "I need to speak to Mrs. Donovan, privately."

She shook her head, once.

The man came to her defense. "Don't look to me like she wants to speak to you. Now, I don't know who you are, but maybe you'd better just leave."

"I'm her husband."

They all took a step back, away from Jackie, and the newly engaged man, Cletis, narrowed his eyes dangerously. "You've done it now, mister."

He watched Jackie regain her composure. A hint of color came back into her face, and her back and shoulders stiffened. "It's all right Cletis. Mr. Nagle, if we could have just a minute . . . "

Everyone backed away slowly, returning to the front of the store and leaving Rory relatively alone with Jackie. At least there was no one leaning over his shoulder.

All the way here, he'd rehearsed for this moment, but now . . . now that he was looking at her he didn't know how to begin.

"Well?" she prompted. "What do you want?"

"I want you to come home," he said softly.

"This is my home."

He'd known this wouldn't be easy. After all he'd said, maybe it shouldn't be. "I'm sorry if I hurt you."

"If?" She repeated incredulously. "Do you by any chance remember what you said to me the night I left your house?"

He remembered too well. The words came to him in nightmares and flashed into his mind in quiet moments. More than anything, he wanted to take them all back, to pretend that night had never happened. But he couldn't.

"I was suffering, and afraid, and I wanted to make you suffer with me. When I saw you talking to that man by the stables, and when I saw you sneaking out of the house with the egg, I believed the worst."

"You didn't ask," she said softly.

He took a single step, closing the distance between them. "You didn't come to me when Luther tried to blackmail you. Why?" Another step.

"I didn't want you to know all I'd been," she whispered. "I was afraid you'd look at me . . . the way you looked at me that night."

"I'd known for a long time," he admitted, "and I didn't care."

"How could you not—"

"Because I love you, and nothing matters to me but today and tomorrow and the years to come. Why didn't you trust me with the truth?"

She didn't answer immediately. Rory held his breath, waiting for the answer that would change his life, either for better or for worse. At first Jackie's face was stern, her eyes ice-cold, but as she searched his own eyes her expression changed, softening, yielding.

"I fell," she whispered. "You were supposed to catch me but you didn't. You let me fall."

He knelt before her, so that they were face-to-face. "In the past three months I have been to Baltimore, Charleston, and every city in between looking for you. I never gave up, not when your banker told me you'd donated most of your money to three different orphanages and closed your account, not when your friend Mina threatened to shoot me with a pearl-handled derringer, not even on those lonely nights when my common sense tried to tell me I might never find you."

"You shouldn't have bothered," she said coolly, and then she shot him a sideways glance. "Mina tried to shoot you?"

"Threatened," he clarified. "I assume you've been keeping in touch with her, because she sure as hell knew who I was and she was none too happy with me." He grinned, just a little. "She's a tough lady, and she cares very much about you."

"I have written her a few times," Jackie admitted.

"You've been doing lots of writing, it seems. When letters came for Sally and Nell and Kevin, I was so relieved to know you were all right."

"Of course I'm all right. I've always done just fine without you, Mr. Donovan, and I will continue to do fine without you."

"You didn't write me."

"I didn't think you'd care."

She was stubborn as always. "Well, I did care, dammit. I read Kevin's letters a dozen times over, and Nell's once, when she allowed it, and I tried to bribe Sally into letting me read hers." The memory of Sally Marsh's condescending refusal still stung.

"How is Kevin?" Jackie asked softly. "Oh, I love his letters, and his handwriting has improved so much I can read every single word."

"He's been working on it," Rory said. "He has front teeth now."

Jackie almost smiled. He could see the subtle change in her, as their conversation took this warm and normal turn. "Does he?"

Suddenly, she seemed to realize what was happening. No, she wouldn't allow him to suck her in so easily.

"I'm glad to hear it," she said stiffly. "Though that information could very well have been shared in a letter."

"Come home and you can see for yourself," he said quickly.

She raised finely arched eyebrows in an un-spoken, cold refusal.

He wouldn't be so easily dissuaded. "I knew it wouldn't be easy to convince you to take me back, so I tried to think of what I could give you to make you understand what you mean to me, what gifts would make you forgive me."

Her eyes widened, and he could see a spark of true anger there. Good. Anger was much better than numbness. "You want to *buy* your forgiveness? How typically Rory Donovan of you. Diamonds, I imagine, or something else cold and meaningless. You are a cretin."

He reached out to touch her cheek but she slapped his hand away. That hand fell to her knee, where he refused to allow her to shake it off. "I have two gifts for you," he said calmly.

"I don't want—"

"Your name," he interrupted, and she clamped her mouth shut. "Is Irene Jacqueline

384

Byrne Donovan, and you were born in New York City on January 24, 1871. You'll be twenty-five on your next birthday. Your parents, Irene and Sullivan Byrne, were hardworking people who were saving every penny they earned for a move west. They wanted their child to have a better life, you see. It was Sullivan who called his little girl Jackie, from the day she was born."

Jackie's striking blue eyes shone bright, but she didn't let a single tear fall.

"Unfortunately, Irene Byrne died giving birth to her second child. The baby died, too. Sullivan did his best to go on without her, but just a few months later he contracted pneumonia. With no family in the city, he trusted the care of his daughter, who was not yet three years old, to a neighbor, a man he hadn't known long but who had managed to gain his trust. He gave this man the name of his sister, who still lived in England, in case the worst should happen."

"The worst did happen, didn't it?" she whispered.

"I'm afraid so." He placed his other hand on her knee and she didn't try to shake him off, this time. "I'm so sorry."

"The neighbor didn't contact the sister in England, did he?"

Rory shook his head. "He was not the kind man Sullivan had thought. Very quickly, he discovered that a bright and beautiful child could be an asset in his line of work."

"It was Luther, wasn't it?"

"Yes."

She took a deep breath and closed her eyes. "Thank you," she whispered. "It . . . hurts, but I'm glad to know that my parents didn't just abandon me." A flash of pain flitted across her face. "But it changes nothing. I still don't have anyone."

"You have me," Rory whispered.

Jackie's eyes snapped open. This time when he lifted his hand to her face she didn't swat it away. His fingers settled over a soft cheek. "You have me," he repeated, "and Kevin, and good friends who miss you very much." He took a chance that Nell had been right all along, and he reached out to place his hand against her stomach. A careful exploration of her gently rounded belly brought a smile to his face. "And we have this little one."

"But you said—"

He placed his fingers across her lips. "I was wrong. I fell, Jackie. Catch me."

For the first time he saw a spark of hope in her eyes, and it fueled the hope in his own heart.

"It was a pretty big fall," she said.

He smiled at her, but she didn't trust enough to smile back. "Time for your next gift. Wait right here." Before he rose he leaned forward and kissed her quickly, taking her by surprise. By the time she had a chance to push him away he was already rising.

If this didn't clinch it, nothing would. He

barely looked at the crowd of people who stared as he passed by. He grabbed the two burlap sacks from the front porch and carried them to the back of the store, placing one behind a shelf where Jackie wouldn't be able to see it.

She was standing now, pacing in front of the stove.

"Sit down, please," he said, issuing a soft order. Amazingly, she obeyed, and he stood before her with the sack in his hand.

He wasn't leaving here without her! Whether she admitted it or not she needed him as much as he needed her. Who would take care of her when the baby came? Who else would love her the way he did? No one.

"You didn't have much of a childhood, and I want to make it up to you."

"You can't give me a childhood, Rory," she insisted impatiently.

"Why not?" He reached into the bag and withdrew a straw hat that was beribboned and festooned with yellow silk flowers. "This is your new lucky fishing hat," he said presenting it to her.

"I don't fish," she said lowly.

"You do now. Kevin picked out a fishing pole for you, but it wouldn't fit in the sack so I left it in his able care."

She studied the hat carefully before setting it aside, depositing it on the seat across from hers.

387

He reached into the sack and brought out the next item, a brand new baseball. "Kevin picked this out, too." He lobbed the ball to her and she caught it with both hands. If he wasn't mistaken there was the beginning of a smile on her face.

Reaching into the bottom of the sack he pulled out the final item, a doll with a porcelain head and a cloth body. "Sally helped me with this one," he admitted. "See? Her eyes are blue, like yours, and she has dark hair, and Sally had the dressmaker make a little dress out of scraps from a gown she made for you. She said you liked the lavender."

Jackie cradled the doll carefully. "I never had a doll," she whispered as her fingers raked gently over the porcelain face. "She's beautiful."

But when she glanced up there was still an unwelcomed stern set to her eyes. "So I have a fishing pole and a baseball that Kevin chose for me, a doll Sally chose for me, and what about the hat?" She lifted the straw hat and studied it critically. "Nell?"

"Yes," he admitted, taking the doll and the hat from her and placing them, together, on the empty chair. "What I picked out for you myself is over here."

He collected the second, heavy sack, and dropped it at Jackie's feet, where it landed with an odd, wavering thud and a rattle. And then he knelt there once again and delved deeply into the bag. His hand came up full, and he dropped the dried beans into her lap before going back for another handful.

"Magic beans," he whispered. "A lifetime's worth." He dumped the second handful of beans in her lap, and went back for more. "Let me make all your wishes come true."

Jackie stared silently down at the beans in her lap, and Rory's heart sank. It wasn't enough. Heaven help him, it wasn't enough to make up for everything he'd said and done to her.

She moved at last, raking her fingers through the beans. Still she didn't lift her head to look at him, and she remained silent. There was just the soft clacking sound of dried beans being stirred against black silk, and then there wasn't even that, as her hand stilled.

What now? God help him, he didn't know what to do now, had never imagined that she wouldn't forgive him.

Very slowly, Jackie slid out of her chair until she knelt before him. Dried beans fell off her lap and onto the floor as she wrapped her arms around his neck and placed her head against his shoulder.

"I love you," she whispered as he encircled her in his arms. "You're the only magic I've ever known."

Rory closed his eyes and held her tight. Jackie gave him his life back with those words.

Her gently rounded belly pressed against him, and he slipped a hand between their bodies to caress the bulge with his palm. Jackie backed up a little and looked down at his hand against the black silk.

"So," she whispered, "what do you think? Are you scared?"

He looked into her eyes, and a wide grin spread across his face. "To be honest I'm a little terrified, but I'm happy, too. How about you?"

"Terrified," she admitted with a smile of her own. "And happy."

Rory plucked a bean from the floor, studied it carefully, and then took Jackie's delicate hand in his own and placed the bean on her palm. He folded her fingers carefully into a gentle fist, and whispered against her lips just before he kissed her.

"Make a wish."

Epilogue

Six years later

Jackie rolled over and into Rory, waking slowly with her nose against his chest and her hands about his waist. "Good morning," she whispered sleepily as he pulled her closer. The early morning light warmed the room, while the gentle breeze through the open French doors added a nice chill.

"Listen to that," he whispered into her ear.

"What?" she strained, but heard nothing.

"Silence," he breathed.

He rolled her onto her back and kissed her languorously, bringing her fully awake in a most wonderful way. "Complete and total silence," he said dreamily as his hand grabbed the bottom of her shift and pulled it to her knees. "They're all asleep."

His words were a jinx, for at that moment Jackie heard the patter of feet in the hallway, and a moment later their bedroom door swung open and five-year-old Nicholas crept to the side of the bed.

"Goodie, you're awake," he said, crawling onto the tall bed to sit beside his father.

Nicholas was a tall child for five, and he was a true beauty, with pale blond hair and clear blue eyes and the face of an angel. Appearances were sometimes deceptive.

In spite of the fact that Nicholas looked very much like his father, he had his mother's adventurous spirit. He was particularly fond of climbing trees and had already managed to shimmy a good way up one of the columns that encircled this house.

The very sight of Nicholas always managed to make Jackie's heart swell.

"Can we go riding today?" Nicholas asked as he jumped up and down on the side of the bed.

"Maybe later." Rory said, still sleepy. He snaked an arm around Nicholas to still his jumping and give his son a hug.

"When can I start racing like Kevin?" Nicholas pressed. "I'm almost as good as he is, and I bet I could beat him if I had the chance."

As if on cue, Nicholas's big brother stuck his head in the opened door. "You'll never beat me in a race, squirt," he said with a smile. At twelve, Kevin was becoming a handsome young man himself. His hair had turned more cinnamon than carrot in the past few years, the size of his ears were now proportionate with his head, and his teeth were white and straight.

"Will too!" Nicholas insisted.

At that moment three-year-old Maggie squirmed past her eldest brother, rubbing her eyes and making straight for her papa. Magnolia Irene Donovan was exquisite. Her dark hair curled gently all on its own, her brandy brown eyes were large and innocent, and her mouth was curved in a perpetual smile.

Rory said she looked like her mother, right down to the curve of her cheek, but Jackie couldn't believe she'd ever been this beautiful.

Nicholas helped his sister up onto the bed, and she crawled into her papa's arms. "My brothers are too noisy," she complained as she settled comfortably into Rory's embrace.

Rory loved all three of his children, but Jackie knew that Maggie held a very special place in her father's heart. A healing place.

Jackie wanted to give her children everything she'd missed. Love, family, safety and security. Together, she and Rory had managed to give their children everything. Well, almost everything. Maggie still needed something Jackie had longed for and never had. Sally Marsh had filled the space nicely for Jackie, but Maggie needed one more thing.

A sister.

They made plans for the day, for study and fishing and perhaps even a picnic, and then the children left the room together. Kevin would head for the stables before breakfast, to check out his new gelding. Alvin had moved on, and Billy Ray was now in charge of the stables. Billy Ray, the odious young man who had so bullied Kevin, had grown into a hard-working man who had a gift for handling horses.

He still couldn't play the harmonica.

Kevin held Maggie's hand as they headed for the stairs, and Nicholas wondered aloud if Nell had made pancakes for breakfast. He was sure he could smell them, even from here.

Jackie slipped from the bed when the kids were gone, and closed the door behind them, quietly slipping the latch into place. She crossed the room and closed the French doors, locking them as well.

Rory reclined on the bed, his hands behind his head, a satisfied smile on his face. Well, what did he expect when he woke her with a kiss like that?

She didn't return directly to the bed, but stood over the case where their treasures rested. The glass that had once protected the Fabergé egg had been replaced by another, larger case. Since it was left unlocked, it was a simple matter for Jackie to reach out and lift the lid.

The egg had been pushed to the back, and it was surrounded by drawings, Kevin's blue ribbons for his equestrian efforts, a porcelain doll, and lots and lots of dried beans. She plucked one bean from the case and closed the lid easily.

Crawling into the bed with her fist closed, she knelt beside Rory. She shut her eyes and made her wish, and then she leaned over and snaked her arms around his neck.

"I want another little girl," she whispered.

Ever obliging, he made her wish come true.

The Indigo Blade
Linda Jones

Penelope Seton has heard the stories of the Indigo Blade, so when an ex-suitor asks her to help betray and capture the infamous rogue, she has to admit that she is intrigued. Her new husband, Maximillian Broderick, is handsome and rich, but the man who once made her blood race has become an apathetic popinjay after the wedding. Still, something lurks behind Max's languid smile, and she swears she sees glimpses of the passionate husband he seemed to be. Soon Penelope is involved in a game that threatens to claim her husband, her head, and her heart. But she finds herself wondering, if her love is to be the prize, who will win it— her husband or the Indigo Blade.

___52303-5 $5.99 US/$6.99 CAN

Cinderfella

Linda Jones

The daughter of a Kansas cattle tycoon, Charmaine Haley is given a royal welcome on her return from Boston: a masquerade. But the spirited beauty is aware of her father's matchmaking schemes, and she feels sure there will be no shoe-ins for her affection. At the dance, Charmaine is swept off her feet by a masked stranger, but suddenly she finds herself in a compromising position that has her father on a manhunt with a shotgun and the only clue the stranger left—one black boot.

___52275-6 $5.99 US/$6.99 CAN

Dorchester Publishing Co., Inc.
P.O. Box 6640
Wayne, PA 19087-8640

Please add $1.75 for shipping and handling for the first book and $.50 for each book thereafter. NY, NYC, and PA residents, please add appropriate sales tax. No cash, stamps, or C.O.D.s. All orders shipped within 6 weeks via postal service book rate. Canadian orders require $2.00 extra postage and must be paid in U.S. dollars through a U.S. banking facility.

Name_____
Address_____
City _____State_____Zip_____
I have enclosed $_____ in payment for the checked book(s).
Payment <u>must</u> accompany all orders. ☐ Please send a free catalog.
        CHECK OUT OUR WEBSITE! www.dorchesterpub.com

Linda Jones
On A Wicked Wind

Hurled into the Caribbean and swept back in time, Sabrina Steele finds herself abruptly aroused in the arms of the dashing pirate captain Antonio Rafael de Zamora. There, on his tropical island, Rafael teaches her to crest the waves of passion and sail the seas of ecstasy. But the handsome rogue has a tortured past, and in order to consummate a love that called her through time, the headstrong beauty seeks to uncover the pirate's true buried treasure—his heart.

___52251-9 $5.99 US/$6.99 CAN